LOVE'S PUZZLE

Olivia gasped. How could Clara, her own sister, sit there so calmly after saying such an extraordinary thing?

Clara observed her sister's bewilderment with tender affection. With all her books, how much—how *very* much—the lovely young woman had yet to learn of the intricate puzzle of love . . .

Elizabeth Mansfield

The Fifth Kiss

BERKLEY BOOKS, NEW YORK

THE FIFTH KISS

A Berkley Book / published by arrangement with
the author

PRINTING HISTORY
Berkley edition / July 1981

ISBN: 0-425-04739-3

A BERKLEY BOOK® TM 757,375

PRINTED IN THE UNITED STATES OF AMERICA

The Fifth Kiss

chapter one

The fog was remarkably thick even by London standards, and Olivia, peering out of the window of her coach, could not be certain at first that the gentleman she suddenly spied there on the street was indeed the one she thought he was. She drew in her breath in a suppressed gasp and threw a quick, uneasy glance at her sister who was dozing beside her, her head nodding gently with the motion of the carriage. Relieved to see that Clara was still asleep, Olivia turned back to the window and pressed her nose against the pane. Yes, the gentleman out there who was so brazenly embracing a lightskirt looked shockingly like Strickland.

But he couldn't be! Olivia *must* be mistaken. The fog (a chilling, enveloping mist that made one feel colder this February night than snow would have done) had made of the nighttime streets of London a cloudy nothingness, and even though the gentleman was standing in a beam of light from the open door of the house behind him—a beam which cut a swath of brightness through the soupy haze—his outline was nevertheless made indistinct by the thickness of the fog. The little scene being played out on the street just beyond the carriage appeared to be shrouded in gauze. In addition, the gentleman's face was obscured by the tousled coiffure of the woman he was so unrestrainedly embracing. The two had evidently just emerged from the house and were engaged in a shockingly fond farewell. The position was too intimate for propriety, and the woman was obviously not the sort of creature a gentleman

1

should be seen with at all. So of course he *couldn't* be Strickland . . . could he?

The coachman was inching his way through the mist very cautiously, and Olivia had ample time to stare down at the man in question. He seemed to be as tall as Strickland and his shoulders as broad. If he were not Strickland, his form was as like as a twin. Still, Olivia cautioned herself, it was decidedly nasty-minded of her to suspect for a moment that Lord Strickland could be the sort to embrace a doxy on the street. She disliked Strickland intensely, but she was not so mean-spirited as to assume that he would be likely to behave in so reprehensible a fashion. She must not permit herself to jump to such an unwarranted—

But she did not finish the thought, for the gentleman lifted his head at that very moment and looked directly at the passing carriage. Olivia gasped aloud and quickly withdrew her face from the window, her heart pounding and her fingers trembling in shock and chagrin. It *was* Strickland after all!

"What is it, Livie? What's the matter?" Clara asked, suddenly awake.

Olivia's breath caught in her throat. She forced a smile. "Matter? Nothing's the matter. Why?"

"I heard you gasp," her sister replied.

"You must have been dreaming." Olivia patted her older sister's hand nervously. "Go back to sleep."

"I wasn't really sleeping . . . just lightly drowsing. I was sure . . ." She shrugged and grinned at the slim young girl beside her. "Well, perhaps I *was* asleep. Your London hours are too much for me. At Langley Park I would have been abed these past four hours."

"You really *have* become a country mouse, haven't you?" Olivia remarked absently, glancing back through the oval window behind them and noting that the scene she'd just witnessed was still visible, the embrace still revoltingly in progress. "I suspect you no longer care for London at all."

"That doesn't mean I don't care for *you*, love. I've truly enjoyed this little visit with you and the family, you know that. But—"

"But you'd rather be back in the country with your babies."

Clara gave her sister a mock-shamefaced smile. "Yes, I

would. *Mea culpa*. Guilty as charged. I admit it frankly—I hate being away from them."

"But *why*, my dear?" Olivia asked, forcing herself to keep her eyes from the rear window of the coach. "You know they're being adequately cared for. You couldn't *have* a better house-keeper than Mrs. Joliffe, and there's Fincher and Miss Elspeth and—"

"Yes, I know. The staff is completely reliable. Nevertheless, the children need their mother at their ages. Perry, even though he's almost seven, is too young to take a scolding without his feelings being hurt. Shy though he is, he does seem to fall into mischief. He's apt to be scolded more than you'd expect, and, somehow, I don't like anyone to scold him but me. And little Amy is only three and hardly understands why her mother has deserted her."

Olivia threw her sister a scornful glance. "*Deserted*, indeed! You've sent them trinkets every day since you've come! Besides, isn't it about time you began thinking of yourself? You haven't come down for a visit since before Amy was born. Four years! Haven't you missed it at all—the bustle, the excitement, the activity of London life—the opera, the political dinners, the witty conversation, the shops and bazaars, the cultural variety, the intellectual stimulation—?"

"No, not a bit," her sister admitted without a touch of shame. "I miss *you*, of course, and Charles and Jamie. But as for the rest, I find 'cultural variety and intellectual stimulation' a bit of a bore. I know that *you*, you little bluestocking, find these things exciting, but I'm too involved in motherhood, I'm afraid."

Olivia frowned. "Yes, you've always been more motherly than anything else," she said with a touch of disapproval. Sophocles had once said that "children are the anchors of a mother's life," and he was quite right. Children weighed a woman down. She loved her sister devotedly, but she strongly objected to Clara's absorption in domestic life to the exclusion of all other matters.

Of course, she had no right in the world to be critical of her sister. Clara was twelve years her senior, and when their mother had died (Olivia was only two at the time), Clara had stepped into her mother's place with remarkable serenity. She'd raised her twelve-year old brother, Charles, her six-year-old brother, James, and her baby sister, Olivia, with a tenderness and wisdom remarkable in a fourteen-year-old girl. Their father, a famous scholar, revered and respected for his brilliant Greek translations, had not been brilliant in domestic matters. He had been of no help at all to Clara during those years. Sir Octavius Matthews had always preferred the solitude of his study to the companionship of his family. Clara had had to deal with the management of the household and the rearing of her sister and brothers entirely on her own. Olivia should feel nothing but gratitude that her sister had always been the maternal type.

A sound of a muffled curse from the coachman interrupted her thoughts, and the carriage came to an abrupt halt. Wollens, the coachman, slid open the little window through which he communicated with his passengers and stuck his head in. "Beggin' yer pardon, Miss Livie . . . yer ladyship. There seems to be a bit of 'n accident up ahead. Now, don't be alarmed. Both of ye just sit right there nice and snug while I 'op down to see what's afoot."

Olivia cast a worried look over her shoulder through the oval window, while her sister lowered the window at her side and peered out ahead of them. "I don't see a thing out there," Clara remarked.

But Olivia could still see Strickland. Although he and his *chère amie* were now at quite a distance down the street, she could dimly make them out. The woman was now standing apart from her paramour and, with his hands in hers, seemed to be trying to coax him back into the house. *Go in, blast you!* Olivia urged him in her thoughts. *Go in or go away! Do you want Clara to see you?* She slid over close to her sister. "Are you sure you can't see anything up ahead?"

"No, nothing. But here comes Wollens now."

The coachman informed them that a carriage had collided with a wagon in the fog and that the street was completely blocked. "But they've righted the wagon an' steadied the 'orses. They'll be out o' the way in a minute or two."

Olivia threw another quick glance over her shoulder, noting with irritation that the miscreant pair was still visible. Would Clara be able to detect the gentleman's identity if she turned around? Olivia rather doubted it, but she nevertheless turned hastily back to her sister, determined to keep her so closely engaged in conversation that Clara would not be at leisure to look behind her. "I don't wish to imply that there's anything wrong, exactly, with being the motherly type," she said, deftly picking up the thread of their conversation before the interruption of the coachman. "But one can carry domestication too far, you know."

Clara smiled at her indulgently. "Can one? And do I?"

Olivia blushed. She was an ungrateful wretch to criticize her sister's loving nature. Clara had been the best sister in the world, motherly at a time when Olivia had needed mothering. Clara hadn't tried to force Olivia into her own mold, either. When Olivia had shown, quite early, that she wanted to study Latin and mathematics with her brothers' tutor rather than music and embroidery with her governess, Clara had permitted her to sit in on Jamie's lessons. Clara had never tried to turn her sister into one of those simpering misses who know nothing but the latest fashions in hairstyles and the feminine tricks to lure gentlemen to their sides.

For ten years, Clara had unselfishly refused all the suitors for her hand. She'd repeatedly rejected matrimony in order to do her duty by her younger siblings. But eight years ago, when she'd fallen deeply in love with her Miles, Charles had insisted that she accept him. Charles had reached his majority by that time and felt completely capable of taking over the management of the family. James was already at Eton, and Olivia, although only twelve, was an intelligent and independent girl. So Clara had married and moved away to Langley Park, her husband's estate in Wiltshire.

But Olivia had not felt—nor did she feel now—any resentment toward her sister for marrying. It had really been all to the good. Clara had made for herself the kind of life for which she was most suited, while Olivia had been permitted to develop her mind and personality in her own way. It was a different way from her sister's. Olivia could read Latin and Greek, she had an interest in politics, in literature and in scientific developments, and she didn't waste her time with dressmakers, milliners, frivolous gossip and shallow flirtations. Clara might call her a bluestocking, but as far as Olivia was concerned, that was just what she wanted to be. Better a blue-stocking than a domesticated brood-mare.

Clara was quite aware of her sister's unspoken disapprobation, but she merely smiled lovingly and put her arm around the young girl's shoulders. "Don't look down your nose at me, love. When you have babies of your own, you'll understand."

Olivia's eyes flickered guiltily. "I wasn't looking down my nose at you, Clara, really. How could I? You've always been my closest and dearest friend. But I shall *never* understand you, you know, for I don't intend to *have* any babies. There are *other* things I want to do with my life."

Clara had heard that declaration before and had no intention of entering into a foolish debate on the matter. Olivia was too pretty and spirited a girl to be passed over in the Marriage Mart, and Clara was convinced that when a man of sufficient wit and charm came along, Olivia would change her tune. Until then, all argument was pointless. "Be that as it may, my love," she said placidly, "I hope you won't be put out with me if I leave for home tomorrow."

"Leave? *Already?* See here, Clara, you haven't been here a fortnight!"

"I know, dearest. But to the babies it must seem like a year."

Olivia had no answer. Nervously, she darted a quick look over her shoulder again. Strickland and his paramour were still there. With a frowning glance at her sister, she sat up straight, folded her hands in her lap and pursed her lips. "I don't suppose one could expect your children's so-consequential *father* to step in and care for them while you're here in London."

Clara's eyes clouded. "Miles is so very busy with his political activities at this season," she murmured apologetically. "You know he has to be here in London at this time."

"Yes, I know. And he's so busy that he hasn't bothered to see you more than twice since you've arrived," her sister answered, unable to keep the sharp edge from her voice.

Clara leaped to his defense. "Come now, Olivia, be fair. Miles knows I came to town to see my *family*, not to visit with *him*. I know you don't like Miles very much, but you mustn't find fault where none exists."

"If neglecting you and your children is not a fault, I don't know what is," Olivia responded sullenly.

Clara studied her sister with her ever-patient indulgence. "*I* don't think he neglects us, and if *I* have no complaints, I see no reason for *you* to provide me with any."

Olivia opened her mouth to retort, but she bit back the words before she could utter them. "I'm sorry, Clara. I didn't mean—"

"No, of course you didn't," Clara said with instant forgiveness, squeezing her sister's hand warmly.

"It's just . . . that I shall have had you with me for so short a time," Olivia apologized. "It's very disappointing."

"Yes, I know. But don't look so crestfallen. If you can tear yourself away from your cultural and intellectual pursuits long enough to pay *me* a visit, I shall make it up to you. Besides, Perry has been asking for his Aunt Livie, and Amy will forget you completely if you don't come to visit her soon again."

Olivia nodded, gave her sister a somewhat forced smile of acquiescence and looked away. Poor Clara! She was so serene in her contented acceptance of the conditions of her life that she seemed to Olivia to be almost bovine! Olivia put a fluttering hand to her forehead. It was unkind to think of her sister as cow-like, but what else was she to think when Clara was positively *eager* to spend her life buried away in Langley Park—a huge country manor house far away from civilization, with no companionship but two demanding children and a few aging servants—and never uttering a complaint while her supposedly-doting husband spent his days in London without her?

And what was worse, Clara considered herself the most fortunate of women! She truly believed that she was the beloved wife of the most wonderful man in the world—a man universally admired not only for his wealth and titles but for his striking appearance, his sharp wit and his gift for politics. Clara, poor thing, had not an inkling of a suspicion of what Olivia now knew to be true—that Clara's life with her husband was, at bottom, an utter sham.

Suddenly the carriage began to roll, and by the time Olivia felt brave enough to glance over her shoulder again she found, to her intense relief, that Strickland and his paramour were no longer visible. She leaned back against the cushion with a deep sigh. Thank goodness Clara had not turned round to discover for herself that her adored husband, the so-brilliant, so-striking, so-gifted Miles Strickland, the Earl of Langley, had been standing back there on the street, brazenly—and with disgusting fervor—embracing a tart!

chapter two

Olivia slept fitfully that night, troubled to the depths of her being by indecision. On the one hand, she felt disloyal to her sister by not revealing what she'd seen. On the other, she was revolted by the prospect of having to play the role of tale bearer—and of such an ugly, distressful sort of tale as that.

Besides, she knew herself well enough to understand that she was not at all comfortable in dealing with matters of the heart. She'd had no experience of love herself, and she knew nothing of married life, not even as an observer. She was vaguely aware that she'd been brought up in an abnormal household. She had no recollection of her mother, and she had difficulty imagining her father in the role of a loving husband, although she'd been told he'd been a devoted one. As a father, Sir Octavius Matthews was a failure, not so much from a lack of warmth as from a pervading absentmindedness and lack of interest. It was as if his Greek studies absorbed so much of his emotions that there was nothing left for his family.

It was not at all the case that Olivia felt neglected or unloved. Her sister had been a most affectionate mother-substitute, and her brother, Charles, a wise and fond surrogate father. Even Jamie, self-centered and hedonistic as he was, treated her with playful affection. Nevertheless, Olivia realized that she had never experienced the normal relationships which existed in a household presided over by a happily married couple who showered each other and their offspring with natural and loving attention.

Olivia had never felt sorry for herself and only rarely yearned for a more conventional existence. But she'd never missed having a real mother as much as she did this night. How comforting it would have been to be able to confide in a sensible, thoughtful, mature woman. But the Mama of her imagination was too vague and indistinct a person to offer advice, and Olivia got out of bed the next morning no more certain of a course of action than she'd been the night before.

The morning was cold and wet, but the weather had evidently not daunted Clara. From across the hall, Olivia could hear the telltale sounds of Clara's stirrings as she packed to leave. Olivia dressed quickly and started across the corridor to assist her, but some instinct kept her from knocking at the door. *Perhaps*, she thought as she turned away, *it would be best to avoid Clara until I've made up my mind about what to do.*

Seeking some sort of help or advice, she wandered down the stairs and into her father's study. Although it was not yet eight, he was already bent over the papers on his desk, hard at work on his translation of Thucydides' *Melian Dialogue*. She crept up behind him and planted a light kiss on the top of his head. "Will you come to breakfast with us, Papa?" she asked as he looked up at her, blinking distractedly. "Clara's leaving this morning."

Sir Octavius looked at his daughter through his spectacles, his eyes foggily revealing his struggle to concentrate on the Athenian envoys in the book before him rather than on this unwelcome interruption. "Is she leaving already?" he asked absently. "I thought she intended to remain for a few more days."

"She's been here over a week, you know," Olivia explained patiently.

"Has she?" He shook his head and lowered his eyes to the pages before him. "I don't know where the time goes."

Olivia persisted in her attempt to gain his attention. "Leave the Athenians for a few minutes, Papa. I want to talk to you."

"Yes, yes, but let me jot this down first. The Melians are saying, 'It is natural in our position to indulge in imaginings.' But 'imaginings' does not truly reflect the quality of the Greek. It should be more like 'phantasies,' I think. Look here, child...what do you think? Shall I use 'phantasies' instead?"

"I think 'imaginings' sounds perfectly clear. But if you are unsatisfied with it, why not try 'fancies'?"

"*Fancies?*" He gazed up at her with a smile she could almost have called affectionate. "That's very *good*! Very good indeed! *Fancies!*" He turned back to his paper and scribbled in the word rapidly. Then, as if his daughter were not there, he went right on reading.

Olivia determinedly perched on the desk in front of him. "Now that you've found your word, Papa, can you not talk to me?"

"Yes, of course, my dear," he said, not looking up. "What is it?"

"I was wondering, Papa, if you . . . that is . . . er . . . have you a liking for Strickland?"

"Strickland? *Clara's* Strickland?"

"Yes, Papa. Clara's Strickland."

"Well, of *course* I like him. Fine fellow, Miles. Very clever on the subject of tariffs and finance."

Olivia snorted impatiently. "I'm not speaking of his Tory politics, but of—"

"Of course," Sir Octavius mused, lifting his head and chewing the tip of his pen thoughtfully, "he's perhaps not expert in Greek philosophy, but if he gave it some real attention, I'm sure...but really, Olivia, must you sit just *there*? You're crushing my papers!"

"Sorry, Papa." She slipped off the desk and straightened the pile of closely written notes. "I wasn't speaking of his *mind*. I meant his *character*."

"Whose character?" her father muttered absently, having returned to his papers again.

"*Strickland's!* Your son-in-law's!" she said in complete annoyance.

"Oh, yes. Fine fellow. Already said so. Now here, in this next line, shall I say 'council' or 'conference'? *Council* connotes a meeting of a body of men who meet regularly—wouldn't you say?—while *conference* sounds like a more spontaneous assemblage. 'Conference,' therefore, seems closer to the facts, I think. Yes, 'conference' it shall be."

Olivia frowned irritably at his bent head. She should have

known better than to expect any help from him. Sir Octavius Matthews had a marvelous mind, but not for family matters. "But you *will* come to see her off, won't you, Papa?" she asked as she walked dolefully toward the door.

"Eh? See whom off?" he murmured.

"Oh, *really*, Papa! *Clara!* She's leaving right after breakfast."

"Well, Olivia, I'm at a crucial place just now." He didn't look up from the page before him. "Tell her goodbye for me. Love to the children . . . good trip and all that." And he waved her away.

She closed the study door behind her and sighed. Her father was a strange sort. He was not a bit gregarious—*living* people didn't seem to interest him. Only dead Greeks engaged his mind. Even at dinner, the only time of day he joined the family, he scarcely ever engaged in conversation; his mind was still occupied with the books that had engaged him during the day— the *Poetics*, or Plato's *Republic* or his favorite *History of the Peloponnesian War*. She was foolish to have expected to receive any assistance from him in dealing with *real* problems. If Thucydides hadn't recorded it, if Aristotle hadn't codified it, or if Plato hadn't ruminated on it, the problem had no reality for him.

She had to turn elsewhere for advice, but she was not sure where. The logical choice should be Charles. He was the most sensible, well-rounded member of the family, despite the fact that he was a thirty-year-old bachelor and so promising a scholar that it was expected he would some day surpass his famous father. But although his head was crammed with learning, *his* feet were planted firmly in reality. She should really talk to *him*. But something made her hesitate.

It was Charles' unfailing, uncompromising honesty that caused her to pause. What if she revealed the story of Strickland's infidelity to Charles, and then they decided *not* to tell Clara? Charles would not be able to hide the truth. He was so straightforward that whatever was on his mind would be reflected in his face. He would try to say nothing to his departing sister but a simple goodbye, but Clara would immediately sense that there was something wrong. Charles was as transparent as glass. Olivia could not afford to chance it. It would be better to speak to her brother James.

Dear, pleasure-loving Jamie! He was not the sort to whom one would ordinarily turn for advice. Although he was the complete antithesis of his father in that he was *all* gregariousness, he was the most superficial and selfish creature in the family. He was so completely occupied with his cronies and the relentless pursuit of pleasure that he came home only to sleep. He had realized early that he had little interest in the subjects that absorbed the rest of the family, and he'd left school as soon as he could. A substantial inheritance from his mother made it possible for him to live a life of dissipation: sporting and gaming with his friends. However, it occurred to Olivia that he might be just the one to help her now. Perhaps his dissipated life had given him the sophistication in worldly matters that Olivia now needed.

She hurried up the stairs to his bedroom and knocked at the door. Of course he didn't answer; he'd probably been up quite late the night before and was undoubtedly still deeply asleep. She pushed open the door and went in. The room was still dark, for the drapes were closely drawn against the light, but through the darkness came the sound of gentle snoring. She went to the bed and shook his shoulder firmly. "Jamie, wake up," she said loudly. "I must talk to you."

Jamie shuddered, turned his head toward her and opened one eye. "Go 'way," he muttered thickly.

"But I need your advice. Urgently. It's about Strickland."

"Don't care if it's 'bout the Prince Regent! Go 'way!"

"Oh, Jamie, don't be such an indolent slugabed. I *need* you!" And she ruthlessly tore the comforter from around him, exposing him to the cool air.

He shivered and groaned. "Give that back at once!" he demanded, huddling into a quivering ball. "I'm freezing!"

"I'll give it back to you if you sit up and talk to me," Olivia bargained, throwing open the heavy draperies and letting in a stream of bleak, grayish light.

Jamie groaned again, heaved himself into a sitting position and reached eagerly for his comforter. As soon as he'd pulled it about him, he cast a bleary eye at the window. "What an odious start for an odious day," he muttered. "By whose leave do you come barging into a fellow's bedroom?"

"By my own leave," his sister declared, perching on the bed. "I think I've stumbled upon a family crisis, and I have no one to turn to but you."

He raised a suspicious eyebrow. "Since when have I been considered useful in a family crisis?"

"Never, as far as I know. But this is as good a time to begin as any. Please, Jamie, don't be so sullen. I've never come to you this way before, have I?"

"No, you haven't. I must say *that* for you." He looked at her with a sudden frown. "What sort of scrape have you got yourself into, Livie?"

"Not I. It's Clara I'm worried about."

"*Clara?* I don't believe it! What's she done?"

"Nothing, you gudgeon. Clara would be the very *last* one of us to do anything amiss. It's *Strickland* who's put us in this coil."

"Strickland, eh? Now what on earth—?" He leaned toward his sister in sudden irritation. "Have you shaken me up like this just to tell me that he's submitted another of his damnable Tory proposals to the Lords?"

"Good heavens, no! I wouldn't wake you for something as commonplace as that! This is much more . . . more personal."

Jamie fell back against the pillow in surprise. "Personal? Now I *am* nonplussed. Speak up, girl. You have me quite agog."

"I wish you will take this a bit seriously, Jamie. It may affect Clara's entire future! I saw Strickland last night . . . on the street . . . with a . . . a . . . *fancy piece!*"

If Olivia expected her news to shock her brother, she was doomed to disappointment. His face remained impassive. "Well?" he asked, as if expecting more.

"What do you mean, well?" she demanded.

"Well, what *else?*"

"Good lord, isn't that *enough*? He was *kissing* her . . . right there on the street!"

Jamie shrugged. "That *was* a bit of bad manners, I suppose, but I hardly see the matter as a family crisis. Is *that* what you woke me up to tell me?"

Olivia gaped at her brother in surprise. "Of course it is! Don't you think it's *shocking*?"

"Not at all. *All* the men in London have fancy pieces."

"*Jamie!*" she cried, not believing.

"They *do!*" he insisted. "Perhaps not often, and some more often than others, but sooner or later all of them—"

"*Stop* it, Jamie!" Olivia put her hands to her ears in horror. "I think you're only saying these dreadful things to take a paltry revenge on me!"

He gave her a look of disgust. "Don't be such a little innocent. London is full of—as you call them—fancy pieces. Why would there be so many if men didn't patronize them?"

"B-But . . . *married* men . . . w-with little children . . . like Strickland?"

"Why not? Strickland is a prime candidate for a liaison. He's here in London, alone, for almost half the year. Where else is he to look for female companionship?"

"If he wants female companionship, he can jolly well go home to his wife!" Olivia snapped, her voice trembling.

"Well, don't fire up at *me*. *I* didn't have anything to do with it."

Olivia glared at him. "Well, whatever the *other* men of London choose to do is of no concern to me. But Lord Strickland is our sister's husband, and I'm at my wit's end as to what to do about it."

"*Do* about it? What *is* there to do about it?" Jamie asked flatly.

"Do you think I should tell her?"

"Tell *Clara*? Whatever for? Keep your nose out of it and your mouth shut. That's my advice." With that, he slid down under the cover, turned on his side and shut his eyes. "Now, I hope you'll take yourself off and let me sleep without further disturbance."

But Olivia hadn't moved. She sat staring abstractedly into the middle distance, her brow furrowed in puzzled anxiety. "Do you really think silence is best? That we should let our sister continue to play the fool, believing that her dear Miles is . . . above reproach?"

"Clara's no fool. She knows all about it," Jamie answered, his voice muffled by the pillows.

Olivia jumped to her feet and stared at the lump under the bedclothes. "*Knows* about it? She *couldn't*!"

"She would if she had any sense."

"Do you mean to say that she knows and meekly *accepts* it?" Olivia asked incredulously.

Jamie turned his head and opened his eyes with a patient sigh. "Yes, my little innocent. That's what, *any* sensible wife would do. And so will *you* when your time comes."

"Never!" she declared vehemently. "I would *never* permit myself to be... betrayed. I think all men are *dastardly*, and I shall never marry any of them!"

She stalked to the door in a fury, but before she grasped the doorknob a horrible thought occurred to her. Slowly she turned back to her brother. "Jamie, you don't mean to imply that *you* ...? No, I won't ask."

Jamie broke into a loud guffaw. "Do you want to know if *I* have a fancy piece?" he asked challengingly, lifting his head and grinning at her mockingly. "Well, now—".

"*No!* Don't tell me! I don't want to know... now or *ever*!" And she fled from the room, slamming the door behind her.

chapter three

Charles sat at the breakfast table with his two sisters, looking from one to the other with a brow wrinkled in puzzlement. Something was amiss, he knew, although not one word was said to indicate that anything at all was out of the way. Yes, it was quite true that Clara had decided to cut short her visit, but that decision did not surprise Charles; he'd suspected from the first that Clara wouldn't be able to stay away from her children for an entire fortnight. No, her *departure* couldn't be the problem. As a matter of fact, Clara looked completely serene and untroubled. It was *Olivia's* manner that had aroused his suspicions.

Like most men, Charles harbored the illusion that he was inscrutable. It would have irritated him beyond measure to know that his sisters could quite easily read his face. He would have been utterly dismayed if he'd realized that Olivia had refrained from seeking his advice merely because she'd feared that his thoughts (which were so clearly reflected in his expression) would reveal themselves to Clara.

If anyone had asked Charles, he would have said it was *Olivia* whose facial expressions were transparent. Her large, green-flecked brown eyes sent out distinct signals of light and shadow which revealed quite plainly to anyone who knew her just what she was thinking. In addition, her fair, almost translucent skin gave evidence of the slightest flush of emotion. Thus Charles, watching her from across the table, was very much aware that something was troubling her deeply.

Olivia, his "baby" sister, was Charles' pride and joy. He had taken a father's pleasure in her transformation from a chubby child to a lively, willowy, warm young woman—and a scholar's satisfaction in the development of her mind from a willful, precocious youngster's to a reasoning, free-thinking, well-read adult's. Their peculiar family situation had thrown the two of them together more than might have been the case in an ordinary brother-and-sister relationship, and they were in the habit of speaking to each other with frank and affectionate intimacy. If something was troubling her now, why hadn't she come to him?

It was obvious that she was disturbed about something. The color in her cheeks was high (an unmistakable sign of anger), her eyes were clouded (indicating confusion), her remarks abstracted (revealing that her mind was absorbed elsewhere) and her plate of eggs untouched (signifying that she was upset). But before Charles could discover any clue to the source of the trouble, Clara set down her teacup with an air of finality and rose to take her departure. Charles and Olivia immediately followed her.

Their exit from the breakfast room was a signal to the servants that the time of leave-taking had arrived. Immediately, a great bustle of activity commenced: the servants scurried about gathering up those bandboxes and packages that had not yet been loaded aboard the carriage; the outer door began to swing open and shut as the two footmen, the coachman and Clara's abigail rushed in and out, each one convinced that one of the others would be certain to leave something behind; and Clara turned from Olivia to Charles and back again, directing toward each of them a number of reminders, admonitions and appeals for an early visit to Langley Park. At last, the trio moved out the door and down the stone steps to the carriage.

They made an ill-assorted group as they stood at the bottom of the steps exchanging affectionate embraces in the wintry rain. A passing stranger would not have surmised that they were intimately related, so different did they appear in character and station. Clara, the eldest, looked every inch the wealthy country matron. She was dressed for travel, her motherly form well covered by a velvet pelisse and a large-brimmed bonnet which protected her from the elements as effectively as an umbrella. The bonnet also managed to emphasize the fact that she was the shortest in stature of the three. Charles looked tall only in comparison with his sisters. He stood only five-feet-seven in stockinged feet, but his slim figure and his hair (which was receding from his forehead in two points on either side of his head and was prematurely silvering at the temples) usually gave him a look of dignity and importance beyond his thirty years. Today, however, he hadn't bothered to put on a greatcoat or hat, so the shabbiness of his coat, the disarray that the wind and rain made of his hair and the hunch of his shoulders against the cold made him look more like an impoverished tutor than a gentleman of substance and respectability. Olivia, the youngest, was only a bit taller than her sister, but she would probably have been the one that a passing stranger would have noticed first. The elements had tousled her short, dark curls into wavy tendrils that blew about her face and whipped up the color in her cheeks to an even brighter red than had appeared at the table and, dressed as she was in only a morning robe, that imaginary stranger might very well have taken her for the very sort of woman who'd occupied her thoughts all morning—a beautiful courtesan.

Appearances notwithstanding, the three *were* related, and they faced each other fondly as they said the final goodbyes. "Bestow a kiss on the lazy Jamie for me, and say goodbye to Papa," Clara ordered as she was helped aboard the carriage. Then the coach set off down the drive and turned into the street. Clara waved at them lovingly all the while, and it was not until the carriage disappeared from view that Charles and Olivia turned to go inside.

They ran up the steps quickly and shut the door behind them, glad to take shelter at last from the chilling drizzle. Charles, noting with relief that the servants had all gone about their business, faced his sister with firm decision. "All right, now, Livie," he accosted her, putting his hands on his hips, "let's have it. What's troubling you?"

Olivia, who'd been about to make for the stairway (wishing for the opportunity to indulge in some solitary reflection in her bedroom), turned to her brother in surprise. "Whatever do you mean, Charles?"

"Something's been on your mind this morning. Now, don't

try to deny it, my dear. I can read it in your face. Are you going to tell me what it is, or do you intend to sentence me to spend the day inventing all sorts of imaginary and troublesome explanations which will leave me overwrought, distressed and too distracted to work?"

Olivia cast him a rueful glance. "No, of course I don't," she said, taking his arm and walking with him to the downstairs sitting room which he had long ago taken over as his private study. "I intended to tell you about it anyway, sooner or later."

The room was smaller than their father's study and not nearly as cheerful. Sir Octavius' study had been appropriately and lovingly decorated by his late wife. It was full of her bright touches—sheer draperies which let in the light, colorful floral paintings on the walls, floral chintz upholstery on the chairs, ample bookshelves, a wide fireplace framed with exquisite tiles from Holland and a goodly number of silver candelabra to brighten the work area. But the small sitting room which Charles had adopted for his own had not had the benefit of his mother's delicate touch. The panelled walls and narrow windows made the room gloomily dark, the wall decorations consisted of a pair of dingy portraits of once-famous racehorses, the inadequate bookshelves were crammed to overflowing, and the stacks of books and papers which could not be fitted into them were piled on the tables, the chairs, the windowsills and every other available surface, including the floor. In the midst of all this untidiness—so large that it dominated the room and singular in its meticulous neatness—stood Charles' desk. It was a source of constant amusement to Olivia, for the desk was an island of tranquility in a sea of chaos. Charles' explanation was simple: he could not write amid disorder. When his desk became crowded, he simply piled everything which was not in immediate use into one huge stack and placed the stack on the floor. When Olivia would point out to him that this method of organization could not continue to serve his purposes indefinitely, Charles would respond with a careless promise to "sort through everything one of these days."

Charles closed his door and picked his way through the disorder to the fireplace, where he rummaged through the items on the mantel for his pipe and tobacco. Olivia, meanwhile, brushed the raindrops from her shoulders, removed the books from the seat of the room's one upholstered armchair, placed them on the floor and sat down. Charles crossed to his desk and sat down behind it. After a moment of silence, during which he puffed at his pipe vehemently until he'd ignited the tobacco satisfactorily, he glanced across the room at his sister. She was sitting tensely in her chair, her eyes lowered to the fingers clenched in her lap and her lips pursed thoughtfully. She seemed, for the first time in her life, to be almost afraid to speak. "Well, aren't you going to say anything?" he prodded anxiously.

"I don't know how to:...I wonder..." She looked up at him with sudden purposefulness. "Jamie *can't* be right, can he?"

"Probably not. But, my dear, what are you talking about? Has Jamie done something foolish?"

"No, this has nothing to do with him. But he *did* say..." She shook her head in troubled doubtfulness.

"Well? *What* did he say? If that clunch has upset you with one of his tiresome pecadillos, I'll—"

"I told you this has nothing to do with Jamie. It's only that he told me . . . he said that . . . that all gentlemen have had, at some time or other, something to do with . . . er . . . ladies of the muslin company. Is that *true*, Charles?"

Charles couldn't believe he'd heard her properly. "What?" he asked, blinking at her stupidly. "Did you say...*muslin* company?"

"Yes. That's a proper expression, isn't it? For . . . er . . . opera dancers and doxies and that sort?"

Charles frowned and bit down hard on the stem of his pipe. "Why on *earth*," he demanded, "did he tell you a thing like that? What sort of subject is *that* to discuss with a delicately nurtured female?"

Olivia raised her brows in offended dignity. "Delicately nurtured indeed! Really, Charles, what nonsense! I was under the impression that we could talk about any subject in the world! Did you not always tell me that I might pursue any topic about which I had some curiosity? You never said anything about its suitability for females."

"Perhaps I didn't," Charles muttered, "but I...that is, I meant only *scholarly* subjects, of course. Any fool would know that such a...! Good lord, Livie, I didn't think you'd show an interest in a sordid subject of *that* sort."

"And I didn't think, Charles," Olivia retorted in irritation, "that you would turn out to be a *prig*. Of *course* I'm interested in that subject. *Anybody* would be. Aren't you?"

Charles glared at her, puffing furiously at his pipe. "Never mind about me! This is not a subject fit for a lady, no matter *what* I may have said before! And Jamie was completely buffleheaded to have discussed such a matter with you."

"He *didn't* discuss it with me. *I* discussed it with *him*."

"Don't quibble."

"It's not a quibble. *I'm* the one who broached the subject."

"You? But...why?" His brows came together in a worried frown. "Has Jamie gotten himself into some sort of fix with a...a...?"

"No. Not Jamie."

"Thank goodness for that," Charles sighed, leaning back in relief. "You mean you had merely a...*theoretical* discussion, is that it?"

"No, it wasn't," his sister declared bluntly. "But I *would* like to understand the theory before I tell you the substance. *Do* all gentlemen have fancy pieces in their care?"

Charles, nonplussed, puffed at his pipe in some confusion. He didn't know how or what to answer. This was not the sort of subject he felt comfortable discussing with his young sister. However, he had formed the habit of responding to her questions with candor and forthrightness, a habit which had worked out well in the past. Perhaps it would be best, he decided, to try to maintain that tradition. "I suppose not *all*," he answered with a shrug.

"Well, then, how many *do*? *Almost* all? Half? Two in ten?"

"Really, Livie, this is most indelicate! Besides, how can I know? I don't suppose anyone's ever studied the subject...or published data—"

"Can't you guess?" she persisted.

"No, I can't. It's not a subject on which I feel qualified even to theorize," he answered shortly. "Now, will you stop these silly questions and tell me the 'substance' of all this?"

"Oh, very well. But I'm beginning to realize that there are a great many very interesting matters about which I am sadly ignorant." She got up from the chair and went to the fireplace, pausing to stare into the flames before continuing. "I saw Strickland on the street last night... with a lightskirt. He was kissing her."

"Oh, I *see*." He gave his sister a penetrating glance. "You were, of course, quite horrified. And rightly so."

She lifted her gaze from the fire to his face. "Aren't *you* horrified? He is, as Shakespeare said, 'falser than vows made in wine.'" She studied her brother's eyes for a long moment. "No, you're *not* horrified! And neither was Jamie. Does that mean, Charles, that you men *condone* such behavior? Or that you *yourself*...?" She paused, unable to find the courage to pursue the thought.

"No, it does *not* mean any such thing!" he answered promptly, giving her a wry grin. "That's how I know that not *all* gentlemen so indulge themselves."

Olivia gave a small sigh of relief. "I'm glad, Charles. I *knew* you were too fine a person to... But then, isn't it shocking that Strickland has taken one?"

"Perhaps it is," Charles said thoughtfully, "but I wouldn't judge him too harshly if I were you, Livie. I live a rather monkish life, you know. But Strickland is right in the thick of society, facing all sorts of stimulation and temptation, while his wife is miles away in the country tending her babies. It's not very surprising, under the circumstances, that he should seek—"

"Not surprising for a man of his ilk, I suppose," Olivia cut in coldly, "but quite unforgivable all the same. Why, I would sooner find an excuse for *you*—or even *Jamie*—to take yourselves a *chère amie* than for Strickland! *He* has a *wife*!"

"No one is asking you to find excuses for him, my dear. It is, after all, none of your affair."

"Isn't it? What about Clara?" she demanded.

"What about her?"

"Shouldn't she be told?"

"*Told?*" Charles echoed in horror. "Whatever for?"

Olivia made an impatient little gesture with her hand. "I don't know. But I cannot abide the thought of her innocent adoration of that *rake*! He's making a complete fool of her!"

Charles fondled the bowl of his pipe as he studied his sister with concern. "I can quite understand how you feel, Livie, but you're fair and far off on this subject. No matter how attached you may feel toward your sister, her *marriage* is not your concern. It is a private matter between man and wife. You are too young and inexperienced to comprehend the complexities of such relationships—"

"Humbug!" his sister said cuttingly. "This is the first time, Charles, that I've ever heard you resort to an *ad hominem* argument of that sort! Too young to comprehend, am I? If you ask me, the truth of the matter is that you're too *cowardly* to wish to deal with this problem. These sordid personal matters *embarrass* you!"

"*Now* who's indulging in *ad hominem* arguments?" he promptly retorted. "Let us try to discuss this rationally, if you please. You are arguing that Clara should be told so that Strickland cannot make a fool of her, is that right?"

"Yes, I suppose you may phrase it so."

"Well, before *whom* is he making a fool of her?"

Olivia shrugged. "Before anyone who knows that he's involved with a doxy."

"And who knows it?"

"How can I say? Half of London, perhaps."

Charles shook his head scornfully. "Balderdash! We would certainly have heard some gossip if that were the case. I am convinced that Strickland is clever enough to manage his affairs with discretion."

Olivia glared at him. "But *we* know it!"

"Yes, but Strickland can scarcely make Clara a fool in *our* eyes, can he?"

"No, I suppose not," Olivia admitted, returning to her chair and slumping into it.

"Then your argument is overset," Charles concluded triumphantly.

"Not quite," Olivia persisted, sitting up and leaning forward in urgent concern. "*I* managed to discover the truth, didn't I? I, who don't go about in society a great deal. Then is it not logical to assume that some others may also have discovered it—and much more readily than I?"

"Yes, perhaps," her brother granted, "but until the matter is a subject of gossip, there is very little harm being done to

Clara. Does the possibility that one or two people may know the truth justify your going to your sister with a tale that is certain to give her pain?"

Olivia put her elbow on the arm of her chair and rested her chin in her hand. "No, of course not. You're quite right. I'm undoubtedly being excessively foolish about this."

Charles smiled at her fondly. "Not foolish, exactly. You're merely permitting your distaste for Strickland's behavior to affect your judgment."

"Distaste?" Olivia raised her eyebrows and slowly rose from the chair. "*Distaste?* That's much too mild a word, my dear Charles. Much too mild a word. What I feel for Miles Strickland is complete and utter disgust. No...more! An overwhelming *loathing*! Yes, a loathing . . . a revulsion so . . . so sickening that I shall probably not recover until I've had an opportunity to tell him *exactly* what I think of him!" Matching action to her words, she strode to the door, kicking aside whatever books and papers were stacked in her path.

"Livie!" Charles exclaimed, shocked. "You're behaving quite immoderately."

"Yes," she said, pausing at the door and looking back at him disdainfully. "I suppose I am."

"I'm sure I needn't caution you, my dear, against doing anything so foolish as speaking to Strickland about this," he admonished.

"No, you needn't. I wanted your advice about *Clara*. But as far as *Lord Strickland* is concerned, I'll follow my *own* counsels, thank you. So you may keep your cautions to yourself."

"Livie, you can't mean that you—?" He lifted himself from his chair, but the door slammed behind her just as he'd raised himself halfway between sitting and standing. He dropped back down into his chair again with a grunt. "No, she wouldn't . . . she *couldn't* do such a thing as that," he assured himself aloud, and he puffed at his pipe with deep, reassuring breaths. After all, he knew his sister. She was not the sort of girl to indulge in outrageous, headstrong, ill-conceived bouts of mischief. And that was just what a confrontation with Lord Strickland would be.

But he assured himself that Olivia was above such misconduct; she was too self-controlled, too sensible. Therefore, there was no need to follow her. He need do nothing but turn his attention to his work and put the entire matter of his sister's explosion of temper from his mind. It was nothing but a tempest in a teapot—that was all. If he knew his sister at all, she would have regained her equilibrium by dinnertime.

But Charles did not know his sister as well as he thought.

chapter four

Miles Strickland, the Earl of Langley, was attempting to shave. One would suppose that, having shaved himself since his youth (and that was a greater number of years ago than he would wish to count, his lordship having turned thirty-five just a month earlier), he would find no great difficulty in accomplishing so mundane a task. But with his valet hovering uselessly at his right elbow (overly eager to supply shaving soap or to swab his lordship's face with a towel at a moment's notice) and his friend, Arthur Tisswold, leaning over his left shoulder (busily arguing politics with Strickland's reflection in the shaving mirror) Strickland was finding it almost impossible to complete the chore. When he'd nicked his chin for the second time, he turned to Tisswold in annoyance. "How many times must I *reassure* you, Arthur? We are in no danger of losing the government to Grenville, to Grey or to any other Whig. So you may take yourself off with an untroubled mind and leave me to complete my shaving before I do my chin a serious injury."

"Don't see how you can be so certain," Sir Arthur insisted stubbornly, not budging an inch from his position—neither his political stance nor his stand just behind Strickland's left shoulder. "Now that Parliament has given final confirmation of the Regency, Prinny's bound to feel free to let in some of his old friends."

Strickland had been hearing the same argument repeated for over a year. In January of 1811, Parliament had passed the

Regency Bill, and since then the political "sages" had repeatedly predicted that Prinny would appoint some of his old Whig cronies to the cabinet, with Grenville, Grey, or his favorite, Sheridan, as Prime Minister. But here it was, more than a year later, and with Parliament's confirmation of the bill in the Prince's pocket for more than a month, and *still* the Tory, Spencer Perceval, remained as Prime Minister with his cabinet intact. The Whigs were growing angrier and more disappointed with each passing day as the Prince seemed to grow further and further away from his old Whig associates. Nevertheless, many of Strickland's Tory circle still trembled at the fearful anticipation of a change of government. Couldn't they see how the Prince had withdrawn from his Whiggish friends? Why, at this very moment, Prinny was probably closeted in his sitting room at Carleton House reading scriptures with Lord and Lady Hertford, the Toriest of them all. Of what were Tisswold and the rest of them so afraid?

But Arthur continued to voice his concern. "He's *bound* to feel more secure now that his appointment has been confirmed. A coalition cabinet is the very best we can hope for."

"Rubbish," Strickland said shortly, trying to concentrate on the dangerous cleft in his chin. "With Fox dead, whom can he choose? Certainly not Grey or the other Foxites—they've antagonized him past repair. And I've already explained about Grenville's stand on Catholic emancipation—Prinny would never accept that. So please, Arthur, go about your business and let me be."

Sir Arthur Tisswold, older than Strickland by at least a decade, studied the younger man with admiration. It was wonderful how shrewdly Miles was able to evaluate even the most complicated of political situations. He would have liked to pursue the subject, to get Miles' view of Grenville's position in greater detail, but it was obvious that his friend was growing impatient. Tisswold frowned at Miles' reflection in the mirror and passed a hand over his own chubby, smoothly shaven cheeks. "Don't see why you have to shave yourself in any case," he remarked peevishly. "There's your man standing right there at your side, ready and willing to do the job. Why don't you let *him* shave you, as any right-minded gentleman would do?"

The valet nodded vigorously. "That's what I've been tellin' his lordship these past twelve years, Sir Arthur. I've told him time and again, 'Why must you stand there leanin' down into the mirror,' I've said to him, 'when you can be sittin' down, all nice and easy, while I—'"

"Stubble it, Gaskin," Strickland said shortly. "You haven't been able to persuade me to change my habits in all these years, so don't think because you've found an ally in Sir Arthur here, that you'll change me now." He wiped the long razor blade carefully with a cloth, pushed it into the handle that doubled as a sheath, and handed it to Gaskin in exchange for the towel. "I've been shaving myself since I was a lad, and I don't intend—"

A discreet knock on the dressing-room door interrupted him. "Come in," he said in annoyance, patting his nicked chin carefully.

Walker, the butler who ran his establishment here in Mount Street, put his head in the door. "There's a lady downstairs to see ye, me lord," he said, a look of disapproval quite plain on his face.

"A lady?" his lordship asked, his eyebrows rising in surprise.

"Yes, sir. An *unescorted* lady."

Strickland frowned. No ladybird of his acquaintance would be so bold or so foolish as to call on him here. "Did she give a name?"

"Yes, me lord. Miss Matthews, she said."

"Matthews? *Olivia* Matthews?" Strickland's brows rose higher.

"She didn't offer 'er Christian name, me lord. Do ye wish me t' ask?"

"No, no. It must be she. I wonder what the chit—! Just tell her, Walker, that I'll be down directly."

The butler withdrew, the valet turned and busied himself with the cleaning up, and Arthur picked up his hat and stick with a grin. "Have you found yourself a *new* one, old fellow? I thought you'd taken *La Delicieuse Binard* under your protection."

"So I have. My caller must be my sister-in-law. I wonder what the blasted little bluestocking wants with me."

"A bluestocking, is she? You have my sympathies," Arthur remarked.

"Keep your sympathies for yourself, old fellow, for you'll have to meet her on your way out," Miles taunted.

"Eh? What's that you say?" Arthur's smile vanished instantly. "Don't wish to meet her at all! Never know what to *say* to those literary females. If you don't mind, Miles, old chap, I'll take my leave through the kitchen door. Can't abide ladies of excessive cultivation, y'know. Never could. If you ask me, ladies should never even be taught to *read*."

Strickland gave a snorting laugh. "A sentiment worthy of a true Tory mind. You're the archetype for the breed, Arthur— a veritable pattern-card!"

Arthur Tisswold ignored the touch of irony and bowed deeply. "I take that as a compliment, my lord, and I thank you for it. What better breed is there in all the world?"

"What indeed! Well, good day to you, Arthur. Gaskin will show you down the back stairs, if you're determined to retreat in this cowardly way from the attack of a mere slip of a girl. I'll see you tonight, at White's."

After the door had closed behind Sir Arthur and the valet, Miles' ironic smile faded. His brows drew together in a puzzled frown. Olivia Matthews was the last person in the world he would have expected to pay a call on him. In all the eight years of his marriage, she had never done so. In fact, they barely managed to be civil to one another. Miles had sensed from the first that the pedantic little chit disapproved of him. Whiggish and literary, she was an ardent reformer and had no patience with his Tory views. The fact that he was a force in the Lords and a man of considerable influence in governmental circles made no impression on the girl; she judged all Tories to be either self-serving knaves or thick-headed fools, and he didn't know—or care!—into which group she placed him.

He, for his part, disliked her every bit as much as she disliked him. He found her to be officious, smug, pretentious, crotchety, and so unconformable as to be positively eccentric. The girl had a rather pretty face (and a graceful, even admirable, figure under the puritanical clothes she chose to wear), but even a head of springy curls and a pair of fine, intelligent eyes did not make up for her sanctimonious manner and sharp tongue. He could understand why his wife was so attached to her (for Clara had been almost a mother to the girl), but he could not bring himself to show the slightest affection for his sister-in-law. He hoped that she would find a good, strong fellow to wed—one who would handle her with the proper firmness and beat her into submission. But such an eventuality was not at all likely. She would more readily marry a meek, scholarly, bespectacled weakling who would instantly submit to her overbearing and shrewish domination and find himself imprisoned in a life of henpecked misery.

What was even more likely, however, was that the girl would not marry at all. She'd been "out" for two seasons and had not deigned to accept any of the offers she'd received. The strange creature obviously preferred to remain single, to pursue the life of a literary eccentric, and to leave herself free of the encumbrances of wedlock so that she might pay long visits to her sister at Langley Park whenever the spirit moved her. He positively abhorred her visits to his country home. She had a way of staring at him disparagingly from across the room that he found quite disconcerting, a way of arguing politics at the dinner table with such passion that he found his appetite quite deserting him, and a way of suggesting changes in his manner of running his household that he found infuriatingly meddle-some. No sooner would she arrive at the Park than he would find an excuse to take off for London.

But never before had she sought him out here in his London house. Her brother James had occasionally dropped by to ask for a loan, and Charles (who was a rather good sort despite his Whiggish views) had visited once or twice to discuss governmental matters, but Olivia—what could *she* possibly want to see him about?

Good lord! Was it *Clara*? Had something happened to Clara? No, that was unlikely, for Clara had dropped him a note just yesterday, saying that she was returning to Langley. But...could she have had an accident on the way? No, he reasoned...if that had been the case, *he* would have been the one notified rather than the Matthewses.

However, the possibility made him uneasy, and he snatched up his coat. Running quickly from the room, he pulled it on as he clattered down the stairs. He found Olivia in the drawing room, standing before the window and gazing out on the gray, drizzle-shrouded street. "Has something happened to Clara?" he asked hastily.

She turned round and faced him with an expression of cool disdain. "My, my!" she drawled sarcastically. "Such sincere concern for your wife quite touches me. I would *almost* feel impelled to shed a few tears, except that I couldn't help but notice that you called at our house only twice during her entire visit."

Miles gritted his teeth. The girl was infallible in her ability to set him on edge. "From your tone of voice," he said coldly, "it is obvious that you have *not* come to bring me tragic tidings. In that case, we may as well be comfortable while you come to the point. Won't you, dear sister-in-law, take a seat?"

"No, thank you. I shall not be staying long."

"As to that, you may please yourself, ma'am. But *I* should like to sit down, you see, and since I cannot do so while you stand, I'd be quite obliged to you—"

"I have no wish to oblige you, sir," she said, nevertheless crossing the room to the sofa, "but I *shall* take a seat in order to avoid further discussion of this piddling subject." And she sat down stiffly at the edge of the sofa, as far from him as she could place herself.

With a smirk of satisfaction, Miles took the armchair opposite. "Now, Olivia, you may come to the point. To what do I owe the honor of this visit? It must be a matter of some urgency to have brought you here unescorted."

"My lack of escort has nothing whatever to do with the urgency of my visit. I *never* go about with an escort in the daytime."

"Really?" He looked at her with a pitying smile. "It is my understanding that *proper* young ladies are taught to refrain from going about unescorted at *any* time. Surely your abigail could serve—"

"I have no need, my lord, of instruction on ladylike behavior from *you*. I am quite well looked after by my family, and if *they* see nothing to disapprove of in my behavior, it is completely inappropriate for *you* to concern yourself with it."

"Very well, my dear. We shan't spend another moment

discussing your behavior. Can you tell me just what it is we *shall* discuss?"

"*Your* behavior, my lord," she said bluntly.

His lordship's right eyebrow shot up, giving his face an expression of icy disdain. "*My* behavior, ma'am?"

Meeting his eye, Olivia felt a twinge of misgiving. Strickland had a glinty expression which could freeze her to the marrow. His steely gray eyes, under their heavy black brows, gave the impression of being able to look right through her. His face was long, the cleft chin strong and his cheeks were etched with lines that deepened when he frowned. He had thick, unruly black hair which was shot with streaks of gray and which tumbled untidily over his forehead even when he was most carefully groomed (which at the moment he was not). His face, in repose, might be considered by some to be—as her sister always claimed—fatally attractive. A line of Shakespeare's flew into her head: "*Oh, what a goodly outside falsehood hath!*"

Yes, she supposed he was handsome in normal circumstances, but when he was angered, as now, Strickland's face had a decidedly menacing aspect. It was no wonder that, in a recent political cartoon, the artist had characterized him as a hawk sitting on the Prime Minister's shoulder and whispering into his ear. Since then, the *cognoscenti* had been calling him the *Tory Hawk*, and Olivia could now see that the appellation was perfectly fitting. She clenched her fingers in her lap and, forcing herself to keep her gaze steady, answered him bravely. "Yes, my lord. Your own reprehensible behavior."

Keeping his eyes fixed on her face, he leaned back in his chair and smiled sardonically. "If you are referring to the infrequency of my visits to Clara this past week, may I remind you of your own words a moment ago—if Clara sees 'nothing to disapprove of in my behavior, it is completely inappropriate for *you* to concern yourself with it.'"

Olivia flushed. "Your point, my lord, your point . . . even though it is not *that* behavior which brings me here."

"Oh?" He looked at her with a sudden air of interest. "My dear child, while I admit to being consumed with curiosity about just what it is I *have* done to occasion this unexpected visit, I should like to bring to your notice that my point applies equally to *any* misconduct of mine: it is completely inappropriate for you to concern yourself with it."

"Nevertheless," she persisted stubbornly, "I am convinced that it *is* my concern . . . in a way."

"Well, then, go on, if you must," he said with a shrug.

Olivia's fair complexion gave mute evidence of her discomfort—she flushed again. "I've given a great deal of thought to . . . just how I should say this, my lord . . . but in the end I decided that a simple and direct statement would be best," she said, valiantly trying to keep her eyes steadily on his.

"By all means," he nodded, his lips curling with a slight trace of amusement. "A direct statement is always better than roundaboutation."

"Well, then," she said firmly, taking a deep breath, "I saw you last night . . . from my carriage window. You were standing on the street, and you were . . . er . . . engaged in an intimate encounter with a . . . female . . ." Her voice petered out as she watched his expression change from amusement to stoniness.

There was a moment of icy silence, during which Olivia was sure that the beating of her heart could be heard all over the room. His steely eyes never left her face, but his face took on the menacing, hawkish look that had so frightened her before. "So," he said when the silence threatened to become unendurable, "you *saw* me. What do you expect me to say now? Did you think I would make a denial? I haven't the slightest intention of doing so."

"There would be little point in your doing so, my lord. I saw you quite plainly."

"Then what is it you hope to gain by telling me this?"

"The answer should be obvious. I hope to gain your promise to . . . to *stop*."

He leaned back in his chair and regarded her coldly, his nostrils flaring. "Do you realize, my dear, that you are indulging in *black-mail*?"

It was her turn to be surprised. "Black-mail? I don't know what you mean."

He sneered. "How innocent you look! Since you are doing the *deed*, you must be familiar with the word."

"No...I am not *at all* familiar with it," she said, non-plussed. "I have never heard it before."

"Black-mail, *Ma'mselle Naiveté*, is an act of extortion—the word comes from Scotland, I believe—in which the victim (in this case, I) is forced by the black-mailer (yes, *you*, my dear) to pay a price (usually quite high) in exchange for the black-mailer's promise of silence on a private matter which would cause the victim embarrassment or difficulty if the matter were publicly known."

Olivia stared at him openmouthed. "Why, that sounds ...horrible! Almost *criminal*!"

"Yes, does it not? Black-mail, my dear, is a loathsome practice, indulged in by the vilest of scurvy fellows who bleed their victims dry by preying on their most intimate secret lives. They dangle the promise of secrecy before their victims like a carrot on a stick, while pocketing the most extortionate sums—"

Olivia gasped as the import of his words sank in. Then she slowly rose from her seat, her eyes blazing in fury. "Are you suggesting that I...I have come here to extort *money* from you?"

"I said a *price*. The price need not be money. You *did* come to offer your silence, did you not?"

She stared down at him for a moment, but then dropped her eyes to the floor. "Well, I...I *was* going to promise not to tell Clara " she admitted, biting her underlip in embarrassment.

"And that silence was to be given in *exchange* for my acquiescence to your terms, am I not right?"

"Terms?"

"Yes. That I 'stop' my reprehensible behavior, wasn't that it?"

A wave of humiliation swept over her, and she sank down on her seat. "Yes!" she said in a horrified whisper. "That was my intention." She lowered her eyes in shame. "I suppose . . . that *does* make me a . . . a . . . ."

"A black-mailer." He smiled in wicked satisfaction. "Not much better than a common criminal."

But the smugness of his tone and the injustice of his words struck her like a sharp slap on the face. She lifted her eyes and faced him with renewed spirit. "I wouldn't say I am quite a criminal, you know. The price I asked is not intended for my own enrichment. And it is not very high, either."

"Not very high?" he asked incredulously. "My dear girl, it is *extortionate*!"

"Extortionate?" She gaped at him astounded. "I only asked that you give up your . . . liaison . . . and never again enter into such a situation."

"And you don't think *that* is extortionate? My dear little black-mailer, what you ask is a price far higher than mere money. You would extort from me my very liberty."

"Your *liberty*?"

"My right to live my life as I see fit."

She blinked in complete bafflement. "Are you saying that . . . that taking a mistress . . . or having an affair with an opera dancer . . . or whatever it *is* that you're doing . . . is your *right*?"

"I am merely pointing out to you that you've come here to bargain with me like the veriest blackguard . . . like the scurviest of black-mailers."

"But . . ." His accusation made her choke with sudden self-loathing. She *had* come to bargain with him—her silence for his acquiescence. It was undoubtedly an odious thing to do . . . to bargain with him by flaunting her knowledge of his secret immorality. Yet she had not done it to enrich herself. She had done it for the sake of her sister—his own *wife*! And she was asking for nothing more than his word . . . and the recovery of his own decency and moral rectitude. Why, the purpose was really for *his own good*! She looked up at him with imploring earnestness. "Is it black-mail just to expect you to be faithful to your own wife?"

"The conduct of my own life is my own business," he answered with icy deliberation, "and not the concern of anyone else . . . and least of all the concern of an interfering, prying, black-mailing sister-in-law."

His response so revolted her that the last of her feelings of self-disgust fell away. How had he managed to put *her* in the wrong when it was *he* whose behavior was so reprehensible? *Prying, black-mailing sister-in-law, indeed!* She jumped to her feet. "Oh, no!" she cried, her eyes flashing fire. "No, you won't put *me* in the wrong! I admit you're a cunning deceiver. Oh, yes, you are. A regular, scheming flat-catcher, as Jamie would say. And I almost fell into your trap! But I'm not such a flat as you think me. Perhaps I did—unwittingly—attempt what you call black-mail, but my intentions were only to protect my sister. You can't make *me* the criminal here. *I* am not the adulterer!"

He looked up at her, his eyes more menacing than ever, and he slowly got to his feet. "And I won't fall into *your* trap either, my dear," he said, his eyes narrowed. "My wife does not need your protection. Did you really believe your little black-mailing scheme would do any good? Did you think I would permit my conduct to be dictated by a priggish, smug, sanctimonious little bookworm who has more effrontery than sense? You may think again, ma'am."

Olivia whitened. "Are you saying that you intend to continue in your . . . libertinish ways?"

He gave her a contemptuous smile. "Exactly so."

"Even though I am aware of what you're doing?"

"Even so. And you may tell your tale to whomsoever you please."

"Even . . . ?" She gaped at him, appalled. "Even to . . . *Clara?*"

For the first time, his eyes wavered. But almost immediately, his expression hardened, and his steely gaze steadied itself on her face. "As to that, my girl, you may do whatever you wish." He turned his back on her and walked to the door. "I haven't the slightest interest in the activities of tale-bearers," he added, holding the door open for her.

"And *I* haven't the slightest interest in the activities of *libertines*," she flung at him, stung. She crossed the room to the door and faced him once more. "But I *do* care about my sister. And if I decide that it is in her best interest, I shall tell her *exactly* what I saw! Good day, my lord. You needn't bother to show me out. I can find my way."

He inclined his head in a mockery of a bow. She responded with a brief and insolent curtsey, flounced down the hall and slammed out of the front door. He watched her go, a sneer curling his lip. "Damned busybody!" he muttered as he turned and stomped up the stairs.

chapter five

Olivia did not tell her sister what she saw. Nor did she say a word to anyone about her disastrous interview with her brother-in-law. She kept her own counsel, turning the incident over and over in her mind. But the more she thought about it, the greater was her confusion. On the one hand, she was forced to agree with Strickland's assessment of her character; she *had* behaved like a meddler and a tale-bearer. She felt a great sense of shame whenever she thought of her impertinence in going to see him. On the other hand, *her* misconduct did not excuse *his*. He was playing her sister false, and she would have liked to see him suffer for it.

On the other hand, Jamie had said that all London gentlemen behaved in the same way. If that were true—if corruption was so widespread—then Strickland's crime must be judged less harshly; he was merely behaving like the rest of his kind.

On the other hand, it was hard for Olivia to believe that London society was so degraded. And even if it were, a man of character should be able to rise above the foibles of his peers. If Strickland could not behave in an honorable manner, despite the corrupt behavior surrounding him, he was not good enough for her sister.

On the other hand, her sister was convinced that Strickland was the best man in the world. Was it Olivia's place to set Clara straight—and ruin her happiness in the process?

On the other hand, she had used too many "hands" already. Her head was spinning with these circular arguments. She was passing beyond the bounds of logic and was fast approaching the area of unreason. What did she know, after all, about marital intimacy, about the love between man and woman, or about the mores of men in Strickland's circle? She was quite out of her depth in these matters. For the first time since her eighteenth birthday, she regretted not having permitted her family to make more of her come-out. Perhaps, if she'd agreed to let them hold a huge ball (as Clara had wished), she would have been brought to the attention of the *ton* and would have gone about more frequently in society. As it was, the family had held a small dinner party in her honor, she had been squired about for a while on the arms of a few innocuous young men, and the entire enterprise had led to nothing. It was no wonder that she was woefully ignorant on matters of love and intimate relations between the sexes. Therefore, she reasoned, her wisest course of action in regard to *Clara's* problem would be to forget what she'd seen and—as Voltaire might have put it— tend her own garden.

Her own garden, she realized, was empty of appropriate experience. Olivia had not, until now, felt impelled to form close ties with any young man outside the family. As she had explained to her sister so many times, marriage was of no interest to her. She'd been quite content to remain as she was, spending her days in studying the classics of literature and assisting her brother in his researches. But during her conversation with Charles on the matter of Strickland's infidelity, she'd begun to realize the extent of her shocking ignorance in matters of sexual behavior. She found herself curious—and curiously eager to learn a little more of the subject. As the philosopher Spinoza had written, *He who would distinguish the true from the false must have an adequate idea of what is true and false.* Yes, she very much wanted to learn. But to learn, she must enter the lists! She must participate in the hitherto-repulsive game of courtship. She must indulge in those social rituals which involve dalliance, flirtation and coquetry. If she truly intended to satisfy her curiosity on this subject, she must begin to experience these things herself. With a sigh of submission she went to Jamie and hinted that she would like to meet some of his friends.

Jamie was quite pleased at Olivia's apparent willingness to

move from Charles' sphere of influence to *his*, and he promptly arranged for her to join him and a few of his friends on an excursion to the theater at Covent Garden.

It proved to be a rather more enjoyable evening than she'd anticipated. Jamie had chosen his friend, Morley Crawford, to be her escort. He assured her in advance that The Honorable Mr. Crawford was a dashing young man, a great favorite with the ladies and "complete to a shade." He turned out to be a personable young fellow who, though not very tall, was well-built, dandyish in his dress and jovial and lively in demeanor. But he was annoyingly given to offering the ladies in his company excessive, even fulsome, compliments, and after he had told Olivia that her eyes were "speaking" and that she was the wittiest creature in the world (after she had merely remarked of the performance that the actors were not as stiff as their lines), she feared that his company would be very boring indeed. However, his sublime confidence in his own ability to charm her, his ready laugh and his unremitting good humor had their effect, and before she quite realized how he had done it, she found herself somewhat taken with him.

Mr. Crawford, on his part, felt himself challenged. She had shown evidence of a cool reserve that he felt impelled to penetrate. "Besides," he admitted to her brother, "she's a most unusual sort. She don't mince when she walks, she don't giggle and blush when you pay her compliments the way the other girls all do, and she says what she thinks straight out—quite like one of the fellows. And," he added with a hearty chuckle, "she's prettier than I expected, your little sister—she don't resemble *you* in the least. She's perhaps not quite an out-and-outer, but a very pretty little plum."

When challenged, Mr. Crawford was quick to act. The following week he called three times and succeeded in prevailing upon Olivia to ride with him in the park. This was followed by another series of morning calls, culminating with the proffering of a formal invitation to "Miss Olivia Matthews and Mr. James Matthews" to attend a ball being held by his mother in a fortnight's time.

Olivia, more in a spirit of curiosity than with any real enthusiasm (her mind more set on advancing her general education in love matters than in pursuing a specific flirtation), agreed to go. But when Jamie informed her that she would need to purchase a ball gown for the occasion, she balked. "I have no intention of doing any such thing," she declared firmly. "I dislike those foolish, frippery gowns with nothing on top. It would be the greatest waste of time, effort and money, for I would have no occasion to wear it ever again. No, Jamie. Please tell Mr. Crawford for me that I've changed my mind."

But Jamie refused. "It will do you no harm to learn how to comport yourself in a ballroom," he declared. "And it won't hurt you to dress, for once, like a modish miss instead of a frumpish dowd."

"I do *not* dress like a dowd!" she objected vehemently, looking down at the puce-colored jaconet she was wearing at the moment. "What is wrong with my appearance?"

"Everything!" he answered cruelly. "That dress you're wearing is dull in color, outmoded in style by years and years, and is too broad in the shoulders, besides being—"

"Never mind," she cut in, making a face at him. "I quite regret having asked. This dress is completely suitable for my purposes. I don't care to spend my days poring over the pages of *The Mirror of Fashion* or *La Belle Assemblee* just to familiarize myself with the latest designs. Nor do I wish to run up huge bills at some fashionable modiste's."

Her brother hooted. "That, my dear Livie is quite plain. One only needs to take a quick look at you to see that you do not patronize a fashionable modiste's!"

Miffed, she turned her back on him and stalked off. But later, she put her head into Charles' study door and asked if he agreed that she was a dowd.

"A *dowd*? Who said you *were*?" Charles asked, surprised.

"Jamie. He wants me to buy a ball gown so that I might attend Lady Crawford's *fête*."

"Well, why don't you?"

She sauntered in and perched on a corner of his desk. "Oh, it's too great a bother. There would be the expense . . . the search for a pleasing pattern . . . choosing the fabric . . . the fittings . . ."

Charles shrugged. "Well, please yourself, of course. These matters are quite out of my element. But as to the expense,

I would not let *that* be a consideration. Papa can afford it. We're very well to pass, you know."

"Are we?" she asked with sudden interest. "I've never thought much on that subject, although I've always taken for granted the fact that we had sufficient income for our needs."

"More than sufficient. Papa's income may not be remarkable by the standards of, say, someone like Strickland, but it is sizeable. And in addition, you know, you have a legacy from Mama that assures you a comfortable independency for the rest of your life. I daresay you may purchase gowns to your heart's content."

That night she studied herself in her dressing-table mirror with a frown of concentration, and the next day she asked Jamie to accompany her to the modiste's establishment. Since he was the only member of the family with any claim to knowledge of fashion, she needed his counsel. Flattered that there was *something* he could teach his sister, Jamie readily agreed to help. They spent an entire day together, during which he persuaded her to purchase not only a ball gown but a walking dress, a dinner gown, a morning dress, a riding costume, three pairs of shoes, a pair of long white evening gloves, and a Norwich silk shawl shimmering with silver threads. And as a final surprise, he stopped at a jeweler's establishment on the way home and bought her, with his very own funds, a pair of lovely pearl earrings.

Although the necessity of enduring several additional fittings was a nuisance, Olivia made no further complaint, for she had to admit (when she found herself greeting the arrival of each new parcel with eager excitement) that the results of these efforts were rather pleasing. On the night of the ball, she came downstairs in her new gown feeling quite foolishly nervous. The gown was not particularly daring by the current standards of fashion, but it was the most revealing creation *she* had ever before worn. It was made of Persian silk in the color of spring jonquils. It was cut low across the shoulders and bosom, the neckline trimmed with rows of tiny beads. The waist was high and gathered in the center, and the skirt fell away in soft folds to the floor. (She loved the sweep of the soft train behind her; it made her feel queenly as she descended the stairs.) She had put on the long white gloves and the pearl earrings, and she'd draped the silver shawl over her shoulders. Her dark curls had been brushed until they glowed, and the color of her cheeks was high, clearly revealing her inner excitement.

Charles and Jamie, waiting at the bottom of the stairs to get a glimpse of her, beamed. "Now, *that* is something I like!" Jamie said proudly.

Charles puffed at his pipe with brotherly satisfaction. "You look like . . . like . . ." he began, struggling for a simile.

Jamie glanced at him scornfully. "Searching for the name of the correct Grecian goddess, are you?"

Charles grinned. "For an appropriate quotation. The only thing that comes to my mind is Dryden, however, and it must be a paraphrase at that."

"Well, go ahead and paraphrase it," Jamie said impatiently. "We shall have to leave in a moment."

"Livie," Charles declaimed, lifting her hand to kiss, *"you look like another Helen who'll fire another Troy!"*

Olivia giggled. Helen was said to be as tall and fair as Olivia was small and dark. "What gammon!" she said, blushing. But she felt quite pleased with herself as she took Jamie's arm and went with him to the waiting carriage.

Morley Crawford greeted them at the doorway of the Crawford house in Upper Grosvenor Street and added to Olivia's self-satisfaction by revealing clearly that he was quite bowled over. "I *say!*" he exclaimed, gaping at her in awe. "The other fellows will climb all over me to claim a dance with you! You had better promise me *right now* that I may have the first country dance, the supper dance and a waltz!"

James warned her with a wink not to dance with her host more than twice and took himself off. Mr. Crawford pulled her arm through his and led her up the stairs to the ballroom, assuring her all the while that three dances with him would not constitute a *faux pas*. They finally compromised on two dances and his exclusive company for supper.

The ballroom was crowded beyond belief, for Lady Crawford was one of those hostesses who was convinced that a ball was not a success unless it was rated a "dreadful squeeze." There were dozens of young men present, most of whom took admiring note of Olivia's entrance. Her hand was sought for every dance, and as she passed from one young gallant to the next, she discovered that she was enjoying herself hugely. She found no partner whose individual qualities were at all remarkable, but the heady satisfaction of being the reigning belle of the evening was enough to send her spirits flying.

Only one small incident occurred to mar her pleasure. On her way down to supper on Mr. Crawford's arm, she was jostled by a gentleman in a bottle-green coat who was working his way up the crowded stairway. "I beg your pardon," the gentleman said, more by rote than with real regret. They were about to pass each other without further ado when he cast her a quick glance. His eyes lit up in appreciation for a fraction of a second, but in that instant, they recognized each other. It was Lord Strickland. As soon as he realized that the striking-looking young woman he'd jostled was his sister-in-law, his eyes grew icy and his expression hardened.

"Good evening, my lord," Olivia said, smiling at him with satirical politeness.

One eyebrow shot up as he looked her over with cool detachment, taking in every detail of her costume from the earrings to the little silver slippers on her feet. His eyes glinted sardonically, and she felt a blush rise up from her throat to her cheeks. "Good evening," he said with a curt bow. Then, without another word, he turned and went on his way up the stairs.

There was something so insolent in his behavior that she was left speechless. She continued to stare at his back until he turned on the landing and disappeared from her sight. Her cheeks burned with humiliation. How could he stare at her in that hideous, *measuring* way—and then not even take the trouble to *greet* her properly? She would have liked to slap his face!

"Who was *that*?" Mr. Crawford demanded with a growl. "How *dared* he look at you so! I'd like to call him out!"

Since Mr. Crawford had made no effort to defend her honor while Strickland was nearby, Olivia couldn't help but be amused at his belated and exaggerated gallantry. Her anger at Strickland dissipated at once, and she broke into a peal of laughter. "Call him *out*?" she asked, teasing. "For saying 'Good evening' to me?"

Crawford was not accustomed to being treated scornfully.

"Well, I . . . I mean, it was his . . . his *tone*—!" he said defensively.

Olivia instantly realized that she'd offended him. "A duel will not be at all necessary, Mr. Crawford," she said swiftly, trying to placate him. "The gentleman was only my brother-in-law, Lord Strickland."

He gaped. "Strickland? You don't mean . . . the famous Tory Hawk?"

"Yes, I believe he is sometimes known by that epithet."

"Good God! Is *he* your brother-in-law?" He looked at her with something very like awe.

"Yes, he's my sister Clara's husband," she said, turning to continue down the stairway, a wave of annoyance at his obvious veneration washing over her.

"You don't *say!*" he murmured admiringly, following her down. "Mama must be in transports. She hardly expected to nab so large a prize at her annual squeeze."

"*Is* he a prize?" Olivia asked, stopping and looking back at him in surprise.

"Oh, yes, indeed! Rarely accepts purely social invitations, they say. Likes political gatherings or card parties, not *this* sort of thing. But if he's your relation, Miss Matthews, why was he so rude to you?"

Olivia waved her hand dismissively. "Oh, we just don't get on. We haven't liked each other from the first. Don't trouble yourself over him, Mr. Crawford," she advised, and she quickly changed the subject.

But all through supper, over the lobster patties, the cheese buns, the French nougat, the little apple *soufflés* and the champagne, Olivia found herself dwelling on her brother-in-law's humiliating stare. What had his sardonic expression meant? It was as if he'd instantly concluded that her change of style in dress announced loudly that she'd placed herself on the Marriage Mart. Was he laughing at her? Was his insulting expression saying that she would always be a priggish bluestocking, no matter what she wore? If only she could *show* him . . . !

But show him *what*? What was it she would like to prove to him? She could find no answer, and, to pull her mind from this most unpleasant preoccupation, she focused her attention on her escort. When supper was over, she told Crawford that she'd had enough of the dancing and would rather sit down somewhere with him where they could chat in privacy.

Morley Crawford smiled a bit smugly at the suggestion, and he murmured something into her ear to the effect that he was delighted beyond words. He led her to the library, to a small sofa in a secluded corner of the room where a chance intruder would not be likely to notice them at once. He took a seat beside her and tentatively slid his arm along the back of the sofa behind her.

"I suppose, Mr. Crawford," Olivia remarked with her disconcerting directness, "that you've known a great many young women."

Mr. Crawford was both surprised and flattered. "Did your brother tell you that?"

"No, although he *did* describe you as 'dashing.' I assume that 'dashing' means that you've had . . . er . . . some experience with the ladies."

Crawford preened. "I daresay that I . . ." He shrugged with becoming modesty and looked down at his knees. "Shouldn't say this, I suppose, but I *am* reputed to have some . . . er . . . ability to make myself agreeable to the fair sex."

"I'm not at all surprised," Olivia said, looking him over with cool dispassion. "You have an obliging manner and a most pleasing appearance."

Both her words and her tone were sincere and honest, but Crawford found them somewhat discomposing. He'd never before met a girl so very frank and outspoken. "Thank you," he mumbled in growing perplexity. "You are . . . too kind."

"Have you often been alone with a young lady . . . just as we are now?" she asked, eyeing him speculatively.

"Well, I don't know if I'd say *often*," he ventured cautiously, wondering rather dazedly where this was leading, "but from time to time . . ."

"What did you talk about on those occasions?"

"*Talk* about? Why . . . nothing that signifies. Mere . . . commonplaces . . ."

"Such as . . . ?" she persisted.

He shrugged again. "Oh, you know. All the usual things. How amusing the party is . . ."

"How amusing the party is?" Olivia echoed interestedly. "I see. And...?"

He floundered about for an answer. "Oh...I might ask if they'd seen Kean as Richard Second."

"Ah, yes. And then...?"

"Then I might say...er...how charming they look..."

She cocked her head and grinned at him. "Were you going to say that to me?"

"Well, *yes*," he said, a bit on the defensive again. "And I would have meant it, too! You *do* look charming. Very lovely, in fact."

"And what do the other young women usually say to that?" she asked curiously.

"They generally say, 'Thank you, sir.'"

"Like this? Thank you, sir."

"Well, they flutter their eyes a bit when they say it."

Olivia tried again. "Thank you, sir," and she fluttered her lashes at him.

"That's the way," he said with an approving grin.

"And then what happens?" she pursued.

Mr. Crawford was warming to his role as teacher. "Then I usually say, 'You have lovely hands.'" He picked up one of her hands and held it in his.

Olivia stared at their joined hands for a moment and then broke into a laugh. "Oh, I see! How clever of you, Mr. Crawford. It's a *ruse*, isn't it?"

He dropped her hand at once and stared at her aghast. "A *ruse*?"

"To take the lady's hand. I think it's quite delightfully devious, Mr. Crawford. You needn't be embarrassed. Here, take it again and let's proceed."

He took her hand again with a cautious hesitancy. "Pr-Proceed?"

"Yes. What do you do next?"

"Well, I...I..." he mumbled, reddening.

"Please don't mind my curiosity, Mr. Crawford. I'm most truly interested. Just behave as you would do ordinarily."

"But...this is not quite ordinary, you see," he objected.

"No? Why not?"

"I...er...don't usually speak quite so...openly...about my intentions."

"No? Does speaking of these matters spoil things somehow?"

"Yes," he admitted. "The...*mood*, y'know."

"I'm sorry. I should have realized...I should have been warned by Shakespeare's Helena, for she says that we ladies *cannot fight for love as men may do; we should be woo'd, and were not made to woo*. But, Mr. Crawford, if I promise to refrain from my shocking bluntness, may we not proceed from this point in the usual way and restore the mood? Here you are, seated in this secluded spot with a lady, her hand tucked into yours. Now, then, what follows? Do you kiss her?"

He made a slight gurgling sound in his throat. "S-Sometimes..."

"Then go ahead, please," she said, lifting her face to his.

He blinked at her. "Do you *mean* it? *Now?*"

She nodded.

His eyes lit up. "Well, if you're *certain*..." He leaned toward her with dramatic deliberation, but, as their eyes met, he seemed to freeze.

"What is it?" she asked in surprise. "Is something amiss?"

"I...*can't*! Not while you're staring at me."

"Oh, I'm sorry. What shall I do?"

"I think you should shut your eyes."

"Really? Why?"

"Don't have the foggiest, but...most young ladies do."

"Very well. But *do* get on with it," she urged, shutting her eyes and lifting her face to him again. He leaned down and planted a gingerly kiss on her lips. When he'd finished, she opened her eyes and stared at him. "Is that *all*?"

Mr. Crawford's eyes were startled, and his expression revealed that he'd taken decided offense at her question. "*All?* What do you mean?"

Olivia dropped her eyes to her hands. "I think I expected something more . . . more . . ."

"More exciting?"

"Yes."

He frowned. "Well, I *warned* you that we were not proceeding in quite the ordinary way..."

"No, of course not," she said, patting his hand soothingly.

"And besides," he added, defensive once more, "a fellow doesn't ordinarily stop at *one*."

"Doesn't he? Do you mean you'd like to...do it again?"

He looked at her earnestly. "That is usually the procedure."

"Go ahead, then," she agreed, closing her eyes and leaning toward him.

He squared his shoulders, set his jaw and—much more boldly this time—slipped an arm around her and kissed her with fervor.

She neither resisted him nor responded, and poor Morley Crawford, who had in the past been either wildly resisted or warmly encouraged for this type of effort, didn't know what to make of this strange impassivity. He held her close until it seemed foolish to continue, and then he let her go. She opened her eyes and regarded him with a steady, contemplative gaze. "Well, thank you, Mr. Crawford," she said, nodding politely. "That was very...interesting." She got briskly to her feet and started toward the door.

A bit shaken, he jumped up and followed her hastily. *"Interesting?"* he croaked. "Never heard anyone describe a kiss as *interesting* before."

She looked back at him. "Oh, dear, I suppose I shouldn't have said that. I should have said 'exciting,' shouldn't I?"

"Well, *wasn't* it?"

She shook her head. "I'm afraid I...didn't find it so," she said gently.

His mouth drooped sulkily. "It was because of all that *talking* about it, I daresay. *Told* you that wasn't at all the thing."

"No, I suppose it wasn't."

"Of course not. Spoils the...mood, y'know."

"Yes, perhaps. but I think..."

"Yes?"

She walked slowly to the door. "I have the feeling that it was something *else* that was amiss. Something more ...fundamental."

"But...*what*?" he asked urgently, following her.

She paused, her brows knit thoughtfully. "I don't know," she said at last. "I only wish I did." With a deep sigh, she bid him goodnight and went to find her brother.

chapter six

Morley Crawford's self-esteem had suffered a blow, and, as a result, his attentions to Olivia ceased abruptly. Jamie, not knowing the details of the episode, blamed his sister for "cutting the poor fellow to the quick" and refused to provide her with another of his friends on whom to experiment. But fortunately for Olivia's researches into the nature of love and passion, a few of the gentlemen who'd danced with her the night of the ball were brave enough to call. They made an unpromising group, however, and Olivia, without feeling very sanguine about her choice, gave encouragement to only one—a rather plump and serious young baronet, Sir Walter Haldene. She chose him because he claimed to be a scholar, and she persuaded herself that the relationship had brighter prospects than the one with Morley Crawford because she and Haldene had more interests in common.

It didn't take long, however, for her to discover that Haldene's scholarship was more imaginary than real. His knowledge of Latin was shallow and of Greek nil; his views of politics were so naive as to be almost silly; his reading was narrowly parochial and his understanding superficial. Worse still, whenever they discussed a subject on which they disagreed, he would pontificate on his position with irritating doggedness. This combination of pedantry and stubbornness was not only inhibiting to true intellectual growth but stained the rest of his personality like a drop of ink in a saucer of milk.

As these qualities began to manifest themselves, Olivia tried to discourage Haldene's attentions. But Sir Walter persisted with the tenacity of a leech. So great was his self-esteem that he was incapable of taking the hints that she dropped with increasing frequency. Finally, on a rainy afternoon when he was paying his third call in as many days, Olivia took him into the sitting room, firmly urged him to take a seat on the sofa, sat down beside him and told him flatly—although with all the politeness she could summon—that she did not wish him to call again.

His reaction was totally unexpected and shocking: he threw his arms around her, crushed her to him and, muttering a number of incoherent endearments, pressed his lips to hers. His grip was like iron, and Olivia had to endure a seemingly interminable embrace before she was able to push him away long enough to catch her breath and scream.

After Charles had angrily ushered him from the premises, Olivia took refuge in her bedoom to regain her composure. She had been kissed for the second time, and she'd found the experience more repugnant than the first. If she were to draw conclusions from those two examples, she would have to say that lovemaking was a most unpleasant activity. But she knew from books and from the attitude of the world that this was far from the truth. Thus, she concluded, her experimentation had led her farther afield than she'd been before she started. The secrets of love and passion, she decided, were too complex to uncover by this sort of trial-and-error method. Until she could find a way to pursue the experiment in a less hazardous manner, she would put the whole matter aside.

She returned to her usual, secluded way of life, and, as the days and weeks passed, the importance of the subject seemed to diminish. Even her feelings of disgust toward her brother-in-law seemed to abate. By the time two months had passed, she began to believe that she could finally face her sister with sufficient equanimity to keep from blurting out Strickland's repulsive secret. With the coming of April—as spring made itself felt in the new green growth on every tree—she at last accepted her sister's often-repeated appeal to her to pay a visit to Langley Park. But before she left home, she made herself a stern promise to permit no word of Strickland's misconduct to pass her lips during her stay with her sister.

• • •

Whatever misgivings may have lingered in Olivia's mind as the carriage approached the Park were dissipated by the sight of the manor house through the carriage window as the equipage turned into the curved drive. No matter how many times she'd seen it previously, she still felt a thrill of pleasure at the sight of it. Langley Park was considered to be one of the most beautiful of country estates, and the reason was apparent as soon as one turned into the gate. The drive was lined with trees, but every few minutes one could catch glimpses of the house through gaps in the foliage. The three-story building was a large, square edifice with a slightly projecting entrance framed by high double columns. The unusually tall windows and the impressive columns that flanked the entrance made the manor appear lofty and majestic. Built in the Palladian style (a style Olivia usually felt was too massive and imperial for a country house), the building was so perfectly proportioned and so ingeniously scaled to suit the surroundings that it managed to combine both warmth and dignity in its lines. With respect to the house, at least, Olivia mused as the carriage drew near the entrance, her sister was a fortunate woman.

No sooner had the carriage drawn up to the door when her sister came out and flew down the stone steps to welcome her. Clara looked thinner than she'd appeared when Olivia had last seen her—so much so that Olivia felt a constriction of her heart at the first glimpse of her. But Clara enveloped her in so joyous an embrace that Olivia was given no suitable opportunity to remark on her sister's altered appearance. Then she was led into the huge entrance hall while Clara chattered on gaily about the exciting plans she'd made for her visitor's enjoyment during her stay, not giving Olivia a moment in which to catch her breath. Immediately upon crossing the threshold, Olivia was set upon by her nephew, who appeared out of nowhere and flung himself into her arms with a glad cry of "Aunt Livie! Aunt Livie! You've *come*!"

Miles Peregrine Strickland, the someday-to-be sixth Earl of Langley, known in the family as Perry, was an unusual seven-year-old. Although in appearance he somewhat resembled his father, his nature was distinctly his own. Shy and highly strung, he tended to shun strangers, to prefer indoor to outdoor amusements and to find more pleasure in the company of females of any age than of boys of his own. He lived a great deal in a world of his own imagination, which he permitted very few to share. His father was remote and awesome and often away from home. His mother was a sometime companion, but she was often too busy with household matters to listen to his chatter. Miss Elspeth, the governess, was a willing audience for his fancies, but she often was shocked by the gory nature of his stories and tried to divert his mind to more "wholesome" matters. His little sister was his favorite companion, for she listened with wide-eyed fascination for hours on end to his tales of bloody deeds in phantasmagorical places. But his Aunt Livie had a special place in his heart. She was the only one who not only *understood* his tales but entered into them with such enthusiasm that she added details of her own contriving which blended perfectly with his own. Her presence in the household promised happy hours of tale-spinning and joke-making that they two—and they only—could share.

"Have you met my first knight, Sir Budgidore?" he asked, pointing to the empty air beside him.

Olivia did not blink or hesitate a moment. She dropped a bow toward the space indicated. "How do you do, Sir Budgidore," she said, offering her hand for the imaginary knight's imaginary kiss.

Perry laughed delightedly. "He's blushing," he confided to his mother. "Sir Budgidore thinks Aunt Livie is very pretty."

At that moment, little Amy danced into the hallway, and, running right through Sir Budgidore, held up a pair of eager arms to her "Auntie Wivie." Only four, the entrancing little girl had a great deal of difficulty pronouncing her consonants, especially her "s" sounds which she made into "th," and her "r" and "l" sounds which sounded like "w"s. "We've been waiting aw *day!*" the child exclaimed, submitting contentedly to her aunt's embrace. Amy, with her light, silky hair and huge gray eyes was the embodiment of a ray of sunshine. Her disposition was like her mother's—all agreeable placidity. And since her appearance radiated such sweetness that no one in the household had the heart to refuse anything she asked, she never had to shake herself from her customary tranquility. She showered affection on her mother, her father and everyone else with equal warmth, but each member of the household had a particular and personal reason for favoring the child: Clara took keen delight in the similarity of their dispositions; Strickland marvelled at her ability to sit a horse (for even at the age of four she had already surpassed her brother in her ability to ride); Miss Elspeth found her ability to learn quite remarkable (for, like so many governesses, she was more apt to see talent in Amy's ready obedience than in Perry's strange unconventionality); and even Fincher, the staid and impassive butler, would relent and beam as he watched the tiny girl use her spoon at the tea-table with all the grace and finesse of a "real lady."

Olivia swept her sunny-spirited little niece into her arms and kissed her cheek. Then, tossing her over her shoulder, she reached down a hand to Perry. "Come up to the nursery, you two. We must become reacquainted. And tell Sir Budgidore to come, too." With Amy gurgling happily into her ear, Perry chattering away about how Sir Budgidore had come into his life, and Clara following contentedly behind, Olivia climbed the stairs to the third-floor nursery and spent a delightful afternoon in childish play. It was not until the housekeeper, Mrs. Joliffe, took the children away for their evening meal that the two sisters were finally alone.

They made their way down to the second floor toward their bedrooms to dress for dinner. While they strolled down the long hallway, Olivia took the opportunity to ask her sister if all was well with her.

"Why do you ask?" Clara countered, throwing her sister a quick look and then dropping her eyes.

"You are becoming quite thin," Olivia said, aware of a sudden sting of alarm.

"Yes, isn't it delightful? One or two more months of my diet and I shall be as slim in the waist as I was when Miles and I were married," Clara said, giving her sister a bright smile.

Olivia studied her sister sharply. "I don't see why you should find it necessary to reduce your waist. I find you quite satisfactory just as you are."

"But *you*, my love, are not a man," her sister said, slipping an affectionate arm around Olivia's slim waist.

"Are you starving yourself to please *Strickland*?" Olivia demanded in irritation.

"Now, who *else* would I wish to please?" Clara retorted promptly.

Olivia stopped in her tracks and faced her sister angrily. "Did he dare to call you *fat*?"

Clara laughed. "No, of course not." She continued down the hall, leaving her sister frowning after her. "It was entirely my own idea. But do come along, Livie. I've given you the corner room down at the end of the hall. It has a view of the garden, and you'll be able to gaze down on all the spring flowers. Here we are. Mrs. Joliffe has unpacked your things, so you won't have anything to do but change your dress. Do hurry. All this talk of dieting has made me feel completely famished."

Olivia could sense that her sister was being evasive, but she did not press her further. They had always respected each other's privacy. However, as the days went by, it became increasingly clear that Clara was ill. Sometimes Olivia noticed that she would suddenly stiffen, as if seized with pain. Some mornings she did not get out of bed, and Olivia would notice that Mrs. Joliffe ran in and out of her mistress's bedroom bearing teapots and medicines and looking long in the face. But if Olivia dropped in to see her sister as such times, Clara would sit up in bed with a smile and say, "It's only the headache, my love. I'll be up and about in an hour or two."

Olivia's days were spent with the children. In the mornings she often took Amy riding while Perry attended to his lessons. In the afternoons, she and Perry would immerse themselves in a game of pretense. He was King Othar with a round table of knights, among whom Sir Budgidore was the favorite. Olivia took the role of Gorgana, the wicked enchantress whose evil designs for the overthrow of King Othar's court Perry would ingeniously outwit. Sometimes, Clara would carry her embroidery frame up to the nursery and sit with her sewing as she smiled indulgently at their foolishness. And Amy would perch on her little chair and listen to their dramatics with the fascination of a completely uncritical, worshipful playgoer.

Clara's plans for traveling about to see the nearby sites of historical interest, for visiting neighbors and for holding ceremonial teas in her sister's honor were for the most part abandoned as the days took on a pleasantly lazy contentment. Olivia found the peace and tranquility of the days surprisingly to her liking. She did not miss the bustling stimulation of London nearly as much as she thought she would. She suddenly understood why her sister disliked being away from her home for long. There was a great deal to be said, she realized, for the joys of domestic life.

But then Lord Strickland unexpectedly arrived. Olivia could hear, even from the third-floor nursery where she was ensconced at the time of his arrival, the great bustle of servants, the shouts of the grooms, her sister's squeal of pleasure as his lordship's carriage drew up to the door. Tremors of excitement spread through the household from the kitchen to the stables as special menus were planned, formal uniforms were donned, horses were groomed, the second largest dining room opened, his lordship's suite of rooms aired, and the children washed and brushed and dressed to greet him. Olivia was convinced that there would not have been a greater fuss if *royalty* had descended on the house.

Even Clara's normal placidity was affected by her husband's arrival. She became more animated and energetic than Olivia had ever seen her, bustling about the house making certain that his lordship's breakfast was kept warm, that his shirts were immaculately laundered, that the children were ready for him whenever he asked to see them, and that his every wish was instantly and flawlessly granted. Her extraordinary efforts in his behalf, surprisingly, did not seem to tire her. Her eyes shone, her step was light, she dressed herself with more than her usual care, and, Olivia noted, she even rouged her cheeks—an artifice which Olivia had never before known her to use.

It was plain that Strickland was far from delighted to see his sister-in-law on the premises, and since Olivia was equally discomfitted by *his* presence, she went to her sister's bedroom and announced that she would return to London the next day.

"I won't hear of it," Clara said firmly, jumping up from

her dressing table. "You promised to give me a *month*, and you've been here less than a fortnight."

Olivia sighed. "But surely you don't want me *now*, with Strickland at home."

"Of *course* I do! It is not often that I have my *dearest* ones around me. Having you all here together is what I love above anything."

"Strickland would not agree with you," Olivia said frankly. "You *know* we don't get on at all well."

"Yes, I know. But I think it's foolish on both your parts to hold one another in dislike when you would each find much to admire in the other if only you would open your minds."

"Well, we won't, so there's little use in forcing us to live under the same roof. I really prefer to go, Clara."

Clara seemed to droop as she turned and walked back to her dressing table. "Please don't go," she said quietly. "I . . . I *need* you here."

"*Need* me? I don't understand."

Clara stared at the reflection of her sister in her mirror. "Please, Livie . . . I don't want to explain it all just now. But Miles will be staying for no longer than a week. That is not too much to endure, is it? And when he's gone . . . I shall tell you all."

"Tell me *what*, Clara?" Olivia asked. The alarm she'd felt when she'd first arrived returned in full measure. "Is something wrong?" She came up behind her sister and put a hand on her arm. "Are you ill?"

Clara patted her hand and turned to face her again. "Let's not talk about it now. Only promise me you'll stay."

There was nothing Olivia could do but agree. To please her sister, she asked no more questions and endeavored to put the problem out of her mind. Her sister evidently wanted to enjoy her family's proximity, and Olivia didn't wish to detract from her happiness. Whatever it was that troubled her could wait for another week.

For the next two days, Strickland treated his wife's guest with cold but meticulous politeness. He inquired about her health, asked if she found her room satisfactory and requested that she send his best wishes to her family when she wrote to them. Beyond that, they said little to each other but "good morning" and "good evening," and they took care to stay out of each other's way. The most unendurable times occurred during their dinners together. Clara tried valiantly to keep a stream of conversation flowing, but her husband's monosyllabic answers and her sister's lowered eyes and occasional sarcastic comments made her attempts pitiful failures. They all would then lapse into awkward silence and were glad to escape from the table as early as possible. Olivia always took herself off to bed soon after dinner, hoping that Clara and her husband would then be able to enjoy what was left of the evenings in their own company.

Three days after his lordship's arrival, Olivia returned from a walk through the gardens to discover Miss Elspeth crouched on a ledge behind the stairs leading to the nursery, weeping bitterly. "Good heavens, Miss Elspeth," she asked in consternation, "whatever is amiss?"

"Oh, M-Miss Olivia," the young woman sniffed, trying to control her sobs by dabbing at her cheeks with her soaking handkerchief, "I'm afraid I . . . I . . . shall be given my notice . . . although his lordship didn't actually *say* I shall be given the sack, but . . ."

"The sack? Why? What have you done?"

"His l-lordship s-says . . . I'm not fit to . . . instruct M-Master P-Perry . . ."

"Oh, dear!" Olivia sank down beside the distraught governess and put an arm around her shoulders. Elspeth Deering was a sweet-faced, soft-spoken, gentle young woman of twenty-six or -seven who, now that Olivia thought about it, was just the sort to drive her short-tempered brother-in-law to distraction. For Elspeth Deering could be described in one word—wispy. Her hair, her clothes, even her manner of speech seemed to trail off behind her in little, left-behind wisps. A strand of hair would always slip free of its pins and need tucking in, or her sash would come undone and trail along behind her. Even her sentences would peter out in a lost direction or a mire of contradiction.

Elspeth was the daughter of a now-deceased country vicar and had been quietly reared and properly educated, but her character had no force. Her knowledge of literature was only adequate, but her mastery of the pianoforte commendable and her talent for drawing almost remarkable. Clara was quite satisfied with her devotion to her charges, and the children, in their turn, were very fond of her. But Olivia had to admit that her background, while suitable to educate a girl, was inadequate for a boy who would be entering Eton in a few years. She studied the governess's bent head worriedly. Given Strickland's impatience with weakness and vacillation, and his desire to see his son properly prepared for his future schooling, it was not surprising that he'd wish to dispense with her services. She could quite understand Miss Elspeth's alarm. "But his lordship didn't actually *say* he would sack you, you say?"

"N-No, not in so many words... but he was highly d-displeased by the course of study Perry is c-currently embarked upon. No L-Latin, you know . . . and no his-history . . ."

"But Perry is only *seven*. Surely it's a bit early for Latin and history. Perhaps in two or three years, his lordship can hire a tutor to drill the boy in those subjects—"

"Yes, that's just what L-Lady Strickland t-told him. But he *insisted* . . ."

"Insisted that she find a tutor *now*?"

"Y-Yes! Oh, Miss Olivia, what am I to... I mean... where am I to turn, that is, if... ?" Her voice grew faint and trailed off in its usual wispy way.

Olivia thought for a moment and then got to her feet. "You are to wipe your eyes and go about your business. I don't think you'll be sacked at all. If I know anything of my sister, she intends to keep you on, tutor or not tutor. After all, there is still Amy to be educated. And *both* children still need you, even if Perry will be having lessons from a tutor as well. So stop reddening your pretty eyes."

The governess wiped her eyes with trembling fingers. Olivia noticed that the fingers were long and finely shaped and that her face had a sensitive delicacy. She was obviously a young woman of deep feelings, and Strickland was a *boor* to have handled her so thoughtlessly. For the thousandth time in three days she wondered why her sister had fallen in love with—and married—such a blackguard. She tucked up a fallen lock of Miss Elspeth's hair with sympathetic gentleness.

Elspeth looked at her gratefully. "Are you certain they will k-keep me on, Miss Olivia? After all, his lordship may not *wish* to have two of . . ."

"I am *fairly* certain that his lordship has no intention of giving you notice. But I shall speak to Lady Strickland on the matter at once. Promise me you'll try not to worry until I speak to you again."

Olivia found her sister in the front hallway, handing her shawl to Fincher as she smiled up at her husband lovingly. The pair had evidently just returned from a stroll. Clara's cheeks glowed from the touch of the spring breezes, and her eyes looked happier than they'd been since Olivia had arrived. Amazed at the effect love had upon her sister, Olivia realized once again how ignorant she was of the mysteries of marital affection. Strickland was away from home most of the time, was arrogant and demanding when he *was* at home, and yet a mere afternoon in his company had given his wife this inner glow! What *was* the magic that love produced that could so transform a woman?

She was about to steal away when Strickland saw her. Hastily excusing himself, he quickly vanished into the library. Clara came up to her sister with a smile. "You look as if you've a weighty problem on your mind," she said airily.

Olivia hesitated. She hated to dispel her sister's happy mood, but she'd given Miss Elspeth her word. "It's the governess, Clara. You're not going to give her the sack, are you?"

Clara's brows rose in surprise. "Give her the *sack*? Of course not! What gave you such a ridiculous idea? Why, Miss Elspeth is like one of the family."

Relieved, Olivia took her sister's arm and walked with her to the stairs. "But will you be hiring a tutor for Perry? I think he's too young to be forced into serious study, don't you?"

Clara sighed. "Yes, I think so, too. But Miles is quite adamant. He said that *he* had a tutor at the age of *six*. Besides, he says that Perry's head is too full of whimsicalities and nonsense. He's probably quite right about that."

"I don't know," Olivia demurred. "I remember having a head full of phantoms and fairy stories when I was his age. I don't see the harm . . ." But Perry was not *her* son, she realized. It was not her place to interfere, and she stopped herself abruptly. Clara could handle the problem of her son's education without her sister's help. But at least she could go back and tell Miss Elspeth that her position was secure.

As the afternoon wore on, however, Olivia became more and more angry with Strickland, chaffing at the arrogant power he wielded over the household. She spent a part of the afternoon with her nephew in the schoolroom and found the boy unwontedly subdued. He didn't want to play their usual game and asked her instead to read to him from a history book. "Father says I should banish Sir Budgidore," he said despondently. "He wants me to study about *real* people."

She began to read, but when she looked up she saw he wasn't listening. He was staring out of the window. Down below, he could see the stable yard where his father was returning from a ride with little Amy on the saddle before him. Perry's expression as he watched was strangely empty and bleak. Olivia, standing beside him, felt her fingers curl into claws. Perhaps Perry didn't want to play King Othar today, but *she* would have liked to play Gorgana, the evil enchantress. There was someone down below upon whose head she would have liked to call curses. Or, better still, she would have very much liked to claw Strickland's eyes out!

chapter seven

Olivia realized, as she descended the stairs that evening, that she was more than half-an-hour too early for dinner, but since she was already dressed, it made little sense to stay cooped up in her bedroom. Besides, she'd finished the book she'd been reading and intended to spend the time before dinner browsing about in the library. She was about to turn the knob of the library door when a strange male voice assailed her ears.

"Right in the lobby of the *Commons*, I tell you! Saw it with my own eyes!" the man was saying.

"*Shot?* Perceval *shot*?" came Strickland's voice. "That's the most unbelievable tale I've ever heard in my life. Who'd want to shoot *Perceval*?"

Olivia froze. Were they speaking of *Spencer* Percevel, the *Prime Minister*? Was he *dead*? Why, that would be . . . *assassination*! Never in British history had a Prime Minister been assassinated.

"Fellow by the name of Bellingham," the strange voice said.

"Bellingham? Who the devil's Bellingham? One of Grey's lackeys?"

"No, no. Not a Whig plot at all. The fellow Bellingham had been imprisoned by the Russians, and Leveson Gower, who'd been our representative there at the time, had done nothing for him. So when this Bellingham came home from abroad, bankrupt and mad as a marsh hare, he was looking for Gower's blood."

"Then why didn't he shoot *Gower*?" Strickland demanded furiously.

"Couldn't *find* him!"

"Couldn't—!" He sputtered in an angry rage that could be heard through the door. "Couldn't *find* him? So he chose the *P.M.* instead? That is the most insane set of circumstances I've ever heard recounted."

"Told you the man was unhinged."

"And Perceval's dead? You're *certain*? *Dead*?"

"As a doornail, old boy. As a proverbial doornail. That's why you must come back to London *at once*! The government is in chaos, the Whigs are pushing at Prinny already, and the party is completely divided on the matter of a successor. Can you leave tonight?"

"Quiet down for a moment, Arthur, and let me think. Perceval dead! An *assassination*! It's not something one can take in all at once."

There was a moment of silence, and Olivia could hear Strickland's tread as he crossed and crisscrossed the library floor. She couldn't tear herself away. Neither could she enter and interrupt a conversation as significant as this one. So she remained where she was and prayed that she would not be discovered.

"I'm afraid, Arthur," Strickland said after a long silence, "I can't go back with you tonight. You'll have dinner with us, of course, and then go back yourself. I'll follow as soon as I can."

"But, dammit, Miles, every moment may cost us a price. Grenville was going to see Prinny this very *afternoon*!"

"Don't panic, Arthur. The best Grenville will get will be a coalition, and even that is doubtful. Lady Hertford is a staunch Tory, bless her Evangelical little heart, and Prinny hangs on her every word. She'll see to it that Grenville's kept out of consideration."

"But we *need* you, Miles. You may be the very person the party can rally round!"

Olivia almost gasped aloud. Strickland for *Prime Minister*? The country would be *doomed*!

But his next words dispelled her fears. "I? Don't be a fool! I'd make the worst possible Prime Minister. You know how

I set up everyone's bristles as soon as I open my mouth. We need someone whose abilities are cohesive rather than divisive."

"But, Miles, you could learn—"

"No, Arthur. When you get back, try to rally them around Liverpool."

"*Liverpool?* Good God, man, why Liverpool?"

"He's not our greatest talent, perhaps, but Castlereagh is as abrasive as I am and would not find enough support. Nevertheless, Castlereagh himself will support Liverpool, and *that* support is what we need."

"Yes, I see your point. But why can't you come with me? You can maneuver matters so much better than I can."

"I shall not be more than a day behind you. I can't take such abrupt leave of my family at this time. My wife has not been well, you see . . . and there are some matters of estate business to which I must attend—"

There was a sound of footsteps on the stair, and Olivia drew away from the library door hastily. Walking to the foot of the stairs with elaborate nonchalance, she looked up to see her sister coming down. "Ah, *there* you are, Clara," she said innocently. "I just came down and . . . er . . . thought I heard voices in the library."

"Yes, love, you did," Clara informed her. "Miles has a visitor from London, I've been told. Come along and let's meet him."

She was about to tap on the door when the two men emerged. Strickland made his friend, Sir Arthur Tisswold, known to his wife and sister-in-law, and the group repaired to the drawing room to drink some wine before dinner. "Tell the ladies your news, Arthur," Strickland urged.

Tisswold, with appropriate dramatic embellishment, recounted the dreadful story of the Prime Minister's assassination. The shock so upset Clara that she had to be helped to a chair. As Tisswold fanned her face with a newspaper, Strickland made her drink a sip of brandy, and Clara quickly revived. Her collapse had one fortunate consequence: in the stir, no one noticed that the news of the assassination was not as great a shock to Olivia as it should have been.

When the shock waves receded and Clara had recovered

sufficiently to get to her feet, she led the way to the dining room, with Olivia following and the two gentlemen bringing up the rear. Just before the men entered, however, Arthur Tisswold pulled his friend aside. "Who's the pretty little chit?" he asked in a rumbling undertone. "That's not the little bluestocking who came calling at your quarters a few months ago, is it?"

Clara had sent Olivia to hurry the gentlemen in, and Olivia had been about to recross the threshold when she heard the tail end of Tisswold's remark and paused.

"Yes, I suppose so, since she's the only bluestocking with whom I'm acquainted," Strickland responded.

"Why didn't you *tell* me she was such a taking little puss? I wouldn't have had to leave by the back stairs if I'd known," Tisswold said with a chuckle.

Olivia, who suspected that Strickland's response would not be nearly so pleasant to overhear, interrupted them at that point to say that her ladyship was waiting. Sir Arthur gallantly offered her his arm, and they went in to dinner.

The subject of the assassination occupied their thoughts and their conversation all through dinner. After the ladies' curiosity about the details of the madman Bellingham's wild revenge on the English government had been sated, they turned their attention to the question of poor Perceval's successor. The two men explained the various choices available to the Regent in appointing a new Prime Minister, and Olivia took satisfaction in arguing heatedly in favor of the Whig, Lord Grenville, much to Strickland's irritation and Tisswold's amusement. When she thought about it later, Olivia had to admit to herself that, although the subject of the assassination was grisly and the prospect for the government grim, their dinner conversation that evening had been the most interesting she'd ever had in Strickland's company.

It was not until much later that night, after Tisswold had left for London and the household had retired, that Olivia began to recall the *other* events of the day. The political upheaval in London had made her forget all about poor Perry's misery. She felt a renewed bitterness toward her brother-in-law, whose arrogant decisions were made without the slightest challenge. It was fortunate for England that Strickland couldn't run the government in the same way he ran his household. He had enormous power in both places, but in the government he could only maneuver behind the scenes and was forced to face opposition and challenge everywhere he turned; whereas in his household, he had only to give his orders and he was obeyed without argument. What was even more irritating in *this* instance, however, was that he was just as likely to get what he wanted from the Prince Regent as he was to get his way at home. He would manage to maneuver the Regent into accepting Lord Liverpool as Prime Minister almost as easily as he would manage to force a tutor upon his helpless son. If the British government was not too great for Strickland to control, what hope was there for a little boy like Perry?

She found herself too disturbed to fall asleep. She tossed and turned for what seemed like hours. Finally, she sat up and lit a candle. She would have been soothed by reading, but she'd not managed to get into the library to select a new book. Feeling wide awake, and convinced that the entire household had by this time fallen asleep, she got out of bed with the intention of running down to the library to find a book. She slipped on a loose dressing gown over her nightgown and, in the dim light of the single candle and the dying fire, looked about for her slippers. But she could find only one of them, and, impatiently, she gave up the search. No one was likely to be about, she reasoned, and she recklessly decided to slip downstairs in her bare feet.

She flitted down the dimly lit hallway and stairs with quick, light steps, finding the corridors as deserted as she'd expected. But when she opened the library door and slipped inside, she discovered, to her embarrassment, that the room was occupied. Lord Strickland sat at the library table, a small oil lamp lighting a number of ledgers and papers spread out before him, a decanter of brandy at his elbow and a half-empty glass in his hand. "Oh!" she exclaimed, backing out of the door awkwardly. "I'm sorry. I didn't know—"

"Don't be an idiot, Olivia," Strickland snapped. "I won't bite you. If you want something, come in."

Not having any experience with men who imbibed deeply in spirits, she failed to recognize that he showed some symptoms (a ruddy color in his face and a certain glitter in his eyes) of slight inebriation. As for the rudeness of his manner, she simply attributed it to his natural temperament rather than the effects of the bottle. The sharpness of his tone had its usual effect on her. She put up her chin and entered defiantly. But he ignored the angry toss of her head and the rebellious set of her mouth. He merely took another swig of brandy from his glass. She was awkwardly aware of her dressing gown and bare feet. "I . . . couldn't sleep," she explained. "I came down for a book."

"Then go ahead and get it." He gestured with his glass in the direction of the bookshelves.

"I don't wish to disturb you, my lord," she said, hesitating.

"You don't disturb me," he answered, turning back to his papers, "so long as you go about your business and don't stand there behind me staring at the back of my head."

She drew herself up. "You *flatter* yourself, my lord. I don't stare at you at all!"

She crossed the room as purposefully as bare feet permitted and began to scan the shelves. But feeling his eyes on the back of *her* head, she hastily pulled out a book without really seeing the title and turned back toward the door to make a hasty exit. However, his lordship had other ideas. With a malicious smile, he put down his glass, got to his feet and barred her way. "Let's see what you have there," he said rudely, pulling the book from her grasp. He looked at the book's spine, his smile widening to a leer. *"A Practical Treatise Upon Christian Perfection?"* he read. "Why, my dear *girl*! What need have you for *this*? I was under the distinct impression that you'd already *achieved* perfection."

She reddened, but she met his leering eye with a rebellious look in her own and snatched the book back. "Yes, I have. Isn't it ironic, my lord, how this sort of work is always read by those who need it least?"

He guffawed. "And ignored by those—like me—who need it most, isn't that what you mean? *Touché*, dear sister-in-law, *touché*." He walked back to the table. "Well, go along, girl. Don't let me keep you from your so-stimulating reading." He picked up his brandy glass and held it out to her in a mocking salute. "I suppose I should bid you goodbye. I shall probably be gone by the time you rise in the morning."

"Really?" she murmured with a touch of malice. "What a pity! We shall all be devastated by despair."

He lifted his glass to his lips and eyed her over the rim. "Sharp-tongued little witch, aren't you?" He took a swig of brandy from his glass and wiped his mouth with the back of his hand with deliberate vulgarity. "It's a cruel blow to me, my dear, that you take delight in my departure," he sneered, "but I shall try to bear it bravely." Then, turning away, he added drily, half to himself, "There'll be wailing enough from the rest of the household when I leave."

The arrogant conceit of that last remark made her furious. "Perhaps not as much as you'd like to believe," she retorted viciously.

"What?" An eyebrow rose sharply. "What do you mean?"

"Not everyone will be wailing, you know," she went on, unable to control her tongue. "Your *son* will not be sorry to see you go."

His eyes darkened, his jaw tensed, and she saw with cruel satisfaction that she'd made a hit. "Oh?" he asked, setting his glass down carefully. "Are you trying to suggest that there is some conflict between my son and me? I was not aware of it."

"No, I don't suppose you were," she taunted, turning to go.

"Just one moment, ma'am!" he commanded harshly, his voice stopping her in her tracks. "If you have something to say to the purpose, *say it*! I can't abide these womanish hints and innuendos."

"Very well, my lord, since you ask so *nicely*. You have, with your usual sensitivity and tact, managed to disparage the boy's studies, uproot his routine, destroy his imaginary playmate, darken his good spirits, and threaten to force upon him a tutor and a course of study which are completely unnecessary and for which he is completely unready. In short, you've made him utterly miserable!"

He stared at her. "What sort of jibberish is this? Uprooted his routine? Darkened his spirits? Made him miserable? Have you lost your mind?"

"No, I've neither lost my mind nor my heart, both of which faculties I find no evidence of *your* having used in dealing with your son."

Strickland clenched his teeth in fury. "By what *right*," he demanded, his eyes turning icy, "do *you* venture an opinion about my dealings with my son?"

"No right, I suppose. Except that I love the boy."

"What damnable presumption!" He fixed her with a look of frozen scorn. "And who are *you*, ma'am to wave your love for him in my face?"

"I'm his *aunt*!"

"And *I'm* his *father*!" His fury changed his icy glare to an angry, heated flash that seared her through. *"Love!"* he muttered mockingly, turning away in disdain. "You're merely using the word as an *exoneration*—a sentimental and mealy-mouthed excuse for interfering in matters that are not your concern!"

She felt herself waver against the force of his scorn. "Perhaps I *am* interfering where I shouldn't . . . but I've spent more time in Perry's company during these past few weeks than you've probably spent with him this past *year*! And therefore—"

"Confound you, woman, have done!" he burst out, wheeling around. "First you sermonize about my character as a *husband* and now as a *father*! Is there no *limit* to your effrontery?" He slammed his fist down on the table with such force that the glass toppled over, and the brandy seeped out on the papers and began slowly to drip down to the floor. "I don't need *you* to moralize about my conduct, ma'am! Do you hear me?"

"Yes, I do hear you," she answered, a sudden awareness that he might be somewhat foxed making her strangely calm. "And so, I imagine, do the servants. Lower your voice, my lord. And stand aside, if you please. Let me mop up that brandy before it ruins the table and stains the rug." She pushed him aside and, pulling a handkerchief from the bosom of her nightgown, began to wipe up the spill.

"Hang the table, and hang the rug!" He came up behind her and snatched the handkerchief from her hand, tossing the sopping square of lace-edged dimity across the room so precipitously that she gasped in surprise. Before she could recover, he seized a handful of her curls and, with cruel fingers, forced her head around so that she faced him. She gasped again, in shock and pain, finding herself staring up into his furiously

burning eyes. "I want no help or advice from you on any matter—is that clear?" he demanded, spitting out each word with devastating precision.

But she couldn't answer him. She could neither move nor speak. His fingers held her hair in so tight a grip that the pain seemed to pull tears from the corners of her eyes. His arm was pushed against her back, inexorably forcing her body to twist around and fall against him.

"Is that *clear*?" he asked through clenched teeth, his eyes hotly angry and his mouth hard.

She made a frightened sound in her throat—a pleading little moan that begged him to let her go.

But he ignored it. "I hope you fully understand this, ma'am. I shall not permit any more of your blasted, infernal meddling," he went on ferociously. "You are not to concern yourself with my life . . . or with the lives of the members of my family. Find yourself something else—something in your *own* life!—with which to concern yourself . . . instead of tampering with mine!" He glared down at her as if he would have liked to crush her in his hands. "Damnable spinsterish *busybody*!"

She stared up at him dumbfounded, noting the fiery eyes, the taut mouth, the angry muscle working in his jaw. She could no more tear her eyes from his face than her head from his grasp. Yet she was no longer aware of the pain of her hair being pulled. She could feel only a pulse beating wildly in her neck, and a constriction in her throat as if her breath had frozen within. "Let me go," she begged in a choked voice.

There was no sign that he'd heard her, although his eyes were fixed on her face with an almost unbearable intensity. His voice, harsh and threatening, lashed at her once more. "What you need," he growled, "is a man—a husband—who'd beat you daily! *Daily!* Who'd bend you over his arm, like this, and who'd handle you as a wench *should* be handled—like *this*!" She found herself being lifted forcibly from the floor until her face was level with his . . . and his lips were pressed hard against hers.

How long she lay in his embrace she couldn't tell. Time seemed to freeze as her blood seemed to freeze. She felt no pain—only the pressure of his chest against hers, his arm against her back, his fingers twisting her hair, and his mouth on hers. She felt neither anger nor disgust. Instead, she seemed to be living through some sort of cataclysmic experience—like a driving storm or a tidal wave—which, while it filled her with the terror of imminent destruction, offered her also a sense of being completely, totally, shockingly alive. And she thought, wildly, as one does in a storm when surrounded by lightning and with the boom of thunder in the ears, that she would come through it—*if* she came through it—somehow *enlarged*.

All at once, the fingers in her hair loosened, and he let her go. As soon as her bare feet touched the floor, she fell back against the table, shuddering, stunned, and waiting for her whirling brain to steady itself. He was staring at her with eyes as dazed and shocked as hers. Then, muttering a curse under his breath, he swung himself around, turning his back on her. "Let that be a warning to you, girl," he said hoarsely. "Stay away from me!"

"*W-Warning?*" she echoed stupidly, still shaken.

"Stay out of my affairs!"

She stared at his back while, all unaware, she rubbed the back of her hand over her mouth which seemed suddenly to have been spread with a burning and deadly poison. "Good *God*," she thought in horror, "this is my *sister's husband*!" An overwhelming feeling of revulsion, which had somehow been kept at bay since the first moment he'd taken hold of her, came sweeping over her. "You . . . *blackguard*!" she whispered, appalled.

He turned to face her, lifting his hand in a gesture she couldn't read. He seemed about to say something, but changed his mind and walked unsteadily to the table, where he righted the glass, picked up the brandy decanter and poured out a generous drink. Leaning on the table with one hand, he lifted the glass with the other—unable to hide a slight tremor as he did so—and drank the brandy down in one gulp. "Go to bed," he said quietly, not looking at her.

Without another word, she turned and ran to the door, her feelings churning inside her in chaotic confusion. Nevertheless, she was sharply aware that his eyes were on her. At the door, she turned and faced him again. "You *are* a blackguard," she repeated in the same quietly horrified voice. "A decadent, villainous, devilish *monster*!"

Then she walked out, closing the door silently behind her. Standing alone in the hallway, she began to tremble from head to toe. There was no question in her mind that the words she'd just said to him were completely justified. He *was* a monster. Then why, she wondered, did she, herself, feel so dreadfully, frighteningly, sickeningly guilty?

chapter eight

Mrs. Joliffe tapped at Miss Olivia's bedroom door and, hearing a muffled "Come in" from within, entered briskly, threw open the draperies and said cheerfully, "Good mornin', Miss."

The brilliance of the springtime sunshine that burst into the room and spilled across her pillows made Olivia wince. She sat up with a groan and shaded her eyes. "Is it very late, Mrs. Joliffe?" she mumbled sleepily.

"Almost ten, Miss Olivia," the housekeeper answered with a touch of reproof.

"*Ten?* It *couldn't* be!" Olivia squinted at the housekeeper in disbelief.

Mrs. Joliffe smiled indulgently. "Everyone's breakfasted but you, Miss. Not that I'm complainin', mind. It won't be a bit o' trouble fer Cook to fix you some eggs and a nice pot o' tea. I wouldn't have waked you at all, except that it's been more'n two hours since his lordship left fer London—"

"His lordship's . . . gone?" Olivia felt a flush rise up her neck as the memory of the occurrences of the night before flooded into her consciousness.

"Afore eight this mornin'," Mrs. Joliffe said. "What with all that terrible business in London, he *had* t' go, y'see. *Terrible* business, that, wasn't it? An *assass-ination*! Never heard the like in all my days! But his lordship gave me this fer you afore he departed, an' I didn't know but what it might be important.

I already waited more 'n two hours, and so I tho't I better wake you." She held out a note.

Olivia felt herself grow pale. She took the note from Mrs. Joliffe and stared at it apprehensively. Most of her encounters with Strickland of late had been more than a little upsetting. What had the man in store for her *now*?

As Olivia peered worriedly at her name scrawled in a slanting hand across the envelope, Mrs. Joliffe remembered something else. "Oh, aye, I almost forgot. Here's your handkerchief, Miss." She put her hand into her apron pocket and pulled out the freshly laundered square of cloth and lace.

The bewildered girl gaped at her. "My *handkerchief*?"

"Aye. Gaskin, his lordship's man, did it up for you this mornin'. I *told* him I'd do it with the reg'lar washin', but he said it was Lord Strickland's orders that he should do it at once."

Olivia took it dazedly. "But, why?"

Mrs. Joliffe shrugged and went to the door. "Couldn't say, Miss Olivia. The ways o' gentleman ain't never been clear to me. Never been clear to me at all. Now, if you won't be needin' me, Miss, I'll be off to her ladyship."

Still shaking her head over the strange ways of gentlemen, the housekeeper left the room. Olivia studied the handkerchief for a moment, thinking that the ways of gentlemen were strange to her, too—and then she put it aside. What an unfathomable person her brother-in-law was, to be sure. She turned her attention back to the note. Why had Strickland written to her? The letter must surely concern the scene they'd played the night before, but what could he wish to say about an incident which was best forgotten? Did the note have something to do with Perry? Would his lordship be so cruel as to order her to stay away from the boy? Or . . . had he written to her about . . . Something Else.

It was the Something Else which had kept her awake half the night, that had caused her to sleep in nightmarish fitfulness for a meagre few hours and that had made her awaken in sluggish thick-headedness, miserable and crushed with the weight of a barely explainable guilt. The Something Else was the most troublesome part of the entire occurrence in the library the night before. That Something Else was *not* the fact that her relationship with her sister's husband had gone from bad to worse (although she couldn't deny that the relationship was a problem); and it was *not* the battle that had been waged over differing viewpoints concerning Perry's happiness and best interests (although this was surely the most serious situation to have come up between Strickland and herself). No, the Something Else was a completely personal and probably trivial matter that she was ashamed even to *think* about: it was the fact that Strickland's kiss had upset her. The kiss had been the third she'd experienced, and it had overturned all her beliefs about love and passion—all the admittedly inconclusive theories she'd so carefully managed to accumulate.

The first kiss had been dull, the second mildly revolting... but *this* one had been nothing short of shattering. Were the sensations she'd felt during this third experience *typical* of the feelings which kisses inspire? Is *that* what kisses were *supposed* to do?

She rather doubted it. The experience had been too frighteningly intense. Nevertheless, there had been something profoundly exciting about it, and she'd realized at once that it was an experience she would want to seek again—a realization that had filled her with guilt. There was something decidedly improper about having been so stirred up by one's own *brother-in-law*.

Nevertheless, the fact remained that only Strickland, of the three men who'd kissed her, had been able to stir her emotions so thrillingly—and by performing a physical act which had been executed in more or less the same way in all three cases. They had all pressed their lips to hers. Why was her reaction to the third instance so remarkably different from the other two?

Olivia was not so stupid as to ignore the fact that her feelings for the gentlemen involved had differed widely *even before the act of kissing*. She had therefore theorized that those preliminary feelings had adversely affected her emotional response to the kisses themselves. She had concluded that one reacted to a kiss in the same general way that one reacted to the man who performed the kissing. She'd been indifferent to Morley Crawford as a man, and her response to his kiss had been one of indifference; she'd been slightly revolted by Sir Walter

Haldene, and her emotions during his embrace had reflected that.

But she *hated and despised* Strickland, yet the feelings she'd experienced when *he'd* kissed her were completely unrelated to her feelings for the man himself. How could *that* be explained? And what good were her theories now?

It was extremely puzzling. Was there something in Strickland's wide and libertinish experience as a lover that made him more expert—and thus more effective—in kissing women? Would she have felt the same if *another* libertine had embraced her? Did *Clara* feel what she'd felt when Strickland embraced *her*? (Good heavens, if she *did*, it was *no wonder* she'd married him!)

But all the theorizing, all the worrying, all the cogitation during the sleepless hours of the night had provided no answers; they'd simply multiplied the number of questions. At last she'd given up and, still wrapped in a most distressful guilt, had fallen heavily asleep, beset by dark, fearsome, half-remembered dreams of struggling to keep from drowning in a churning sea while a creature of unrecognizable visage clamped strong arms about her in an endeavor either to pull her out or to drag her under.

Now it was morning, and here she sat bathed in the incongruous brilliance of the sunlight which could not dispel the dark shadows in her mind, all the while holding his note in her hand and feeling too cowardly to tear it open.

But eventually curiosity overcame timidity, and she opened the envelope. The crested notepaper within was covered with a sharply angular, almost illegible, slanted scrawl which somehow brought Strickland's face very forcibly to mind. The note began simply with the word *Olivia*—no other words of salutation had been added. He then went on: *Lady Strickland will not permit me to leave the premises until I have penned, in her words, "a proper apology" for having quarreled with you last night. Here, then, is that apology, although probably far from "proper." Apologizing is something I have never learned to do with good grace. I do admit, however, to behavior that was less than gentlemanly. My recollection of the occurrence is somewhat hazy, but if I manhandled you in any way, it was*

the result of having dipp'd too deeply into the brandy before
you, barefoot and belligerent, arrived on the scene. However
it may have been, you have my assurance that such behavior
on my part will never be permitted to recur.

As to the substance of our disagreement, on the other hand
(that is, the dispute over the education of my son), I have
nothing further to add to what I've already said. I trust you
will not again question my authority in this matter. Strickland.

Olivia read the letter in disbelief. Was *this* supposed to be
an *apology*? *I do admit, however, to behavior that was less*
than gentlemanly. How very decent of him! Less than *gentle-*
manly? His behavior had not only been less than gentlemanly—
it had been positively *depraved*! How *could* he have written—
"if I manhandled you . . ." ? *If*, indeed! That evasion might be
a satisfactory way for him to explain the situation to his *wife*,
but did he think it would fool *Olivia*? And that weak excuse
about being drunk! Perhaps he *had* imbibed more than he should
have, but he'd not been drunk. And his recollection was not
the *least bit* hazy. She was certain of that. She'd seen his eyes
when he'd released her last night—he'd been almost as shaken
as *she*! And she was certain that he remembered the entire
incident. He'd *assaulted* her, that's what he'd done! And he'd
been in full possession of his faculties when he'd done it. If
this were a "proper apology" he would have *admitted* it.

She crushed the note into a tight ball and threw it into the
wastebasket. But a moment later, she hopped out of bed, picked
it up, smoothed it out again and re-read every word. It made
her angrier than her first reading had. She'd a good mind to
show the thing to Clara! Let her *see* what a scoundrel she'd
married!

But on reconsideration, she decided against it. Of *course*
she wouldn't show Clara the note. In fact, she was surprised
that Strickland had seen fit to tell his wife a *word* about the
incident. Why had he done it? And how much had he told her?
Had he mentioned the "manhandling?" She suspected that he'd
told her only about the quarrel. Oh, well, it was for the best.
What good would it do for Clara to know that her beloved
Miles was a libertine? The same impulse that had probably
guarded Strickland's tongue had also guarded Olivia's in the

matter of what she'd seen a few months ago on a London street . . . and it was the same impulse which would keep her silent now.

She read the note through once more, shaking her head in bewilderment. Then her eye fell on the laundered handkerchief he'd so scrupulously returned. For Strickland, she supposed, this really *was* a kind of apology. Perhaps he was truly ashamed of what he'd done. Well . . . no matter. He'd promised that it would never happen again, and she was certain he meant it. The entire incident was best forgotten.

Carefully, she tore the paper into dozens of tiny pieces and threw them into the basket. That made an end of the incident. The matter was disposed of. She only wished that she could as easily dispose of her memory of it.

When Olivia came upon her later that afternoon, Clara was at her desk in the upstairs sitting room, writing a letter of inquiry to Strickland's business agent asking him to find a suitable tutor for Perry. When Olivia saw what she'd written, she couldn't keep back an expression of annoyance. "Do you always obey your husband's orders so meekly?" she asked in obvious disgust.

"Most of the time," Clara admitted serenely, looking up at her sister with a warm smile. "His orders are usually meant to promote the welfare of the family."

"Are they indeed?" Olivia asked, her voice dripping sarcasm. "Even in this case?" Without waiting for a response, she flounced away and threw herself upon the loveseat near the window.

Clara sighed and put down her pen. "He told me about your quarrel on this matter, Livie. And while I can't help but agree with your feelings—for Perry is such a *little* boy—I must admit that the child has an overly active imagination. Perhaps Miles is right in believing that the boy is too withdrawn from reality."

"Balderdash!" Olivia muttered unsympathetically.

"No, it's not balderdash. Perry really is—as Miles claims— too closely surrounded by females. Miles says a boy should have a *man* to talk to," Clara argued gently.

"Then let his *father* spend more time with him!" Olivia flashed back.

"But you know that isn't possible. Besides, Miles says—"

"*Miles* says! *Miles* says! I never would have believed, Clara, that you'd turn out to be the sort of wife whose every opinion is formed by what her husband says!"

Clara laughed. "Don't be a spiteful cat, love. What Miles says is often wise and good."

"Wise and *good*?" Under the circumstances, this was much too much for Olivia to swallow. "Your Miles is a damned—!" She stopped herself from going on by forcibly clamping shut her jaws.

Clara looked at her sister with shrewd insight. "What is it, Livie?" She got up from her chair and came to sit down beside her sister. "Are you still smarting because of the altercation with Miles last night? Was he *very* dreadful to you? Please try to forgive him. I know he can be very rude, sometimes, but he truly means well."

"He does *not* mean well... at least, not always!" she burst out, unable to help herself. "Honestly, Clara, it makes me *livid* to hear you speak of him in that... foolishly adoring way! Can't you be his wife without blinding yourself to his faults?"

"I'm not blind to his faults, Livie. Not at all. I just view them from a different perspective than you do. I know he has faults—quite serious ones. But they are not inconsistent with his being a man of strong character... or a man of honor."

"*Character? Honor?*" Olivia looked at her sister with eyes stricken with pain. "Oh, Clara... I can't *let* you..." She paused, hesitated, and turned away. "What if I told you that... that I know Strickland is *not* a man of honor?"

Clara put a gentle hand upon her sister's shoulder and turned her back, looking at her with wistful intensity. "You've heard that he has a mistress, haven't you?"

"*Clara!*" Olivia could scarcely believe what she'd heard. "How did you . . . ? How can you . . . ?"

"I've known for some time. But who told *you*, Livie?"

Olivia lowered her eyes miserably. "I . . . I *saw* him with her . . . one night . . . on the street."

Clara lowered her hands to her lap, her fingers trembling slightly. "I see. Was she... very beautiful?"

"I couldn't see her face," Olivia murmured, her chest constricted in pain. She took one of Clara's hands in hers and squeezed it in heartfelt sympathy. "But I could see, even in that one glimpse of her, that she was a . . . a lightskirt."

"Could you?" Clara shook her head sadly. "Poor Miles."

"Poor *Miles*?" Olivia snatched her hand away from Clara in sudden fury. "Poor *Miles*? Clara, have you lost your *mind*? You are speaking of a . . . libertine! A debauched scoundrel who has been playing you false! And you say 'poor *Miles*'?"

"Yes, my dear. For he has been forced to seek the arms of the very sort of woman he cannot abide . . . and it's all my fault."

Olivia blinked at her sister stupidly. "Clara, I don't know what you're talking about. *Your* fault? How can it be?"

Clara drew in her breath and then expelled it in a slow, wavering sigh. "I'm afraid this will be difficult for you to hear, my love," she said slowly, looking at her sister with a troubled frown. "You are very young and . . . inexperienced . . . and we have never spoken of . . . such matters. But there's a reason why I believe it is time that I told you the whole."

Olivia felt her pulse begin to race. What dreadful tale did her sister wish to reveal that required so forbidding a preamble? Something in her sister's life was decidedly out of joint. But if she was to be of any help to Clara at all, she would have to be sensible and brave. She faced her sister squarely and put her hands on the older woman's shoulders. "Look at me, Clara. I'm no longer a child. And you yourself have always said that I'm not deficient in intelligence. If there's anything you think I ought to know—no matter how painful—then *tell* it to me."

"Yes, love," Clara agreed, taking her sister's face between her hands and giving it a long, loving scrutiny. "You are quite right. You're old enough, and bright enough, and loving enough to be brave and sensible about . . . about what I must tell you." She kissed her sister's cheek, dropped her hands back into her lap and sat back against the cushions. "You see, Livie, my dearest, marriage is perhaps the most . . . intimate of partnerships. And Miles and I were, during the first few years, learning to become the most lovingly intimate of couples."

"*Were* you, Clara?" Olivia asked wonderingly, trying without success to imagine her placid sister locked into Strickland's embrace, being swept away on an emotional tidal wave . . .

"Oh, yes," Clara assured her, a nostalgic smile turning up the corners of her mouth. "We were very contented then. But after Amy was born, I . . . I was not the same."

"Not the same? Do you mean you no longer . . . *cared* for him?"

"Oh, no, not that. I loved him as much as ever. But it had been a very difficult lying-in . . . and an even more difficult delivery . . . and my *body* was not the same. I was full of pain. I couldn't . . . I could no longer be a true wife to him. Not in the fullest sense. Do you know what I'm saying?"

"Yes, I think so. You were ill, is that it?"

"Yes, I was ill . . . too ill to behave as a loving wife to my husband, and more seriously ill than I wished him—or anyone else—to realize."

Olivia's eyes widened in shock. "Clara! Why didn't you *tell* me—?"

"Wait. Let us not rush ahead with the story. We were speaking of Miles. I did not wish him to know about my illness, you see. I didn't want him to give up his political activities, to fill the house with doctors, to treat me with pity . . . all the things that serious illness seems to bring about. I didn't want *anyone's* pity. So I told him only that I had no more interest in . . . in those physical relations which are so basic to true contentment in married life. In other words, Livie, I permitted him to believe that my love had cooled."

"Oh, Clara!" Olivia sighed, much moved.

"Can you understand what that meant to Miles, my dear? Do you have enough maturity to comprehend the difficulty of his position?"

"No, I'm afraid I don't," Olivia admitted. "Just because his wife is no longer . . . er . . . *compliant* . . . is not sufficient reason for a man—if he *is* a man of honor—to turn into a *rake*."

"Then you know nothing of men, my dear. Miles is a man of strong desires, of full-blooded passions. He couldn't understand why I had suddenly cooled to him. He was furious . . . yet he was as proud as he was angry. He never again spoke to me about the matter. He's been as scrupulously devoted to me and the family as he ever was. He's not permitted my name to be dragged into scandal. Yet he must have had a great need to find an outlet for his passions. Can't you feel for him? Still loyal to his marriage, he would not permit himself to indulge in a relationship with a woman of his own class—although there are many men who are not so fastidious, and many women who would welcome his attentions. If he's found himself a mistress from among a class of women he would normally disdain, I cannot find it in my heart to blame him."

Olivia lowered her eyes and bit her lip. Perhaps her sister didn't blame him, but Olivia couldn't help but *despise* him. A man need not be the slave of his passions. If he had any sort of character, he would have endeavored to control his passions and eschew the sort of self-indulgence of which Strickland was guilty. Even if he'd been led to believe that his wife no longer loved him in that way, he was still *married*. Honor and loyalty should have taken precedence over desire. How can he have believed himself to be a man of honor otherwise?

"I see by your expression that you don't agree with me," Clara said with a sigh. "But, Livie, you have much to learn about marriage. When a wife deserts her husband's bed, she hurts him in many ways. She deals a blow to his pride, to his self-esteem, to the essence of his manhood. Don't you see?"

Olivia considered the matter. "But, Clara, if that is true, why did you *lie* to him? Why didn't you tell him that you were ill and that as soon as you were well, your lives could return to the happy intimacy that you'd had before?"

"Because, my love, I knew that I would *never* be well. Never again."

Olivia's heart stopped for a moment, and her face paled. "Clara!" she gasped. "Clara . . . *no!*"

Clara reached for her hands and held them tight. "Don't look like that, Livie. Hold on to yourself. I *need* you to be *strong*. That is why I've told you all this. I don't have very much more time, you see. And although I've tried to arrange things so that my family will continue to thrive after I'm gone, I'm very much afraid that I haven't succeeded very well. There are parts of the family's structure that may fall to pieces. And only you, my dearest Livie, can be counted on to keep things together."

Olivia stared at her sister in white-faced horror. "What do

you *mean*? You don't have much more time to...to *live*? But...it can't be *true*! It *mustn't* be true!"

Clara didn't answer. She merely sat quietly, looking down at the hands folded in her lap and waiting for the shock waves to pass. But Olivia couldn't face the fact at first. *Perhaps this isn't happening*, she told herself. Perhaps it was only a terrible dream, and she would waken and find the whole scene disintergrating into the mists where all dreams disappear. Or perhaps Clara was mistaken. Perhaps another doctor . . . another medicine . . . "Oh, Clara," she whispered brokenly, "are you *sure*...?"

But Clara's eyes were fixed on hers, level, steady, unwavering, and she knew there was no escape. How could she have been so blind not to have read the message in back of those courageous eyes? How had she not guessed her sister's tragedy—a tragedy developing right before her eyes? How could she have permitted her sister to carry this shocking burden *alone*? With a cry, she lifted her arms, and the two sisters embraced, letting the tears flow in sorrow, in grief, and in relief that the burden could now be shared. So they hugged each other close, painfully close...as if they were hanging on to each other for dear life.

chapter nine

Clara had only one wish—a most urgent desire to live out the few months remaining to her in as normal a manner as her illness would permit. She wanted to avoid tension in the household. She wanted no shadow to cloud her children's eyes when she played with them. She wanted no pity or unwonted attention from the people around her. To that end, she made Olivia promise to tell no one about her illness. No one—not her father, not her brothers, not Strickland, not *anyone* was to be informed. Only Mrs. Joliffe (who had guessed a long time ago that her mistress was seriously ill), the doctor and Olivia were to know the truth. Olivia was not at all certain that this secretiveness was for the best, but despite a nagging reluctance, she did as her sister wished.

Olivia would never forget as long as she lived the amazing courage her sister demonstrated as she passed her days with seeming serenity, never acknowledging her pain, rarely taking to her bed, always welcoming the children's company and taking part (as much as she was physically able) in the activities of the household. For Olivia, watching her with aching heart, it was an inspiration—a demonstration of the enormous gallantry which the human spirit can sometimes muster in time of stress.

In order not to arouse suspicion, Clara did not permit Olivia to overstay her visit. At the appointed time, Olivia returned to London. But she came back as often as Clara permitted for short visits, especially when she knew that Strickland would be away from home. It was only in Olivia's company that Clara could relax her rigid self-control and permit herself to speak truthfully about her pains, her problems, her fears and her desires for the future of her family. The two sisters became closer than they had ever been, the pain of their imminent separation making the pleasure of being together more poignant and meaningful.

On the first of her return visits, Olivia was surprised to see that the advent of the new tutor had not made a significant difference in the daily routine. Mr. Cornelius Clapham was a studious young man whose eyes, behind their silver-framed spectacles, had a warm twinkle. A little below average height, the tutor was quick and nervous in his movements, his step was sprightly and his long fingers constantly twitched as if from an excess of energy. Although his hair was scraggly and his lips thin, he had an agreeable face lit by a ready smile, and everyone seemed to have taken a liking to him. Olivia, who had so violently objected to a tutor's presence in the household that she was prepared to detest him, had to admit that his presence seemed to be doing Perry no harm.

Mr. Clapham took over Perry's schooling during the afternoons. He was a patient, indulgent teacher, and Perry was an eager pupil. Olivia, on paying a visit to the schoolroom, was pleased to discover that the tutor had no objection to the presence in the classroom of Sir Budgidore. The teacher even addressed a number of his comments to the invisible knight, asking him to impart bits of history in his ear or to repeat the declensions of the Latin verbs that Master Perry had confused. "Sir Budgidore is better at history than I," Perry confided to Olivia proudly, "though I'm catching up to him in Latin. Don't you think Papa will be pleased at how well I'm doing in Latin?"

Olivia assured him that his Papa would be proud as a peacock, but in her heart she was not at all convinced. She had never known Lord Strickland to unbend enough to pay *anyone* a compliment, so she very much doubted that his son would have the satisfaction of a kind word from his arrogant father.

However, Strickland evidently had been right about the tutor. Perry was certainly thriving under his tutelage. Olivia was humiliated to realize that she'd made that scene in the library—and been subjected to that unnerving embrace—all for nothing. His lordship had been right, and she'd been an interfering fool.

Olivia came away from the schoolroom very favorably impressed by Mr. Clapham's scholarship and his handling of the little fellow. He was a natural teacher—affectionate, patient, knowing and kind. "He even has a touch of humor, though it's a pedantic, dry sort," she told Clara later. "At least you have nothing to worry about on that score. Perry is in good hands."

Clara smiled in agreement. She had gone to bed with a book to spend a restful afternoon, and she now leaned back against the pillows and studied her sister with a teasing glint in her eye. "So Miles *was* wise in this matter, wasn't he?" she asked triumphantly.

"Not necessarily," Olivia demurred. "He was more lucky than wise. If his agent had not found such a good specimen in Mr. Clapham, the entire situation might have been quite different."

Clara sighed. "How can I convince you to change your opinion about Miles?" she asked wistfully.

"Why does my opinion concern you? What difference can it make to you whether I approve of your husband or not?"

Clara cast a quick look at her sister's face and then looked away. "It makes a difference to me. A great deal of difference. I had hoped that..." But she fell silent and turned her head away.

"What had you hoped?" Olivia asked curiously.

"Nothing. Never mind." She looked back at her sister with her quick, soothing smile. "I'm glad you find our Mr. Clapham to your liking."

"Yes, I do like him. In fact, I think I should like to encourage a match between him and Miss Elspeth. Wouldn't they make the most perfect pair?"

Clara shook her head and smiled in disparagement. "You're not the sort to be a matchmaker, Livie. You haven't the knack."

Olivia drew herself up in offense. "How can you say that? What's *wrong* with my matchmaking?"

"Your match is too obvious, don't you see? People don't take to each other in such neat, comfortable patterns."

"Don't they? Why not?"

"I don't know. The strangest sort of people attract each

other. No one can say why. But our Elspeth, who is just the right age for Mr. Clapham and has enough in common with him to make it appear that they would be *ideally* matched, is the only person in the whole household who holds Mr. Clapham in dislike."

Clara was quite right. Miss Elspeth had turned up her nose at Mr. Clapham the moment she laid eyes on the tutor. She never said a civil word to him, despite the fact that they both spent the greater part of their days on the third floor in the children's wing. The moment the tutor would appear in the schoolroom doorway for his afternoon lessons with Perry, Miss Elspeth would snatch up Amy's hand and scoot from the room, leaving a trail of hairpins or a forgotten scarf. Like a cook who can't abide having another chef in his kitchen, Elspeth couldn't bear the presence of the man she felt was a *rival*. It brought a bitter taste to her mouth to realize that she had to share her Perry with this *usurper*. She could see no good in him at all. To her, he was a nervous, fidgety, pretentious, encroaching *bore*, and the less she had to do with him the better.

As for Cornelius Clapham himself, he was completely indifferent to Miss Elspeth's view of him. His mind was on his lessons, his own scholarship and the child in his charge. The colorless little governess who dressed them in the morning, supervised their meals and took them out to play did not interest him in the least. If anyone had suggested to him that Miss Elspeth could be a potential wife, a potential lover or even a potential friend, he would have gaped in amazement. For he had his eye on another female entirely. At the first glimpse of Miss Olivia Matthews he had completely lost his head and heart.

He knew, of course, that Miss Olivia was quite above his touch. She was a lady of quality, high-born and rich. He was a nobody, without rank, title or wealth and with nothing to recommend him but a fairly prepossessing appearance, an honest nature and a good education. He had no property to his name and no prospects of ever being much better off than he was at this moment. A lady of Miss Matthews' sort would never even deign to notice him.

But a man could dream. And in his dreams, Olivia Matthews played a leading role. Her face hovered over his desk when he bent over his books, it shimmered in the sky when he gazed out of the window, it smiled over his bed when he stared up at the ceiling during the night, and it haunted his dreams during his sleep. He imagined her sitting with him before a fire, listening to him as he read her the lyrics he'd written in her praise. He dreamed of her in a bridal gown, standing before the vicar of a church, gazing fondly at him as he took his place beside her. He fancied himself embracing her as they stood high on a crag, the wind blowing about them and the stars beaming down on them. But never by word or deed did he reveal to anyone that she was the soul and substance of his waking dreams and his secret life.

Olivia's comings and goings were observed by Mr. Clapham with an interest more intense than that of anyone else in the household. When she returned to London his life lost its color. When she came back to Langley Park, his spirits soared. During the rest of that spring and the summer that followed, poor Cornelius Clapham's emotions were lifted and depressed too frequently for his good, for Olivia came and went a dozen times. Her visits to Langley became very frequent, for during that period Strickland was often away from home. Ever since the assassination of Perceval in May, the government in London had been in turmoil, and Strickland's presence was required. Even though the Prince Regent had appointed Lord Liverpool to the post of Prime Minister in June (after a month of inde- cision, procrastination and confusion), the appointment had really pleased nobody. Strickland, who had been instrumental in pushing the Regent to his decision and in forming the cabinet, felt it necessary to be on hand during the early days of the new ministry. Clara had said nothing to her husband to give him a moment's concern, and he therefore pursued his life in his usual manner. This was what Clara wished him to do, in spite of the fact that she missed him greatly. So Olivia posted up to Langley Park whenever she heard Strickland was in town, hoping to give her sister some comfort.

Olivia instinctively rebelled against Clara's stubborn in- sistence on secrecy, especially as the summer wore on and Clara's condition worsened perceptibly. But Clara was ada- mant, and Olivia let her have her way. She did her best to make the time happy for her sister, arranging for the children to spend time with their mother during the hours when Clara felt relatively well, taking them out on picnics or excursions when their mother was ill, keeping the atmosphere of the household as cheerful as she could and supporting her sister's spirit when it weakened. It was a taxing and difficult time, and often, when she fell wearily into bed at night, she wept herself to sleep.

When the strain became unbearable—as it did from time to time—she would go to the stable and take out Strickland's most spirited gelding for a brisk gallop. Nothing was so soothing to her spirits as flying across the fields on the back of the magnificent, glossy-coated horse. Strickland had named him Pegasus; it was an apt name, for the creature did indeed seem almost winged as he galloped with graceful ease over hill and field. Olivia had been an indifferent horsewoman until this summer, but now she seemed to ride by instinct. On Pegasus' back, she could feel the rhythm of his movements, her body relaxed, and she learned to move with the motion of the animal. It was remarkably invigorating to speed across the landscape, feeling the wind beating at her face, hearing its whistle at her ears and seeing the trees whipping by in a blur of green. For those few moments, she could stop her thoughts, dull her worries and surrender to the sensation of motion—pure, natural, death-defying motion.

She had no idea that, while she indulged herself in this one pleasure, she was being observed. At first from the schoolroom window, then from the stable loft and finally from behind a hedge that divided the two broadest fields, Cornelius Clapham watched her with adoration. It was on horseback that she looked most like the girl of his dreams—her eyes shining, her cheeks rosy from the whip of the breeze on her face, some strands of curls escaping from beneath her little riding hat and flowing back from her face. It was a sight that took his breath away.

As time went on, the watcher grew bolder. He took a hiding place behind a tree not far from the stables. From there he could see her when she was starting out or just reining in, closer and in slower motion than he'd been able to see her from his other vantage points. Whenever he noticed, from the schoolroom window, that Higgins, the groom, was saddling Pegasus, he would set Perry at some engrossing task and steal out to take his place behind his tree.

On an afternoon in late summer, when Olivia was drawing near the stables after a rather longer gallop than usual and had just tightened the reins to indicate to Pegasus that it was time to slow down, she was abruptly distracted by a glimpse of a white face peering out at her from behind a tree. In fright, she gasped and, already having been tightening the reins, gave them a jerk that pulled too sharply on the horse's bit. The unsuspecting animal neighed loudly and reared up on his hind legs, throwing his rider off his back and making a dash for the safety of the stable. Poor Olivia flew through the air, landed in a painful heap on the ground, and fainted.

When she drifted back into consciousness, her first awareness was of a wet cloth being applied to her forehead. Then she heard a voice whispering near her ear in a tone of agony, "Miss Olivia, Miss Olivia, *speak* to me!"

She blinked her eyes open. "Mr. C-Clapham? Is that *you*?"

"Oh, thank *God*!" he sighed in relief, pulling her to him in a clumsy embrace.

Her mind was only slowly beginning to return to its normal awareness. She realized that she was lying on the ground, that there was a painful bruise in the region of her left arm and shoulder, and that the tutor was inexplicably cradling her upper torso in his arms. "What happened?" she asked confusedly.

"It was all my fault," the tutor said, looking down at her in abject misery. "I frightened the horse."

Olivia shut her eyes and tried to remember what happened. "No . . . it was *I* who frightened the horse," she said slowly. "I was startled by a . . . a face."

"Yes," the tutor muttered. "Mine."

Her eyes flew open. "Yours? But, Mr. Clapham, whatever were you *doing*?"

The fellow bit his lip in shame. "I was . . . watching you," he admitted.

"I don't understand. Why?"

Mr. Clapham was twenty-eight years old but had never been in love before. What little he knew of love came to him from Greek drama and Roman verse. But from that reading he had the distinct impression that love grew out of just such dramatic scenes as this. Fate had dealt him a unique opportunity for a moment of intimacy with the woman of his dreams, and he was not a man to let the chance go by. *Carpe diem*, Horace had advised. This was his opportunity to seize the day, and seize it he would. "Can't you guess?" he asked looking down at the girl in his arms with a meaningful intensity.

"No, I can *not*," Olivia said with a touch of asperity, feeling suddenly quite uncomfortable and wishing to be helped to her feet. She pushed at his enfolding arms so that she could sit up.

But Mr. Clapham had decided to seize the day. His hold on her tightened, and his eyes glowed with longing. Before she knew it, he lifted her tightly against his chest and kissed her with fervent ardor.

Olivia made a furious sound in her throat and struggled to disengage his hold on her. But the tutor's grasp was stronger than she'd expected. With a painfully throbbing shoulder, and a head still swimming from her fall, she was not capable of resisting so tenacious an embrace. She could feel the trembling of his arms and the rapid beating of his heart. Although she was furious with him and annoyed at herself for having fallen into this fix, she was aware of the urgency of his embrace and the tenderness of his kiss. It moved her somehow.

But when he lifted his head, she pushed him forcefully away from her. "Mr. Clapham," she exclaimed, "have you lost your *senses*?"

His heart was hammering in his chest and his blood pounding in his ears. He'd gone too far to retreat now. "I *love* you," he declared, and he reached for her again, his chest heaving in his attempt to catch his breath.

"Don't you *dare* do that again!" she snapped forbiddingly. "Stop this nonsense and help me up!"

"But . . . didn't you *hear* me? I said I love you!"

"Rubbish! Are you going to get to your feet and help me up, or must I shout for the groom?"

Turning quite pale, the tutor scrambled up and helped her to her feet. She stood up unsteadily, wincing with pain and rubbing her bruised shoulder and arm. "Are you very much hurt?" he asked solicitously.

"Don't touch me! It's no thanks to you that my *neck* isn't broken!"

"Forgive me, Miss Matthews. I never meant—"

Olivia softened. "No, of course you didn't." She looked at him curiously. "Whatever *possessed* you—?"

Her matter-of-fact manner was quite disconcerting, but he plunged ahead heedlessly. "I told you. I love you."

She glared at him impatiently. "And I said *rubbish*! How can you love me? We've barely exchanged a dozen words."

"But that doesn't signify. I've loved you from the f-first moment I laid eyes on you."

Olivia ceased massaging her arm and stared at him in astonishment. "Have you really? How very strange. We're not even *friends*."

"Must people be friends to be in love?" he asked, bewildered by the unexpectedly analytical turn in the conversation.

"I don't know," Olivia said with a thoughtful dispassion. "I had surmised that one must develop *some* sort of amity or *rapprochement* toward the loved one before one could claim to feel such an *enveloping* emotion. That is why, Mr. Clapham, I don't take this declaration of yours at all seriously." She brushed off her skirt and began to walk toward the stable.

He stared after her, nonplussed, and then ran to catch up with her, falling into step beside her. "I . . . I wish, Miss Matthews, that you will not dismiss my feelings for you on that basis," he said in some desperation. "I don't think anyone really knows *how* love comes about. Why, Catullus wrote, *I hate and I love. Why I do so I do not know. But I feel it, and I am in torment.*"

Olivia snorted. "In *torment*? Now, really, Mr. Clapham, this is too silly. Please don't spout Catullus at me. I'm in no mood for foolish quotations. The emotion that you feel is concocted out of the air. It is based on so insignificant an acquaintance that it cannot be worthy of the name of love. Take my advice, Mr. Clapham, and forget the matter entirely."

Mr. Clapham, deflated and depressed, cast her a look of woebegone despair. "I suppose you'll wish me to pack my bags and leave," he murmured sadly.

She stopped and turned to him. "Leave? Why would I wish you to leave?"

"Won't you ask her ladyship to *dismiss* me?"

"No, of course not. Unless, of course, you intend to *persist* in peering at me from behind trees and quoting love poetry to me. Do you?"

He hung his head. "Not if you don't wish me to."

"I don't. So, please, go back to the schoolroom. Perry is undoubtedly wondering what's become of you. If you have the sense I think you have, you will get back to your work and put this incident completely out of your mind."

The incident lingered in Olivia's mind, however. Later that night, as she lay abed waiting for sleep to come, it occurred to her that she'd experienced her fourth kiss. Was there anything to be learned from it? The kiss had not been dull, like Morley Crawford's, nor revolting, like Sir Walter Haldene's. It had been urgent and tender and throbbing with feeling. And it had been obvious, from the tutor's breathlessness and a certain look in his eyes when he'd released her, that he'd been deeply stirred by it. She, however, while she'd been touched and had not *disliked* the experience, could not say she'd been stirred. The embrace had not affected her at all in the way Strickland's had. What *was* there about Strickland's kiss that so differed from the others? It was a puzzle.

But Olivia didn't dwell on the puzzle for long. Strickland's return to Langley Park shortly thereafter sent her back to London before she even saw the tutor again. And by the time she returned to the country, her sister's illness had so far progressed that Olivia could think of nothing else.

By late September, it was so plain that Clara would not last the month that Olivia realized it before she heard the doctor's warning. Clara could no longer leave her bed and was so heavily sedated with laudanum that she slept most of the time. When she did wake, her eyes were foggy and her words slurred. Olivia, heartbroken at the prospect of her sister's passing and terrified of the responsibility of carrying the burden of the aftermath on her own inexperienced shoulders, sent the head groom, Higgins, to London to fetch Lord Strickland to his wife's bedside.

In the meantime, Olivia kept a constant vigil at her sister's side. One evening, when the last rays of the setting sun fell across the pillow, lighting her sister's face with a late-summer amber glow, Clara opened her eyes. "Livie?" she asked, her voice stronger than it had been in days.

"Yes, love," Olivia said, her heart jumping up in senseless hope. "I'm here."

"Isn't it a lovely evening?" Clara murmured, her eyes clear and lucid again. "So cool."

"Yes. The sunset takes your b-breath away." Olivia tried to keep her voice steady and to control her unreasoning elation at seeing her sister so like her normal self.

"Help me to sit up so that I can watch it," Clara implored.

Olivia's first instinct was to object, for Clara had so little strength that any effort exhausted her. But Olivia forced herself to remember that at this late date her objections would be pointless. She immediately bent down and lifted the thin shoulders, piling up the pillows behind her sister's back and propping her upon them.

"Oh, Livie, it *is* breathtaking," Clara sighed, looking out of the window eagerly. Before their gaze, the oranges and reds slowly turned to purple. At last Clara said quietly, "It won't be long, you know, dearest. Not for the sunset, and not for me."

Olivia's unreasoning hope withered, and she pressed her quivering lips together to keep from crying out. Her sister reached for her trembling hand.

"Don't be afraid, love. My mind is quite well prepared. I only wish that I could see Miles. Isn't it dreadful how one wants to have one's cake and eat it too? I long ago decided that I don't want him to see me this way."

Olivia frowned in guilt and indecision. "Are you *sure*, Clara?"

"Yes. It's better this way."

Olivia cast her sister a look of dismay. Had she done the wrong thing to have sent for him? Would Clara hate her for it? Should she warn her sister that her husband was at this very moment on his way to her side? "Clara, I—"

"Hush, Livie, let me speak. It has been such an effort for me to do it of late, and now, suddenly, I feel strong enough. There's something I want to say to you."

Olivia sat down on the bed beside her sister and took her hand. "What is it, Clara?"

"I want you to promise me . . . that you will watch over my family . . . and love them."

"But of course I will! You don't have to ask me that," Olivia assured her.

Clara peered at her urgently. "You must *promise*, Livie! They will need it so. You must promise to . . . to love them . . . *all*!"

Olivia could not keep back her tears. "Don't c-concern yourself, Clara. You have m-my word."

Clara nodded, but she clutched her sister's hand even tighter. "There are so *many* things you must watch. Amy . . . she gets what she wants so easily—she may become quite spoiled. And Perry . . . sweet, unworldly Perry . . . he must learn to live in the real world. You mustn't let him go off to school without the proper defenses. He's so vulner—" The words died on her lips, and her eyes suddenly lit up with a glow that startled Olivia by its joyful animation. She turned quickly in the direction of her sister's gaze. Strickland stood in the doorway.

He was staring at his wife, his eyes stricken, his cheeks like chalk and his lips compressed. "Clara, *what*?"

"Miles! Oh, *Miles*!" she cried, reaching out her arms.

He strode across the room and knelt beside her bed, enveloping her in his arms. Olivia, completely unnoticed, tiptoed from the room and closed the door gently behind her.

For the next few hours, she kept a vigil outside the door, but no sound issued from inside. She lingered about the hallway, wishing to be on hand if she were needed but reluctant to interrupt the encounter within. When Mrs. Joliffe appeared with the supper tray, however, Olivia permitted her to tap on the door, but Strickland's rough voice ordered her away. Later, however, the housekeeper was permitted to enter with her ladyship's medicinal draught. When she emerged, she told Olivia that his lordship had suggested that everyone go to bed.

Olivia undressed and lay down on her bed but couldn't sleep. Somehow she knew that her sister would not last the night. Memories of Clara in their younger years floated through her mind—Clara taking her on her first outing to the Pantheon Bazaar; Clara laughing with her over the antics of a gosling in the park; Clara bent over yards of Florentine silk as she stitched the finishing touches on Olivia's first party dress. And over it all, Olivia saw Strickland's face as it had looked on his arrival, stricken with fear and agony. Did he really love his wife after all? Olivia shook her head, confounded. How ignorant she was about things that really mattered.

There was the sound of coach wheels on gravel, and she woke with a start. She'd fallen asleep. Her room was so dark that she knew the hour must be very late. A carriage was moving away from the house and down the drive. Who was leaving at this hour? She flew to the window and caught, in the faint light issuing from a downstairs window, a glimpse of the doctor's curricle just before the darkness swallowed it up. Her chest constricted in terror.

She threw a robe over her gown and tiptoed down the hall to Clara's room. There was no sound from within. With noiseless caution she turned the knob and opened the door. Inside, by the light of a single guttering candle she could see her sister's form covered by the counterpane. She stood frozen for a moment as the awareness of her sister's death sank into her heart. But when the first shock of loss ebbed sufficiently to permit her to think of others rather than herself, she became aware that someone was kneeling at the side of the bed. It was Strickland, his head lowered on the counterpane and buried by one arm, the other thrown across his wife's body in a gesture of unutterable agony. His shoulders were shaking with choked and silent sobs.

Until this moment, Olivia had not been completely convinced about Strickland's feelings for his wife. His stricken face, when he'd arrived earlier, had really moved her, but later she'd remembered a line from Macbeth: *to show an unfelt sorrow is an office which the false man does easy.* But now she was ashamed of the thought. In his grief, at least, Strickland was not false. Here, without awareness of other eyes on him, his pain and despair were as nakedly revealed and as clearly apparent as a bare black tree against a field of snow. Olivia, fighting back her own surge of anguish, backed from the room and silently closed the door, leaving her brother-in-law to his bitter grief.

chapter ten

Even weeks later, when she was able to review the events after the funeral with some dispassion, Olivia blamed Strickland more than she blamed herself. She had really tried her best. She had meant well. After all, how could she have foreseen the devastating effects that a series of unexpected events would have on the family... especially on her nephew?

The fault, she told herself, was more Strickland's than hers. She had tried, after her sister died, to submerge her own grief and to care for the needs of others. When her father and brothers had returned to London after the funeral, she had remained at Langley Park. She had tried to keep the household on an even keel. She had tried to make the atmosphere cheerful, to encourage the children to play, to urge everyone to cease whispering and to speak in normal tones... even to laugh. But Strickland had interfered in every possible way, as, for example, in the matter of the draperies. He had wanted them *drawn* in every room he entered. She, on the other hand, had insisted that the servants *open* them to let the sunshine in. No sooner would Strickland leave a room when Olivia would order that the draperies be opened. No sooner would Strickland enter when he would order them shut. The situation became positively ludicrous as the servants ran about opening and shutting draperies to obey the contradictory orders they'd received—and always displeasing *somebody*, no matter what they did.

Strickland himself had been like a dark cloud hanging over

the house. He made no attempt to hide the blackness of his mood even from the children. He spent most of his days in the darkened library, ignoring the children, shouting angrily at the servants, shunning all companionship, neglecting to respond to his messages from London, and drinking himself into a stupor every night. He left a trail of resentment and chaos wherever he went, and Olivia felt completely incapable of dealing with the wreckage in his wake. As a result, the servants became more and more sullen, the atmosphere more and more gloomily tense and the bewildered children more and more unhappy.

The children were confused by the absence of their mother, and Olivia had to deal with their confusion all by herself. Perry did not speak of his mother at all, nor did he cry. He seemed to close in on himself, to withdraw, showing the world only a stiff, white face and a lost, uncertain look in his eyes. The look pierced Olivia to the heart, but she didn't know what to do to dispel it. Amy wandered about in bewilderment, asking repeatedly, "But wheaw hath Mama *gone?*" Olivia tried to explain, but Heaven was, to the child, a baffling abstraction. Could her Mama *see* her from so far away? Olivia sat down with the children and gave them a long, carefully considered explanation. Amy listened intently, her large eyes wide in awe. After her aunt finished, some round, fat tears rolled down her face, and she seemed to accept—with at least *some* degree of equanimity—the idea that her mother was watching over her from somewhere in the sky and would always do so. But Perry, Olivia suspected, was not comforted.

Weeks passed in this precariously ominous climate. It was almost inevitable that a crisis would occur. And it did, one evening in mid-October. Miss Elspeth had tapped at Perry's bedroom door to tell him that his supper was ready, but she heard no response. After a moment, she went in. The room was empty. She searched through the entire third floor, even going so far as to enlist Mr. Clapham's assistance in the search, but there was no Perry to be found.

When she informed Olivia that Perry had disappeared, Olivia guessed at once where the boy had gone. Following her instinct, she ran down the hall to her sister's bedroom, with Miss Elspeth following close behind. There, standing at his mother's dressing table, her hairbrush in his hand, stood the unhappy child.

Miss Elspeth sucked in her breath (for his lordship had ordered that no one be permitted to enter the room) and made as if to snatch the boy out of there, but Olivia, with a gesture of restraint, motioned for the governess to wait. She went up to him and knelt down beside him, gently taking the brush from his hand and replacing it. "Perry, love," she said soothingly, "your supper is waiting. Don't you want to have your soup while it's hot?"

The boy gave an almost imperceptible sigh and nodded obediently. Olivia had a sudden desire to see him cry . . . or shout . . . or stamp his foot in refusal. Why was he so compliant? What had happened to the child's spirit?

At that moment, Lord Strickland loomed up in the open doorway. His eyes, darkly forbidding, swept over the boy, the kneeling Olivia and the governess hovering anxiously over them. "What are you doing in this room?" he asked in tight-lipped anger.

"N-Nothing," Perry stammered, his body stiffening in fright.

"*Really*, my lord," Olivia said in some impatience, "there's no need to take that tone—" She hoped that her mild defiance would show Perry that his father was only a man—not a monster—and someone who could be reasoned with.

"I gave specific orders about this room!" Strickland said darkly. "Now get out of here at once! *All* of you!"

Perry turned ashen and backed slowly to the door, his eyes fixed on his father's face and wide with terror. Olivia was appalled. She rose and, turning to the frightened governess, told her quietly to take Perry upstairs. "I'll be up in a moment," she assured her as Miss Elspeth took Perry's hand and scurried to the door. Olivia followed the pair to the doorway and watched them leave. Then she closed the door, put her back against it and faced Strickland furiously. "How *can* you speak to your own child in that way?" she demanded.

"I was speaking to *you*, ma'am. Evidently you didn't hear me. I asked you to go."

"Well, obviously Perry thought you were shouting at *him*." She boldly took a few steps forward, determined to persevere in this attack. "Don't you care *anything* about your son's feelings?"

Strickland ground his teeth wrathfully. "You are doing it *again*, ma'am. I thought I had made myself clear on an earlier occasion (when you presumed to comment upon my management of my son) that I do not wish any interference from you!"

"But I *must* interfere. Can't you see that the child is in *misery*? Are you so deeply mired in your own grief that you have no sympathy for your children's?"

His eyes flashed furiously at her for a moment, and then fell. "Perhaps I am. But they are children. They will soon forget. While I must carry this . . . this lodestone of guilt to my grave." He looked up at her with eyes burning with resentment. "And, dammit, it is *you* who are to blame!"

"*I*?" she asked, astounded.

"Yes, *you*! You and your interfering ways. If you had *told* me that my wife was ill and had let me *prepare* myself and the children for the blow, we would all be in a better state," he said with bitter venom.

Olivia felt her chest constrict. "But Clara *said*—"

"I don't care *what* Clara said. You had no right to withhold such news from me."

A pulse began to beat in Olivia's throat. How could he place the blame at *her* door? She had often asked Clara *not* to keep her illness secret. Was it *her* fault if Clara had chosen to face her illness alone? "I . . . I *could* not refuse to respect my sister's wishes," she argued in self-defense.

"But you *could* take it upon yourself to stand between a husband and his wife, is that it?"

She was stung with a sudden wave of anger. What sort of husband had he been anyway? Faithless, selfish, far away from home most of the time . . . and now, when it was too late, he chose to play the role of husband to the hilt. "How can you blame *me* for stepping between you? You were not very much of a husband to begin with, as far as I can judge," she said in a choked voice.

"Who are you to *judge*?" he snapped back. "What do you know of the matter? You, who are nothing but a callow *spinster* . . . with no knowledge of marriage except what comes from the yellowed pages of your father's books."

She winced. "You do know how to be cruel, my lord. You needn't throw my lack of experience in my face."

"But I *must*, it seems. How else are you to learn the consequences of the actions you've taken in your damned ignorance?"

"But I...I only did what my sister *asked* me to do!" she cried.

His nostril flared in an icy sneer. "Don't hide behind that lame excuse! You could have made your *own* decision, instead of allowing yourself to be led by the pathetic urgings of a dying woman who had mistakenly convinced herself that her best course was to be unselfish. *Unselfish!* Is there anything more selfish than someone who insists on martyrdom? Why didn't you use the mind God gave you? Any *fool* would have known that a husband and wife needed to be together during such a terrible time."

The memory of her sister's face as it had looked when Strickland arrived at her bedside flashed across Olivia's mind. Clara's joy had been unmistakable. Yet she'd said only a moment before that she didn't want Olivia to send for him. Good God, was Strickland *right*? Was Clara's unselfish sacrifice a mistaken one? And had *she*, Olivia, abetted her sister in that mistake?

Agonized tears welled up in her eyes. If she had followed her own instincts, Strickland might have been able to share in his wife's last days. He might have eased Clara's torment...and his own. Olivia's throat burned in pain and guilt. "I'm...sorry. I sh-should have thought..."

"Yes, you should have," was the terse, cold reply.

There was a moment of silence. Strickland turned and walked to the bed, staring down at the pristine neatness of its covers, which only emphasized the terrible emptiness. Olivia stood watching him, overwhelmed with her guilt. How deeply had he been wounded by being kept in the dark about his wife's illness? And how great was her—Olivia's—responsibility for that wound?

Nevertheless, she reminded herself, he was not the *only* one wounded. The entire family had suffered over Clara's death—and perhaps Perry most of all. In all this display of self-pity, bitter recrimination and guilt, were they forgetting the boy?

"My lord," she said tentatively, "I agree that . . . I have made an unforgivable mistake. But I don't think I'm mistaken about Perry. He doesn't deserve—"

"*Damnation,*" he spat out, wheeling around, "don't you ever *stop*? Is there nothing which will keep you from this everlasting interference?"

This sudden vituperation made her jump. "Wh-What? I . . . I only . . ." she stammered.

"You only want to throw my inadequacies in my face. Well, I don't need you to do that, my dear. I can do it quite well on my own."

"I didn't mean—"

"Yes, you did. You *always* mean to put me in the wrong. You've tried to show me in the past that I didn't know how to be a husband, and *now* you want to show me that I don't know how to be a father. Very well, ma'am. You've shown me. But what about *you*? Take a look at *yourself*, my dear. You've been a meddling busybody from the first. You've brought trouble and contention with you whenever you've come on the scene." He turned away from her in disgust. "Have done, woman," he muttered savagely, "and leave me alone!"

Stunned, Olivia clapped her hand to her mouth to stifle the cry that sprang to her throat, and she ran from the room. He had said words like these to her before, but this time they struck her to the soul. Before, they had been merely angry words, spoken in the heat of the moment and not very deeply felt. But this time they were wrung out of the depths of him, and they struck her on the fresh wound of her guilt with the ring of truth.

Trembling, she stumbled to her room and crawled into bed. All night long, she wept. Early the next morning, she packed her things and left the house. A stableboy was prevailed upon to take out the curricle and drive her to Devizes where she would catch the mail to London. As she looked back at Langley Park from the rear window of the carriage, her tears began to flow again. If that house was to be put in order . . . if the children were to be helped over their loss . . . and if Strickland was to recover from his bitter grief . . . the task would have to be done by someone else. Her *meddling interference*—if indeed that was what it was—was at an end.

chapter eleven

Miss Elspeth Deering, governess to Lord Strickland's children, could bear no more. In the four months since Lady Strickland's passing, she had watched the goings-on with quiet dismay, but she'd told herself that it was not her place to say or do anything. All she could do was to care for the needs of the children and try to soothe their fears. But her efforts had not been enough. Without Miss Olivia, matters had gone from bad to worse. And this latest crisis was, for her, the last straw.

She paced about her little bedroom, nervously smoothing back the wisps of hair which had come loose from the knot at the back of her head. She was troubled to the core. She knew that she was not the sort to perform decisive actions. In all her life, she'd been a drifter—floating along with the tide of events without in any way taking control of them. She had done her father's bidding when she was young, and then, when he'd died and she was orphaned, an aunt had found the post at Langley Park for her. She had never been forced to make decisions for herself. Now, for the first time in her life, she was faced with a situation which called out for action, a situation which seemed fraught with danger—not for herself but for her charges, Perry in particular. If she didn't take matters in her own hands, the poor little fellow might be completely undone.

Hastily, she pulled out from her chest of drawers a few necessary garments and stuffed them into a small, shabby leather valise which her father had used to carry his Bible and sermon notes to and from the vicarage. It was too small for her needs, but it was the only piece of luggage she owned and would therefore have to do. As she busily crammed a clean petticoat, a pair of warm stockings, an extra handkerchief and a few other essentials into the corners of the bag, her mind reviewed the events of the past few months with renewed agitation.

She realized now that things had not been so very bad while Miss Olivia had been among them, although at the time they had seemed gloomy enough. But at least the young woman had kept the household in some semblance of peace and order. Then Miss Olivia had had a quarrel with his lordship, during which (according to Tilda, the upstairs maid, who'd claimed to have "overheard" the altercation and repeated the tale to the scullery maid who'd told it to the Cook, who'd ladled out the news, along with the soup, to everyone else on the household staff) he'd called Miss Olivia a meddling busybody. Tilda had reported that his lordship had been monstrously cruel. If the story was true, it was no wonder that Miss Olivia had decided to go back to London. Who could blame her?

But since that day the atmosphere in the household had been grim. The children were miserable, the servants sullen and disorderly, and Lord Strickland himself almost impossible to approach.

Through it all, Miss Elspeth had endeavored to shield the children from the worst of the confusion. In this, she had the valuable assistance of Mr. Clapham. Although she still disliked the tutor personally, she had to admit that he was devotedly protective of the children, especially Perry. He seemed to care for his charge as much as she, and he did his best to keep the boy's mind occupied with pleasant things. She herself spent all her waking hours with the children, soothing them when their mother's absence overwhelmed them, inventing games to keep them amused, making certain that their health, their eating habits, their cleanliness and their outdoor exercises should not be neglected. She noticed that the tutor, too, kept his eyes on them both, almost as aware of their needs as she was.

Therefore she was particularly incensed when, just yesterday, Lord Strickland peremptorily gave Mr. Clapham the sack. His lordship had paid an unexpected visit to the schoolroom and discovered that Perry, with Mr. Clapham's approval and encouragement, was still playing with his imaginary companion, Sir Budgidore. His lordship had fallen into a fury and, right before the horrified eyes of his son, had told the white-faced tutor to pack his things and take himself off the premises within a fortnight. "You have a fortnight and not one more day to find another post, do you hear?" Lord Strickland had declared. "And in the meantime, you are *not* to permit my son to indulge in these idiotic imaginings!"

Elspeth and little Amy, overhearing the commotion, had come running from the nursery to the schoolroom doorway just as Lord Strickland had lurched out. He brushed by Elspeth with a peremptory order to "stop gaping, and get back where you belong!" But before Elspeth turned to do as she was bid, she caught a glimpse of Perry's stricken face, and her heart had dropped down to her shoes.

Her alarm for the boy's state of mind proved to be justified. Later that afternoon, she found Perry sitting beside his empty bed, staring down at the pillow with a forlorn face. "Sir Budgidore is dying," he told Miss Elspeth tragically. "Do you suppose he will go up to heaven like Mama?"

Poor Miss Elspeth was dumfounded. What was the significance in Perry's mind of Sir Budgidore's possible demise? Did it mean he was dispensing with his imaginary playmate because of his guilt over causing Mr. Clapham to lose his post? Or was there something even *more* forbidding in this development? She knew that Lord Strickland would expect her to tell the boy that there was really *no* Sir Budgidore and therefore that he couldn't die . . . but she hadn't the heart to say so. "What makes you think Sir Budgidore is so sick?" she asked gently.

"He told me," Perry said, his underlip trembling. "Besides, you can see how he looks. He can't even get up out of bed." He looked at Miss Elspeth in hopeless misery. "With Mama gone, and Aunt Livie, too . . . and soon Mr. Clapham . . . I don't know whom I shall talk to when Sir Budgidore dies."

"But you still have me . . . and Amy," the governess suggested earnestly.

"Yes. But Amy is so little you know . . . and really doesn't understand about important things like the Round Table. And you are so busy with her most of the time—"

"Not too busy for you, love, if you need me," the governess said tenderly. "Besides, you can't be *certain* that Sir Budgidore won't get better."

"How *can* he get better? No one here knows how to make him well," Perry said despondently.

It was then that Miss Elspeth got her inspiration. She knew at once what had to be done, and she knew that *she* had to set about doing it. "Do you think you can take care of Sir Budgidore for a few days . . . until I can fetch Miss Olivia? *She* knows how to make him well, doesn't she?"

Perry blinked up at her uncertainly, almost afraid to let himself hope. "Oh, *could* you fetch her, Miss Elspeth? That would be the very thing, wouldn't it, Sir Budgidore?" He bent over the pillow to hear the knight's answer and then gave the governess a tentative smile. "He says he feels better already."

Thus committed to take action, Miss Elspeth set about making her plans. She would go to London herself and convince Miss Olivia to come back. She would make Miss Olivia see that Perry's emotions were stretched to the breaking point. His sensitive nature could not endure another loss of someone to whom he had grown attached. At this painful time of his life, he could not afford to lose either his imaginary companion or the tutor whose devotion to him was unquestionable. Elspeth, in her determination to protect the poor, troubled boy from stress beyond his endurance, was about to take the first decisive step of her life.

When her valise was packed, she put on her warmest woolen shawl and her best bonnet and left her room. She checked the adjoining bedrooms to make certain that both children were sleeping soundly, and then she marched courageously down to the farthest end of the third-floor corridor and tapped at Mr. Clapham's door. After a long moment, it was opened. The tutor peered out into the dimness of the hallway from behind his spectacles, blinking in surprise. "Miss Elspeth? Is there anything wrong?"

"There's something I . . . I must discuss with you . . . I mean, I know this is a bit shocking, but may I come in for just a . . . ?" Her voice trailed off in its usual, indecisive manner.

"Yes, please do," he said, stepping back and permitting her to pass into his room. He noted with some surprise that she was attired for the outdoors and carried a valise. "Are you going *away*?"

"Yes. That's why I had to...that is, I must ask you to watch over the children while I'm gone, no matter what..."

Mr. Clapham frowned at her in confusion. He had always found the governess to be a muddleheaded sort, unable to speak with proper clarity. He took the valise from her hand and urged her to a chair. "You must forgive the confusion here, Miss Elspeth. I've already begun to pack my books, you see."

She looked around the small room with interest. She had never visited him before and was surprised at the spartan appearance of his quarters. Her own room was quite pretty, with flowered dimity curtains at the window and some framed paintings on the walls. Mr. Clapham's room, however, was smaller than hers and quite bare of decoration. He'd covered two walls with a number of improvised shelves on which he'd stacked a great many books, but the room contained only the most necessary of furnishings—a small, crowded desk in one corner, a commode with a plain bowl and pitcher near his bed, and the one chair on which she was sitting. On the floor was a box which he had evidently been filling with the books he'd piled on his bed. She suddenly felt quite sorry for him. He must have led a lonelier and bleaker existence than she'd suspected. "That's quite all right, Mr. Clapham. I don't find much confusion here...but I don't know why you're packing so soon. Lord Strickland said a fortnight..."

The tutor sighed. "Yes, but I thought I might as well go now as later."

"Oh, no, you *mustn't*!" Elspeth cried. "You must promise to stay as long as possible. Perry will be heartbroken, you know, if you..."

The tutor frowned unhappily and sank down on the bed. "I know. But he may as well become used to it. And I may as well begin to look for a new post as soon as I can."

"But I'm going to London to speak to Miss Olivia about you, you see..."

"You're going to see Miss *Olivia*?" the astonished tutor asked. "About *me*?"

"Yes. Well, not *only* about you of course, but...I'm sure

she can help you, too, if she . . ."

Mr. Clapham made a nervous, impatient gesture with his hand. "Miss Olivia won't be able to help me. She won't even *want* to, after I . . ." Here *his* voice petered out just as hers was wont to do.

"But why not?" Elspeth asked curiously.

"Never mind. I don't think she . . . thinks very highly of me."

"But of course she does. That is, I always believed that she quite approved of . . . at least, I had the impression that . . ."

"Had you really?" the tutor asked, his eyes brightening. "Had she ever *said* anything to you in that regard?"

"I can't remember anything specific, of course, although I certainly believe that there were several occasions when . . . or one or two times, surely, when she remarked . . . I'm not sure of her exact words, but . . ."

The tutor sighed. "Well, it doesn't matter. But, Miss Elspeth, I don't quite understand why you should wish to take it upon yourself to go to Miss Olivia in my behalf."

"It's not entirely on your behalf, you know. In fact, to be quite frank, it is only in the smallest part in your behalf. I must go for Perry's sake . . . and Amy's too, for things in this house are becoming quite unbearable and are bound to affect *both* children . . . although Perry's situation seems to be the most urgent, if one only looks into his eyes, you know . . ."

"I see." Mr. Clapham eyed her dubiously. "And you're going *alone*? Without anyone's permission?"

Miss Elspeth nodded, biting her lip worriedly. "Yes, I *must*. I shall try to catch the night mail coach at Devizes . . . if I can persuade one of the grooms to drive me there . . ."

"But it's dreadfully cold this evening. The sky is very threatening, Miss Elspeth. It may even *snow*," Mr. Clapham pointed out.

"Oh, I shan't mind the weather. My shawl is very warm . . . and they do say that the mail coaches are so very crowded, one is bound to feel warm in the crush of bodies, don't you agree? And even if it *should* snow, the mail coach usually gets through. But you must promise to keep a close watch on the children while I'm gone, Mr. Clapham. This is the most important task of all. May I count on you?"

"Yes, of course. It is very good of you to take this upon yourself. I quite admire you. And I shall do my very best to watch over the children, so long as his lordship doesn't come up and order me away."

"Oh," Elspeth cried in dismay, "you don't think . . . he wouldn't possibly . . . would he? But he rarely comes up to this floor, and we must hope that . . ."

With the rest of her thought unspoken, she got up from her chair and, squaring her shoulders resolutely, went to the door. The tutor jumped up, picked up her valise and the reticule she'd forgotten and handed them to her. Wishing her Godspeed, he accompanied her down the hall and watched until she disappeared down the stairway before he returned to his room, shaking his head with misgivings. She would lose her reticule before reaching Devizes, he surmised, and she would be robbed of the rest of her possessions before reaching London. She was too bubbleheaded to carry out such a plan. As far as he could judge, Miss Elspeth Deering was incapable of taking herself to the *stable* without mishap. She would never be able to carry off a trip to London, not in a hundred years.

But Elspeth Deering arrived on the doorstep of the Matthews residence in Brook Street before eight the following morning without suffering a mishap greater than losing one of her gloves. The butler answered her knock wearing an expression on his face that said as plainly as words that the hour was far too early to be paying calls. "I wish to s-see Miss Olivia Matthews, p-please," Elspeth told him as bravely as she could while shivering with cold and fright.

"None of the family has as yet come down to breakfast," the butler said reprovingly. "You certainly cannot wish me to disturb Miss Matthews so early."

"N-No, of course not," Elspeth said, looking about her desperately, wondering where she was to go on this freezing morning while she waited for a more appropriate hour to pay her call.

The butler, seeing her shiver again, softened. "I suppose there would be no objection to your waiting inside," he said and reached for her valise.

She followed him into the entryway and down a short hallway. There, at the side of the stairway, he motioned her to a stiff, tall-backed chair and placed her bag beside it. "You may sit here," he said coldly and left her.

She sat down meekly, pulled off her one glove and folded her hands in her lap, uncomfortably aware of having blundered in at an awkward hour and wondering at the reception Miss Olivia would give her. Soon a step on the stairway set her heart hammering. An elderly gentleman came into view as he turned from the stairway and strolled in her direction. She recognized him at once as Sir Octavius Matthews—she'd caught a glimpse of him at his daughter's funeral—and she jumped up and dropped a quick curtsey. Sir Octavius' eyes brushed her face without interest as he walked right past her. "Good morning," he murmured absently, continuing without a pause down the hall and disappearing into a nearby doorway. His indifference to the presence of a stranger in his hallway was completely unsettling. Elspeth began to fear that she should never have come. Perhaps she should run out of this place and fly back to Langley Park before...

But her thoughts of flight were aborted by the appearance of the butler with a breakfast tray. The smell of fried ham reminded her that she hadn't eaten for many hours, and she wondered if the butler was bringing the tray to her. But he did not glance in her direction. Instead, he paraded down the hall to the room into which Sir Octavius had gone. A moment later he emerged without the tray and, still paying her not the slightest heed, marched back to the nether regions of the house.

This lack of attention to her existence was extremely unnerving. Her pulse began to race uncomfortably and her indecision grew. Another heavy step on the stair, however, kept her frozen in her place. This time, a younger gentleman appeared, rounding the stairway in his turn. It was Miss Olivia's brother, Charles Matthews, whose high forehead and keen eyes had excited her admiration when she'd seen him at Langley Park. She felt her pulse race even faster and hoped desperately that he would ignore her as his father had. But Charles stopped in his tracks and stared at the unexpected visitor sitting so stiffly in his hallway, his eyebrows raised inquiringly. "How do you do, ma'am?" he asked politely. "Are you waiting for someone?"

"Y-Yes, sir," Elspeth said, getting up awkwardly and bobbing diffidently. "I've come to s-see Miss Olivia, please."

"Oh, I see." The young man smiled at her reassuringly. "I'm her brother, Charles. I believe I've seen you before. It was at Langley, was it not?"

Elspeth blushed and her hand flew to her forehead to brush away a wisp of hair that had fallen over one eye. "Yes, Mr. Matthews. It is...most kind in you to remember me. I'm Elspeth Deering, governess to Lord Strickland's children, you see, and I..."

Charles waited politely for the lady to finish her sentence, but not another word was forthcoming. "But why are you sitting out here in the hallway, Miss Deering?" he asked when he realized she would say no more. "And why has no one taken your shawl? I think you must be frozen! Come in to the drawing room where there is, I am sure, a nice fire. You can warm yourself while I fetch my sister."

"Oh, no, sir, don't do that! That is, I'm sure you are...very kind . . . but I would not wish to disturb . . . I shall be happy to wait for her right here..."

"No need for that, Miss Deering," Charles said after another brief pause. "If you'll not permit me to call her, you must at least let me make you comfortable while you wait. Please let me escort you to the drawing room."

"Oh...thank you, sir, but I'm quite comfortable...that is, I would not wish to put you out..."

Charles looked at her in some bafflement. Then, with a shrug, he said, "Very well, then, Miss Deering, if you're certain there's nothing I can do for you, I'll take myself off." He made a little bow and continued down the hall. Suddenly he paused and turned back to her. "I say, have you breakfasted? Because if you haven't, I'd be delighted to have your company at the breakfast table."

Elspeth, who had sunk down on her chair as soon as Charles had turned away, jumped nervously to her feet again. "Well, I've not exactly breakfasted," she murmured awkwardly, "but a gentleman who sat next to me . . . on the mail, you know . . . was kind enough to give me some bread and cheese...and I'm not feeling at all hungry . . . although I do thank you for your . . . quite overwhelming kindness...and I don't wish to keep you from your..."

"You have offered me a great many thanks for very little,

my dear," Charles said in amusement, studying the young woman curiously. "You can't pretend that a bit of bread and cheese is an adequate breakfast on a day like this." The girl was a strange creature, he noted. Her conversation was somewhat disjointed, but Charles was touched by the frightened look in her eyes, the redness of her upturned little nose, and the way her fingers nervously twisted her one glove as she spoke. "Oh, come along with me, do! Here, let me take your shawl. If nothing else, you can do with a cup of hot tea to warm you."

Without permitting her to resist, he removed the shawl from her shoulders and threw it over the bannister. Then, taking one icy little hand in his, he pulled her forcibly behind him into the morning room.

When the butler appeared with another tray and found her sitting opposite Mr. Matthews in apparent familiarity, his manner to her became more deferential. She was supplied with more eggs, hot biscuits, ham slices, toast, jam and jellies than she could have consumed in a week of breakfasts. Through all this, Mr. Matthews kept up a stream of polite conversation, pausing only to urge more food on her, intending to set her at ease, but she only became more uncomfortable than before. What would Miss Olivia *think* when she came down and discovered that her brother-in-law's *governess* was sitting at her breakfast table, being treated like an honored guest and taking up her brother's time and attention? In spite of Charles Matthews' urging, she could not make herself eat a bite. She was too fearful of what Miss Olivia might say when she discovered that the reliable Miss Elspeth had deserted her post and had come all this way to London for the express purpose of complaining about the gentleman who employed her.

She had not so very long to stew in apprehension, for Miss Olivia soon appeared in the morning room doorway. She had evidently not been told that a guest was present, for she was absorbed in the newspaper she was holding in her hand. "I say, Charles," she remarked without lifting her eyes, "have you seen this? They've arrested Leigh and John Hunt, simply because of what they wrote in the *Examiner* about the Prince last year. Of all the dastardly—"

She looked up from the paper to find herself staring into

Miss Elspeth's very frightened eyes. "M-Miss Olivia—" the governess stammered, starting from her chair.

"Miss *Elspeth*!" Olivia gasped in immediate alarm. "What are you doing here? Good *lord*, has something dreadful happened at Langley?"

"N-No . . . no!" Elspeth said quickly. She hadn't meant to alarm Miss Olivia unduly. She was doing everything wrong. She must say something reassuring. "Nothing so *very* dreadful . . ." she said awkwardly, belatedly realizing that reassuring Miss Olivia was just the thing she ought *not* to do. Her throat choked up, and her words became mired down in indecision and confusion. To get herself out of the fix, she did the only thing she could think of, the only thing she ever did in times of stress—she burst into tears.

chapter twelve

When Olivia was finally able to extract from the weeping governess a passably intelligible account of the happenings at Langley Park (her efforts at communication with Miss Elspeth considerably hampered not only by the girl's natural incoherence but by Charles' repeated and irritating warnings to "stop badgering the poor chit"), she knew she had to leave for Langley at once. But all sorts of impediments, both natural and man-made, seemed to loom up to bar her way.

The situation was very much like a nightmare—the sort of nocturnal adventure in which the dreamer has an urgent errand at a particular and distant place and is prevented from getting there by all kinds of phantasmagorical obstructions. In this case, her eagerness to take herself to her nephew's side seemed to grow more urgent as one obstruction after another appeared to block her way. First, there was Charles. He refused to let her question Miss Elspeth until the governess had been taken to the drawing room, installed in the wing chair near the fire, given a sip of brandy and permitted to overcome her bout of tears. Miss Elspeth's tears gave Olivia the first indication that she was about to become involved in a nightmare. Charles insisted that she should not question the governess until Miss Elspeth's crying had ceased, but since the young governess would burst into fresh lachrymal outpourings each time Charles said or did something kind (and Charles was behaving more kindly to the young woman than Olivia could bear), Olivia despaired of *ever* seeing Miss Elspeth dry her eyes.

The second obstacle was her own reluctance to return to Langley Park. According to the disjointed report Miss Elspeth gave, his lordship was still in residence at Langley and showed no inclination to return to London. Olivia didn't know if she had the courage to face him again. Her feelings of guilt for having withheld from him the truth of her sister's illness had not abated, but her dislike of his arrogance, his arbitrary domination of the lives of those around him and his Tory views of the world had not abated either. Although she could not forget her sister's entirely different view of his character, and the tenderness and pain in his face when he'd come to her bedside, she still clung to her habitual, unchanging revulsion toward him. Yet sometimes she found herself thinking of him with a dawning, if reluctant, admiration. This confusing conflict of feelings was complicated by her memory of a shattering, illicit and completely disturbing embrace which she could not manage to erase from her mind. To have to face him again was not a pleasing prospect.

But this obstacle would have to be overcome. Her sister's last words to her had been a plea to watch over the family. If Perry needed her, she had no choice but to go to his side. As the picture Miss Elspeth painted of the unhappy boy pierced her consciousness, Olivia's determination to return to Langley hardened. There was no question but that she must leave at once.

No sooner had she made up her mind, however, when the nightmarish impediments began to multiply. Even Nature herself stepped in to make difficulties for her. All during the previous week the frosty air and the heavy skies seemed to presage snow, but not a flake had fallen. Now, however, at the very moment she decided to make her departure, the snow began to fall. By the time her portmanteau had been packed, the roadway was covered with a blanket of white. To leave for Wiltshire in these circumstances would have been foolhardy indeed, for it was obvious that the roads would shortly be impassable. There was nothing for it but to wait until the storm had passed. But the snow did not abate that day, and Olivia gritted her teeth in frustration as she sent a housemaid to ready the spare bedroom for Miss Elspeth.

The wait for the snow to cease falling seemed endless. All

that day and during the interminable night that followed, Olivia seemed to hear her sister's voice asking her to watch over the children. Why, she asked herself repeatedly, had she let her pride—and Strickland's rudeness—drive her from their sides? She slept briefly and fitfully and seemed to hear Perry's weeping as a background to all her dreams.

To her relief, the morning dawned clear. Telling herself that the nightmarish feeling that had haunted her since the governess's arrival would soon be at an end, she hurried downstairs, sent for the coachman and succeeded in convincing him that the roads would be adequately clear by noon and that they could easily reach Langley by eight or nine that night. To her chagrin, however, Miss Elspeth appeared at the breakfast table looking heavy-lidded and ill, reluctantly admitting in response to Olivia's questioning that she had, indeed, caught a chill. "But I don't refine on it too much, Miss Olivia. I shan't permit a slight indisposition to deter me from the journey."

"A *slight* indisposition?" Olivia asked suspiciously, putting a hand on the governess's forehead. "You are feverish, if I'm a judge."

"It's only the slightest flush," Miss Elspeth insisted, edging away from Olivia and throwing on her shawl, determined to prove that she was quite capable of proceeding with their plans. "Do you think we shall be able to depart shortly, or shall we have to wait until the afternoon when . . . er . . . the sun has had a chance to . . . er . . . ?"

Olivia, guiltily aware of the young woman's watery eyes and flushed cheeks, nevertheless tried to ignore the problem. "We shall be on our way by noon," she said firmly.

But Charles stepped in and put his foot down. "You'll not depart at noon, my girl," he declared. "In fact, you'll not depart *at all* today. Miss Deering will return to bed until her fever has completely abated. To go outdoors in this cold while one is feverish would be disastrous."

"Charles is quite right," Olivia agreed reluctantly. "You must go back to bed. But Charles, why may I not leave anyway? Miss Elspeth can follow later, when she has quite recovered."

"But . . . to travel all alone . . . is it quite the thing to . . . ?" Miss Elspeth asked weakly.

"I've traveled alone any number of times," Olivia declared. "I don't see why I can't do so now."

To Olivia's intense relief, Charles made no objection, and the carriage was permitted to depart for Langley at the appointed hour. She sat back against the squabs, wrapped the lap robe about her legs and permitted herself to hope that the nightmare was at last drawing to an end. Because the first few hours of the trip were uneventful—the roads having been made passable by the warmth of the sun and the tracks of the numerous vehicles which had passed over them—she was soon lulled into complacency. She would shortly arrive at Langley Park, ready and able to take her poor nephew under her protective wing and do battle for him. But in the manner of most nightmares, just when one believes that all the fantastic obstacles that can possibly appear have already done so, another one rears up ahead.

As the carriage journeyed farther and farther from London, the traffic grew thinner and the roads more difficult to travel upon. The snow deepened as they moved westward, causing the horses to slow their pace. The trip, which normally would have taken no more than nine hours, now seemed endless. By the time dusk fell, Wollins, the coachman, began to realize that, since they were already several hours behind schedule, they were not likely to reach their destination that night. Fearful that the cold night air would turn the soft snow icy, he suggested to Olivia that they stop at an inn for the night.

Olivia objected stubbornly, for she was impatient to escape from what felt like a deepening mire of delay. But as the night darkened, the road grew slick, and she could feel the horses' hooves slipping against the ice. Reluctantly, she agreed to permit the coachman to pull into the nearst innyard.

The Hare and Horn was a coaching inn, a convenient stopping-place for the feeding of stagecoach passengers but not noted for the nicety of its overnight accommodations. The innkeeper eyed Olivia suspiciously and demanded his money in advance. It was only the appearance of Wollins at the door—for the coachman was an elderly retainer who, because of his dignified demeanor and well-cut livery, gave the innkeeper pause—that saved Olivia from greater disrespect. "Watch yer tongue when ye speak to my mistress," the coachman told the innkeeper severely, "or ye'll deal wi' my fist on yer beak."

"Well, 'ow wuz I t' know she's a lady?" the innkeeper asked in injured innocence. "Wut sort o' lady is it don't 'ave a maid with 'er?"

Olivia colored and ordered her dinner with cold aloofness. In truth, she had never wished for, and didn't employ, an abigail for her own service. She had always been too independent to wish for assistance in putting on her clothes or dressing her hair. But she couldn't blame the innkeeper for looking askance at a lady who was traveling unaccompanied. If she had anticipated spending the night at an inn, she would have brought one of the housemaids with her.

However, the admonished innkeeper immediately mended his ways and served her an enormous, if tasteless, dinner, hovering over her with deferential obsequiousness. He then led her to a bedroom which he claimed was the best in the house but which was small and dank-smelling, with a ceiling so slanted that one could not stand erect on the far side of the bed. She uttered no word of complaint, however, for her eye fell on a soft feather bed covered with a goose-down comforter which was so inviting that it made up for all the other deficiencies. She shut and locked the door and, weary to the bone, quickly stripped off her outer garments and slipped into bed. To her chagrin, she found the comforter smotheringly warm, yet if she attempted to throw it off, she was frozen by the cold air of the room. No amount of poking at the small fire was sufficient to warm the room in the slightest. Surrendering to the inevitable, she crept under the stifling quilt, gritted her teeth and prepared to endure a sleepless night.

Toward dawn, she fell into a heavy sleep, waking to find the sun already high. With a cry of annoyance, she jumped out of bed, banging her head solidly against the low ceiling. Dazed and smarting with pain, she nevertheless dressed hurriedly and ran downstairs to learn from the innkeeper that her coachman was walking the horses around the innyard to keep them warm—and had been doing so for more than an hour. Impatient to start out, she made for the door, but the innkeeper pointed out that he had set out a breakfast of steak-and-kidney pie, bacon, poached eggs, muffins and hot tea especially for her. With a sigh, she sent him out to inform the coachman that she would drink a cup of tea and be ready to leave in a moment. Hastily, without sitting down, she took a swallow of the steaming brew and scalded her tongue. When she at last climbed into the carriage, with a lump swelling on her head and her tongue burning painfully, she wondered irritably what next would befall her on this nightmarish journey.

But no other obstacles appeared until she walked into the hall of the manor house at Langley Park later that afternoon. "You may inform his lordship of my arrival, Fincher," she said to the surprised but obviously pleased butler as she threw off her pelisse and tossed it to him, "but I'll pay my respects to him later. I want to see Perry at once."

Pulling off her gloves, she ran across the huge hall toward the stairway. But as she might have guessed, the last and greatest obstacle appeared to bar her way. At that moment the library doors opened and Strickland himself emerged. "Well, *well*," he said in his usual, sardonic style, "what have we *here*? Can it be Miss Olivia Matthews? This is quite like a scene from *The Prodigal's Return*."

Olivia glowered at him in chagrin. He seemed to loom up before her—one more manifestation in the series of nightmarish impediments to obstruct her path to her nephew's side. He stood towering over her in his shirt sleeves, his neckcloth open, his face unshaven, his entire aspect dark and forbidding. She felt tortured, frightened, foolish and worried; she had a painful lump on her head and a scorched tongue; she was aching in body and spirit and in no mood for arguments. "I shall be available to converse with you later, my lord," she said grimly, "but at the moment I wish you will stand aside. I want to see Perry, and I shall permit *no one*—not even *you*, my lord—to prevent me!"

Strickland blinked at her explosion of temper and stepped backward in surprise. "*Prevent* you, ma'am? Why should I want to do that? What *are* you talking about?"

"I am talking about you, sir. I refuse to listen to another of your speeches about my meddling and interfering. I have no patience for it now."

"But I haven't said anything about—"

"No, not yet. But I'm certain you are forming a speech in

your mind. If you are, I'd be greatly obliged if you'd keep it to yourself until later. In the meantime, I merely wish to point out that I have a perfect right to visit my sister's children, whatever you—"

"But I've never said you *haven't*," the astounded Strickland said.

Olivia was taken aback. "You haven't?"

"Of course I haven't. Have you ever heard me say that you couldn't see the children?"

She stared up at him suspiciously. "Well, then ... if you will let me pass—"

He stepped aside and bowed low, motioning toward the stairway in ironic mimicry of a footman. "Go right ahead, my dear. Make yourself quite at home. This is Freedom Hall to you, I assure you. Freedom Hall."

She gave him one long glance of amazement and ran past him to the stairs. At the first landing, she glanced back. He was standing where she'd left him, looking after her with an expression of surprise still on his face. But when their eyes met, his look changed to one of mocking amusement. He made another bow, more satiric than the first. She put up her chin in annoyance and continued hastily up the stairs.

Neither of the children was in the schoolroom, but the sound of Mr. Clapham's voice brought Olivia to the doorway of Perry's bedroom. She paused on the threshold to watch them before she made her presence known. Amy was sitting at the window, holding a slate on her lap and concentrating on forming letters with such intensity that her tongue was sticking out of a corner of her mouth as if it were trying to aid her fingers. Mr. Clapham was seated at the side of the bed, reading aloud to a supine Perry from Goldsmith's *History of England*. Perry, however, staring up at the ceiling, was not really listening. His eyes seemed to be focused on something far away, and the droop of his mouth gave pathetic and mute evidence of his bewildered unhappiness. The governess had not exaggerated in her description of his precarious state of mind. Olivia was very glad she'd come.

"Gorgana, the enchantress, awaits you," she announced with a mischievous laugh. "How can you remain cooped up here indoors when I've transformed the whole outdoors into a snow-covered fairyland just for you?"

"Aunt *Wivie*, Aunt *Wivie*!" Amy squealed in delight, dropping her chalk and hopping out of her chair. Perry's head turned, his mouth dropped open, and he stared at Olivia in disbelief, while the tutor, his eyes wide in adoring relief, got awkwardly to his feet. Amy flew across the room and was enveloped in a warm hug. Then Olivia went to the bed and sat down beside her nephew. The boy sat up, peered at her for a moment, and then fell against her with a desperate eagerness, hugging her tightly and burying his head in her shoulder. "I thought you . . . weren't coming," he said, choked.

Over the boy's head, Olivia looked across at the tutor, her eyes questioning. He made a shrugging motion, as if to say, "I don't know *what's* wrong with him."

She nodded and looked down at Perry. "Let me take a good look at you, Perry, love," she said, determinedly cheerful. "Amy has grown so much in the short time I've been gone, I can scarcely credit it. What about you? I'll wager you've grown a whole inch."

"You've been gone a *long* time," he corrected, releasing her and looking at her reprovingly.

"Yes, you're right. It seems like an age, doesn't it? Are you sick, Perry? Is that why you're in bed?"

"I don't . . ." Perry began but finished with a small sigh.

"He hasn't felt well enough to get up these last two days," the tutor explained, "but the doctor says he's quite well. Just a bit tired out."

"Papa said I could stay in bed for today, but I must get up tomorrow," Perry added wearily.

"Does something *hurt* you, Perry? Your head? Or your stomach?"

"Just something in here." The boy put a hand on his chest. "It feels so heavy sometimes. Miss Elspeth said it's only the megrims, and I shouldn't mind it. She went to fetch you, you know, when Sir Budgidore fell ill."

"Yes, she did. And here I am."

His underlip began to tremble. "Sir Budgidore died, you know. You didn't come in time."

Olivia pulled him into her arms and cradled his head on her shoulder. "I'm so sorry, love. We shall miss him at the Round Table. Perhaps, tonight, after supper, we can hold a dedication ceremony—dedicate one of the seats at the Round Table to be forever called the Budgidore Chair in his honor. Would you like that?"

Perry lifted his head and looked at her with brightening eyes. "Oh, yes, I *would*. Why can't we do it right now?"

Mr. Clapham cleared his throat. "Lord Strickland has ordered that we . . . er . . . refrain from playing the Round Table game, you know."

"Oh, don't worry about that," Olivia said with matter-of-fact cheerfulness, smiling reassuringly at her nephew. "Everything will be—"

"Er . . . Miss Olivia . . . I wouldn't . . ." Mr. Clapham said, his voice frightened.

Olivia serenely smoothed her nephew's hair from his forehead. "There's not the slightest need to be concerned. I intend to speak to his lordship on the matter myself. This very day, in fact."

"Do you indeed?" came a sardonic voice from the doorway.

"Papa!" little Amy chortled cheerfully, toddling to the door and taking his hand. "Aw we going to wide?"

Strickland, standing in the doorway and regarding his sister-in-law with glinting eyes and upraised brows, merely patted his daughter on the head. "Not today, little one. There's too much snow on the path. Besides, I gather that your Aunt Olivia wishes to have a chat with me."

Olivia, startled, felt her heart begin to race. "Yes, I *do* wish to have a talk with you, my lord. But not just at this moment."

"This is a *very good time*," he said meaningfully, the glare in his eyes an unmistakable order.

Olivia had had quite enough frustration. Her head still ached, her tongue still burned, and her heart was hammering in her chest in fear—a fear that she wanted desperately to hide from Perry's alarmed scrutiny. She put up her chin bravely. "*Later*, sir, if you don't mind. The children and I have a great deal to talk about first."

His lordship's lips tightened, and the muscle in his jaw worked angrily. "*Now!*" he barked.

Perry started, and his whole body twitched in fear. "Don't have a row, Aunt Livie," he urged, his voice trembling. "I d-don't have to play Round Table. It's all right. I don't want P-Papa to be angry with you."

Olivia pulled the boy into a protective embrace, glaring up accusingly at Strickland. "Your father is *not* angry with me. Are you, my lord?"

Before he could respond, Perry gave a choking sob. "Yes, he *is*! I can *t-tell*! He's going to send you away again!"

"I shall do no such thing," Strickland exclaimed, stung. "What sort of monster do you think I am?"

Perry's face came up from Olivia's shoulder. He looked at his father, his face strained and suspicious. "I think I feel sick again," he murmured.

"Here, love, lie down," Olivia said soothingly, smoothing his pillows and easing him down on them. "Your father didn't mean to upset you. We aren't going to have a row, and he isn't going to send me away. Isn't that right, my lord?"

Lord Strickland looked from one to the other in disgust. "Of course that's right," he muttered. Then he fixed a meaningful eye on Olivia's face. "Nevertheless, I would like to exchange a few words with you, ma'am."

Perry sat up fearfully. "But not to have a row?" he pleaded, instantly alarmed again. "Do you promise?"

His lordship's brows drew together thoughtfully. "I don't have rows with everyone I speak to," he said, coming up to the bed and frowning down at his son. "What makes you so afraid we'll have a row?"

Perry looked up at him, his mouth quivering. "Well... I know you don't l-like me to play R-Round Table... but Aunt Livie says it will be all right to play... so there's *bound* to be a r-row, isn't there?"

Olivia squeezed the boy's hand. "Only a difference of opinion, love. It needn't be a quarrel."

"Quite right," Strickland said curtly, "There is no necessity at all for quarreling." He looked at Olivia with a marked diminution of hostility. "Very well, ma'am, finish your visit with the children if you wish. But we shall continue our... er... difference of opinion later. I shall expect you in the library before you change for dinner, if you please."

The tone was cold, but Olivia realized that he'd made a concession. Had he been upset by the boy's obvious alarm? She looked up into his face but could find no answer in his impassive look. "As you wish, my lord," she said, turning her eyes back to her nephew.

There was a moment of silence, and then Strickland left the room. When the sound of his footsteps had died away, Perry sighed deeply. "I suppose we won't be able to have the ceremony after all," he said, his voice dull and hopeless.

"The one for Sir Budgidore?" Olivia asked. "Of *course* we will."

"Really?" Perry looked up at her, scarcely able to permit himself to hope. "Won't Papa tell you not to permit it?"

Olivia's eyes glinted and her fingers clenched. "Your father," she said with a missionary's zeal, "will do nothing of the sort."

The firmness of her tone relieved him. He sat up with a grin and gave his aunt a quick hug. "Then let's do it now," he urged eagerly. "Right now!"

"No, dearest. I don't think now's the time."

"Why not?" His face clouded again. "You said—"

"Yes, but tonight will be better. Right now, you and Amy are going to dress in your warmest clothes, your mittens and your goloshoes, and we're going out to play in the snow."

"Oh, how wovewy," Amy gurgled happily. "Get out of bed, Pewwy, and wet's find Tiwda. We can ask hew to dwess us at once!"

After turning the children over to the housemaid who was temporarily caring for them in Miss Elspeth's absence, Olivia walked out of the room, having promised the children that their afternoon would be glorious, "all sparkling and brilliant and frosty... and we'll make great big footprints in the snow, and toss snowballs, and have all manner of fun." She was followed out by Mr. Clapham. Once in the hallway, he approached her shyly. "I can't tell you how relieved I am to see you, Miss Matthews," he told her.

"Yes, I know, Mr. Clapham. Thank you for the excellent care you've evidently given the children."

He shrugged modestly. "Shall I get dressed and take them

outside? Perhaps you'd rather go downstairs and see his lordship."

"No, thank you. I'll play with the children myself. I intend to see his lordship now, while the children are dressing. Why don't you take a rest for the afternoon?"

"Very well, then, ma'am. If you're certain I won't be needed, I'll go ahead with my packing."

"Packing?"

The tutor's smile faded. "Didn't Miss Elspeth tell you? I've been discharged."

"Yes, she did. But you are not to pay any attention to that. Everything is going to be fine from now on. I shall see to it."

He looked at her dubiously. "I . . . don't think so, Miss Matthews. His lordship was quite definite, you see, when he sacked me. You will have quite enough to . . . I mean, I wouldn't wish for you to . . . er . . . come to points with his lordship on *my* account."

"It will not be on your account but on Perry's. And as for coming to points with him," Olivia responded, her jaw firmly set, "it's about time *somebody* took him on. It's not a good thing for a man to have his own way about everything. It makes him a tyrant."

She went quickly down the hall to the stairway, determined to face the tyrant before her courage deserted her. The tutor looked after her with admiration but nevertheless quite doubtful of her success. "A tyrant he is," Mr. Clapham muttered to himself as he went down the hall to his room. "I wish her luck with him. She'll need it."

chapter thirteen

She paused outside the library door to, as her brother Jamie would say, gird up her loins for battle. She felt ill-equipped for the encounter, for the lump on her head was distractingly painful, and the strain of the past three days was beginning to show itself in the tremor of her fingers and the nervous twitching of a muscle in her cheek. She struggled against an almost overpowering temptation to turn and flee, but she knew she could not. Too much depended on her success in this skirmish. So she tapped on the door and entered.

Strickland was sitting at the far side of the room before a window, reading a letter. The draperies had been opened just wide enough to provide him with a beam of light in which to see. The dimness of the rest of the room contrasted sharply with the bright arc of light in which he sat. He had to peer intently into the shadows to make out who had come in. "Oh, it's you," he muttered, throwing the letter upon a chairside table and getting to his feet. "I didn't expect you quite so soon."

"I'd like to come to an understanding as soon as possible, my lord," she said with more assurance than she felt.

"Good," Strickland said, striding across the room to confront her. "Therefore, I suggest that you listen to me carefully so that your understanding will be complete. You're my late wife's sister, and as such you're always welcome in this house. The children hold you in great affection—as evidently you do them—and I've no wish to suppress or subvert that relationship.

However, I must remind you again that Perry is my son, and I will brook no interference in my management of him. It is *I* who will make the decisions relating to his nurturing, his education, his pastimes and whatever else concerns him."

"Yes, of course," Olivia interjected, taken aback by the cold objectivity of his tone, "but—"

"Don't interrupt, please. We've both given our words that we shall have no row. You need merely *listen*. I have only this to add. You, my dear, must accept my decisions without question and refrain from undermining those decisions in your conversations with the boy and with those I employ to care for him. I hope my meaning is quite clear and that I shall have no need to repeat this speech in the future."

"But . . . may I not even *discuss* with you those decisions of yours which I believe to be in error?" she asked, aghast.

"I have nothing further to say." He went back to his chair and resumed his reading of his letter.

Olivia gritted her teeth in rage. "You cannot *seriously* expect me to—" she began, following him across the room.

He didn't even look up from his page. "That is all I have to say to you, ma'am."

"But on the matter of the Round Table game . . . and the tutor's discharge . . ." she insisted urgently, trying to contain her fury. "Surely we can *discuss*—"

"I'm afraid I've said all I intend to." He stood up, crossed to the door and held it open for her. "Good afternoon, my dear. I hope you and the children enjoy your romp in the snow."

Olivia was so infuriated she could barely breathe. She thought a blood vessel in her neck would burst. "*Ooooh!*" she exploded, stamping a foot in frustration. "You are *impossible!*"

"Yes, I suppose I am. You are, of course, free to discuss *my* shortcomings whenever you like. Although at the *moment* I'm quite busy."

Speechless, seething, and completely at a loss, she stalked across the room and swept out past him, not even favoring him with so much as a glance. Her stormy exit had not the slightest effect on him, however. He merely closed the door quietly behind her.

She wheeled about and stared at the closed door. How *dared* he! He'd treated her as if she were a mere hireling—a maid-servant in his his employ whom he could order about at will! The word "tyrant" was too good for him! She trembled in helpless impotence, wanting to scream, to kick the door, or, better still, to kick *him*!

The sound of clumsy but eager footsteps on the stairs caught her ear. The children clambered down the stairs, barely restrained by Tilda, dressed and impatient for the outdoors. With enormous effort, Olivia pulled herself together, put on a smile and went to meet them. She would have to postpone making a decision about what next she would do in regard to their father. Whatever her next step was to be, it was something that would have to wait.

Later, stumbling through the snow after the children, whose high-pitched laughter struck the cold air like tinkling bells (a sound that was as healing to her spirit as it was to theirs), Olivia found that her mind was unable to refrain from reviewing the latest confrontation with her dastardly brother-in-law. How was she to keep him from stubbornly and autocratically stripping from his son everything in the child's life that made him feel happy and secure? Certainly another confrontation would be useless with such a tyrant, she realized. In all their previous altercations, she'd come away decidedly the loser. What could she say or do to avoid losing again? Perhaps she had to find a more promising way to deal with him than confrontation.

But *every* encounter with Strickland seemed to become a confrontation. How could she make him listen to her without falling into disagreement? While she dodged snowballs, brushed snowflakes from the children's reddened cheeks and rescued Amy from snow drifts that proved to be too deep for her, Olivia's mind probed for an answer. She *had* to discover what it was in their relationship that made them antagonistic from the outset.

A soft ball of snow, well aimed by her nephew, splattered squarely in her face at the precise moment when a sudden insight struck her mind. While the boy cackled in mischievous glee to see his aunt gasp in surprise, topple back and sputteringly eject a mouthful of snow, she—even while blinking and choking—found herself mulling over this new idea. *Strickland saw her as an enemy*!

Olivia had always been aware that her brother-in-law didn't like her...that he thought of her as an eccentric and old-maidish bluestocking. She was also aware that he was infuriated at what he judged to be her interference in his family life. But it had not occurred to her before that her brother-in-law might very well look upon her as a foe—perhaps even a venomous and bitter one. The idea struck with the force of a revelation!

After all, she had accosted him on more than one occasion with accusations of very serious crimes: adultery for one, and the abuse of his son for another. It was perhaps not very surprising that he viewed her with belligerence whenever he saw her. He might very well have felt a need to *defend* himself against her attacks by attacking her in his turn.

Picking herself up from the snow, brushing off her skirts and scooping up a handful of snow to prepare to chase her nephew with a retributive counterattack, she smiled to herself with satisfaction. She had come to a bit of understanding which would help her to find a way to approach her difficult brother-in-law. All she had to do was to convince him that *she could become an ally instead of an adversary*.

But how? Their past encounters had widened the already wide barrier which had existed between them from the first. If only she could make him see that the past must be forgotten, that their mutual dislike must be ignored, and that their differences must be put aside for the sake of the children. Her eyes misted over as she watched the two innocents cavorting through the drifts, pelting each other with handfuls of snow and chortling in the happy, carefree manner that should have been their *usual* spirit but was all too rare for them. If only she could convince Strickland that they must both strive for the same goal—the happiness of these two motherless tots.

"Aunt Livie, let's build a snow fort," Perry called out, his breath visible in the frosty air.

"That's a wonderful idea," she said with enthusiasm. "How do we do it?"

"I don't know. We must shape the snow into blocks—like stones, you know—and set them one on the other."

"Yes, that sounds like an excellent plan," his aunt agreed.

"Do you think we should clear a space first?"

Perry considered the matter. "Would that be a very huge task?"

"Quite huge, I think." Suddenly her heart gave a little leap as she was struck with an inspiration. "What we need is somebody really strong and clever to help us. A strong, grown man."

"Do you think so? Shall I call Mr. Clapham?"

"No," his aunt said, looking toward the house speculatively. "You start to shape the blocks, Perry . . . and get Amy to help you. And I shall go into the house and call for some *real* assistance."

"What do you mean, Aunt Livie? Whom will you call?"

"I think, love," she said with a broad smile, "that I shall call the very *best* person for the task. Your father."

Perry seemed to freeze. "Oh, I don't . . . ! Never mind, Aunt Livie. We don't w-want to disturb Papa."

"We won't disturb him, love. I'm certain he'd *like* to help you with the fort."

Perry eyed her dubiously. "Would he? I don't . . . think so. Besides, he'd get angry if I did something wrong . . ."

Olivia knelt beside him and tightened his scarf about his neck. "Are you *afraid* of him, Perry? There's not the least need to be, you know. He's not a monster. He may *seem* angry sometimes, when he has a great deal on his mind, but he doesn't *mean* to be cross with you. If you remember that you're his first-and-only son, and that he loves you very much, you won't need to feel alarmed if he scowls a bit."

Perry thought over what she'd said. "Do you really think he would *like* to build a snow fort with me?"

Olivia smiled and got to her feet. "I shouldn't be at all surprised. But let me go in and ask him, and then we shall see what we shall see."

She walked briskly into the library without knocking, carrying his greatcoat over her arm and his beaver in her hand. He looked up from his newspaper, startled.

"Will you put on your coat and come out with me, sir? Perry has need of you."

He looked alarmed. "Has something happened to the boy?" he asked, starting from his chair.

"No, of course not. We just need your help. We're playing in the snow, you know. I've brought your—"

"You wish me to come and play in the snow?" He stared at her in revulsion. "*Play* in the *snow*? I think, Olivia, that something has addled your wits."

"I refuse to let you goad me into quarreling with you, my lord. Here—I've brought your hat and greatcoat. Please put them on. Perry wants to build a snow fort, and he needs some help. No one but his father will do for it."

He eyed her suspiciously. "Perry asked for *me*?"

"Yes," she lied. "Does that surprise you?"

"Yes, in fact it does. I don't remember his ever seeking my companionship before."

"Perhaps he was afraid you'd refuse him—as you are doing now."

"Hmmm." He frowned at her sullenly. "You are not suggesting, are you, that I'm so forbidding that my own son—?"

She bit her lip. Didn't he *know* how forbidding he was? But following such avenues of thought would result in another quarrel, and she had another intention entirely. "No, my lord, of course not," she said, looking down at the floor to keep from meeting his eyes, "although you *have* been known to be short-tempered . . ."

He snorted. "With *you*, perhaps. You'd set the temper of a *saint* to boil! But I've not been especially short-tempered with Perry. At least, not that I can remember."

"But you've been short with people in his presence, and that, you know, can be enough to frighten a child."

"Rubbish. Nothing about me to frighten anyone. Perry has always been too timorous—I'd noticed that from his earliest days. Spends too much time with women. Why, even little *Amy* runs up to me with less trepidation than her brother."

"All the more reason for you to spend more time with the boy. How will your son know how to be a man without a proper example?"

He fixed his eye on her again, as if wary of her motives. "Are you trying one of your interfering tricks, ma'am? I hope you are not going to force me to repeat what I said to you earlier."

"In what way can my asking you to join us outdoors be interfering? Come, sir, let me help you on with your coat."

He peered at her cautiously, but she smiled up at him with ingenuous innocence. After a moment, he shrugged. "I'll help myself, thank you," he muttered and pulled the coat from her grasp.

She wanted to jump in the air and clap her hands in triumph. He was going to do as she asked! "Thank you, my lord," she said, barely able to contain her urge to grin.

"You needn't look like the cat with the canary," he added grumpily. "I had intended to go outdoors for a walk in any case. I need some air to clear my head."

She didn't answer but stood meekly watching as he threw on his greatcoat and clapped his beaver on his head. She handed him his long scarf, which he wound round his neck, and they walked down the hall to the drawing room and out the tall doors leading to the terrace. As the brilliant sunlight struck his eyes, Strickland winced. "Good God, it's *blinding*! I shall have to stand here a moment and become accustomed to the light."

"That's because you've been sitting about in darkened rooms for much too long," Olivia taunted unsympathetically.

He glowered at her and determinedly walked on.

She caught up to him and touched his arm. "May I say something before we join the children, my lord?"

"What is it now?"

"I . . . er . . . think it extremely kind in you to agree to come out to play with them, but . . . "

"But?" he asked, steeling himself.

"But—and I hope you will not interpret this as interfering— I would like to suggest that, during this afternoon with them, you refrain from . . . er . . . *lecturing* Perry about anything. Let's just have a bit of pure *playtime* for a change."

"*Lecture?* Why would I lecture him?"

"Well, you do have a tendency . . . that is, I *had* noticed that—"

"Are you suggesting, ma'am, that I *lecture* him—and by 'lecture' I am certain you mean 'scold'—every time I come in contact with him?"

"Not *every* time, perhaps."

"*Thank* you!" He stomped across the terrace and down the steps, Olivia hurrying to keep apace. "You are having a *delightful* time, aren't you, ma'am? Meddling and interfering and criticizing to your heart's content. Very well, you may have your way. I shall not lecture the boy. Is there anything *else* about which you would like to caution me?"

"Yes, there *is* something..."

He stood stock still and faced her. "I might have known," he muttered. "Well, go on!"

"You might try to ... er ... *smile* just a bit, you know, my lord. You have a tendency to glower."

"*Glower?*"

"Yes."

He glowered at her. "It's no wonder. *Anyone* would glower if he had to hear someone *my lord*ing him with every sentence she spoke. I *do* have a name, you know."

Olivia blinked at him in surprise. "You wish me to...call you *Miles?*"

"Why not? You're my sister-in-law, after all, not some toadying governess."

"Very well, my l...Miles. But you *will* be pleasant to Perry, won't you? Even if he doesn't do things quite as you'd like him to?"

Strickland sighed. "Yes, my dear, I shall smile. I don't know why you think it necessary to instruct me in how to play with my own children—I have sometimes done so in the past, you know." He gave her a sardonic look. "I suppose you can't help thinking of me as some sort of monster, but I assure you, Olivia, that I have managed a smile on one or two occasions."

"Have you really?" she retorted, breaking into a grin. "*That* is almost impossible for me to believe." Laughing, she ran off ahead of him, anticipating quite accurately that his response would be to pelt her with a barrage of snowballs.

chapter fourteen

Olivia would not have permitted herself to dream that a day which had begun so badly could end so well. She went to bed that night happier than she'd been in months. She knew that something very important had occurred that afternoon—that, during the time the family had played together in the snow, a turning point had been reached. Olivia was convinced that family life at Langley Park would now begin to improve.

It had been a remarkable afternoon. When Strickland had joined the children in the snow-covered field at the back of the house, his manner had at first seemed stiff. But Amy had welcomed him with her eager warmth, and soon he was tossing his daughter in the air and letting her fall into the snowdrifts gurgling with glee. Perry had hung back warily, eyeing his father with cautious interest and accepting his offer to assist in the fort-building with hesitation. They'd worked together rather silently at first, Perry tense for an expected scolding. But Strickland had been almost pleasant, patiently stacking the snow blocks which Perry had fashioned and giving his son an occasional, awkward smile. At last, encouraged by a lack of friction, Perry had been emboldened to make a suggestion as to the architecture of the entrance to the fort. His father had looked at him with surprise and said the idea was "absolutely inspired." It was probably the first compliment the boy had ever received from his critical sire, and his eyes had glowed with pride.

At that point, Olivia had taken Amy inside, for the child

was almost frozen. She'd not gone out again for more than an hour, deciding to permit father and son to spend time alone in each other's company. She'd come out to find them happily and busily working on the almost completed fortress. Strickland had helped his son to build an elaborate, curved structure with little open spaces in the walls from which a boy could shoot cannonballs of snow at any approaching "enemy," and containing half-hidden little alcoves in which a boy might take shelter from the wind or hide himself from "spies." The two of them had barely noticed that it was already dusk, and only the promise of steaming cups of chocolate could persuade them to come into the house and leave the finishing touches for the following day.

Until he had fallen into an exhausted sleep, Perry hadn't stopped chattering about his fort or his eagerness to continue his work on it the next day. "Do you really think Papa will help me tomorrow?" he'd asked repeatedly, too insecure from past unhappiness to accept this new and pleasant feeling as a sign of good things to come. Olivia had tried hard to reassure him, but she was almost afraid, herself, to hope for too much.

Nevertheless, she had gone down to dinner in a glow of optimism. Determined to do nothing to spoil what had been achieved that afternoon, she'd decided to be scrupulously careful to avoid topics of conversation on which she knew they differed. Since these included politics, the pastimes and manners of the *haut ton*, most poets, all novelists, and almost all their common acquaintance, she was hard pressed to find anything to talk about. Most of the meal was passed in silence, but the success of the afternoon had had such a beneficial effect on her spirit that even the silence seemed to have been congenial.

As she snuggled into the pillows that night, she sighed in relief and self-satisfaction. "Clara," she whispered just before sleep overtook her, "I think we shall pull through after all. Rest easy, love. Rest easy."

But sleep did not come as easily to Lord Strickland, nor were his thoughts nearly as sanguine. Though the afternoon in the outdoors had done much to ease his sickened spirit, he had a great deal on his mind to trouble him. First was his relationship with his son. Olivia had, by hints and innuendo, made him aware that the boy was not comfortable with him. While Clara had been alive, it had not seemed necessary for him to develop a closeness with his son; his own father had always been a shadowy and distant figure in *his* childhood, and he had continued that pattern with *his* son. But he had had an affectionate mother and an independent nature, and he had not *needed* his father's attention. With Clara gone, however, his son's situation was different from his own. Perhaps the boy needed a father's affection to make up for the loss of his mother's. But Strickland was not at all certain he knew how to go about showing that affection.

Strickland was not a bit comfortable worrying over domestic matters; he had never before needed to concern himself with them. His attentions had always centered on his political activities. His wife had run the household so expertly that he'd never given its management much thought. He'd taken care of the business of the estate, but the nurturing of the children and the household cares had been lifted from his shoulders. Now they were his with a vengeance. For the first time in his life, for example, he'd had to concern himself with the servants. There was a feeling of discontent among them. His valet, Gaskin, who had never enjoyed what he referred to as "ruralizin'," had already complained that he did not get along with the butler and had begun to ask impatiently "when your lordship intends to return to Lon'on." The butler, on his part, had muttered about *his* dissatisfaction with the valet, whom he described as "insufferably 'igh in the instep, m'lord," and suggested that he "consider me second cousin to replace th' chap." Mrs. Joliffe had complained to him about the upstairs maid, a wench called Tilda, who was "gettin' ideas above hersel', if ye was to ask me, yer lordship, ever since she's been takin' care o' the little ones." And then there was the matter of the tutor, whom Strickland would have to replace.

All these matters would have been a great nuisance at the best of times, but now, when he was trying to recover his equilibrium after the devastating blow of his wife's death, these problems seemed an intolerable burden. He'd never realized before how much his wife had done to make his home a comfortable, untroubled refuge for him.

Then, on top of all the rest, there was the problem of his sister-in-law. Olivia was an irritating, impudent, presumptuous chit, but there was no question that the children were happier when she was present in the household. She had overstepped her bounds on several occasions, particularly in the matter of keeping his wife's illness secret from him, but he had to admit that she meant well. Her return this afternoon had brought a breath of life back into the house that even *he* had found enlivening. Much as he hated to admit it, the girl had pluck, a redoubtable spirit, and an unmistakable touch of charm. In fact, there had been a moment this afternoon, when they had first emerged into the dazzle of the sunlit snow, when he'd had an unexpectedly powerful urge to . . .

But he would not permit himself to finish the thought. His wife had been gone for less than six months—he would not insult her memory with such thoughts. Of course, he couldn't help remembering the strange request Clara had made before she died—that he try to look at Olivia with *her* eyes. "You two have so much more in common than you dream," she'd urged, "and there is so much each of you can give the other to fill the emptiness—" But he hadn't let her go on. He'd wanted only to talk to her about themselves—to ask for her forgiveness for having been so stupid and so blind. But Clara had given her forgiveness long before he'd asked for it.

Looking back on it now, he wished he *had* permitted Clara to talk about her sister. There was something more she'd wanted to say that he'd prevented her from expressing. Of course, it would have been better for Clara to have said those things to Olivia herself. It was Olivia who disliked *him*, not the other way round. He'd never had much liking for the blue-stocking sort in general, but he had no *particular* dislike for his sister-in-law. She, on the other hand, had always managed to find fault with *him* and didn't hesitate to express her disapproval in the most outspoken fashion. Why, the day in London when she'd accused him of adultery, she'd not even had the grace to be embarrassed. What other female would have had the temerity, the lack of discretion, the *bad manners* to speak to him on such a subject?

He chuckled, remembering it. She'd held her head so high and her back so rigidly straight; she'd tried so hard to appear worldly—and had only succeeded in looking vulnerable and childlike. If his urge to throttle her hadn't been so strong, he would have thought her adorable.

But again his thoughts were circling dangerous ground. He had to take care. He'd been keeping himself isolated for so long, he was perhaps too vulnerable to the attractions of a vibrant young girl. It hadn't escaped his mind that, once before, he'd so far forgotten himself that he'd taken her into a quite-passionate embrace. He hadn't understood then—and he didn't understand now—those secret wells of his *psyche* from which that momentary passion had sprung. At that time he'd sincerely believed he disliked the girl. That night he'd been rather unnerved by the depth of his response to the embrace. He really must make certain that such an incident did not occur again. As a matter of fact, there was something decidedly unsettling in having the girl take up residence in his house now that Clara was gone.

Good Lord! He sat up in bed with a start. Where had his brain been sleeping? There was something decidedly *improper* in her residing at Langley Park now! The tongues of the ladies of the *ton* would certainly be set wagging if they got word of this unconventional household arrangement. Whatever had her family been thinking of to permit her to return to Langley unescorted? He might have expected such indifference from her father—Sir Octavius was not aware of *anything* which had occurred after the fall of Rome—but *Charles* should certainly have known better.

Well, he himself could easily rectify the situation, he realized, and he lay down on his pillows again. He need merely send for a female relative to take up residence with them. All he had to do was decide which relative to invite.

After more than an hour of cogitation, Strickland had limited his choice to two females. One was his aunt, Mrs. Eugenia Cardew, a childless widow living in Derbyshire. She was a large, mannish woman, stubborn and opinionated, whom he utterly disliked. The other was Clara's cousin, Hattie Burelle, a spinster of advanced years who was small, thin and took the most negative view of every question. Strickland found it difficult to decide which of the two was the more intolerable. Neither of them, he surmised, would be likely to refuse an invitation to reside in the luxury of Langley Park for a time, but neither was likely to add any joy to the household. In the end, he chose his aunt Eugenia because he knew her well enough to make the request without embarrassment. Without waiting for dawn, he got out of bed, sat down at his desk and penned a note to her.

Thus it was that, a few days later, Olivia was startled by the arrival of an antiquated traveling coach bearing a formidable visitor. Mrs. Cardew bustled into the house, her shocking, dyed-red hair covered by an enormous feathered hat, bearing in her arms a large fur muff and a jewel case. She was followed by three heavily laden footmen, and she immediately took the house by storm. "Olivia, my dearest child, how good to see you in such high bloom. Your cheeks are positively glowing," she began, her hoarse and mannish voice booming through the hallway.

Olivia, having just come in from an outdoors excursion with the children and Strickland (an activity that was now a happy, daily event), urged the youngsters to kiss their great-aunt and hurry upstairs to shed their outer garments before coming down to tea, all the while glancing wonderingly at Strickland who was welcoming the new arrival in more cheerful spirits than Olivia would have believed possible.

"I hope you've put me in the blue bedroom, Miles," his Aunt Eugenia was saying, giving her hat and muff to the butler but keeping her jewel case to herself. "I cannot abide any of the bedrooms on the north side—drafty barns, all of them. As you see, I've brought only a few of the barest necessities with me, not having had sufficient time to do anything but toss a few things into the boxes and trunks I had at hand—" Here she paused only long enough to signal the overburdened footmen to take her things upstairs. "So you shall have to send someone for the rest of my paraphernalia as soon as my housekeeper sends us word that she's completed the packing. I hope you won't mind if, in the meantime, my dinner dress lacks the proper formality. I've brought my jewel case, of course, but a number of my best shawls, my turbans, my blue Persian silk gown and any number of other items of importance had to be left behind in the rush. And speaking of dinner, I hope you intend to keep country hours and serve dinner at an early hour. I dislike having to wait for dinner until eight or nine, you know, as one does when in town. One goes to bed with the food still undigested in the stomach, and it makes for all sorts of discomforts and for bad dreams as well. Country hours, Miles, my dear...I shall insist on that! And, Olivia, I hope you don't make a *practice* of having the children down for afternoon tea. We can make an exception today, of course, but not as a daily thing. Tea is quite my favorite time of the day, you know, and children, no matter even if they are as delightful and agreeable as Strickland's, *do* have a tendency to cavort about and make noise. Their presence at the tea-table does seem to make the occasion quite dreadfully chaotic, don't you agree?"

"Well, no, I don't, Mrs. Cardew. You see, I feel—"

"You must call me Aunt Eugenia, as Miles does, my dear. I am not the sort to stand on strict formality in matters of address. Formality has its place, but we are going to be *family*, are we not? And excessive formality among family members makes life so difficult, don't you agree? But *do* come upstairs with me, my love, and help me to settle in. Miles, you may go about your business. Olivia and I shall deal famously and shall manage without you, you know."

She took the girl's arm and led her forcibly to the stairs, continuing to ramble on ceaselessly. Olivia had time only to look back helplessly at Strickland, but since he met her pleading look with one of sardonic amusement, she found small comfort there.

Eugenia kept Olivia with her for almost an hour, maintaining a steady stream of observations and opinions of how a country house should be run—from the appropriate time to serve breakfast to the times of day one should visit the nursery. The more she spoke, the more Olivia felt the necessity of biting her own tongue, for Eugenia's ideas were almost all in direct conflict with her own. But it was not until Aunt Eugenia let fall a chance remark that "it was quite about time that Strickland sent for me," that Olivia's patience snapped. "*Sent* for you, ma'am?" she asked, stiffening.

"Why, yes, my dear. And very proper that he should have done so. Running a house like this can scarcely be the province of a mere child like yourself. It will be my place to take some of the burden from your little shoulders."

Olivia excused herself abruptly and, with teeth tightly clenched to keep herself from bursting into tears, flew downstairs to the library. Breaking in on Strickland without so much as a knock on the door, she confronted him accusingly. "If you've been so dissatisfied with the running of the household that you felt it necessary to send for *reinforcements*," she cried, "you could at least have had the courtesy to *warn* me!"

"But I'm not at all dissatisfied with the running of the house," he said calmly, getting to his feet.

"Then *why* on earth did you send for her?" the bewildered Olivia demanded.

Strickland rubbed his chin, a bit nonplussed as to how to answer. He had not anticipated the necessity of explaining to his hot-tempered but naive sister-in-law the impropriety of their continuing to reside at Langley as they did when Clara was alive. "I . . . er . . . *often* invite relatives to visit the Park," he said lamely.

"A *likely* tale! Clara told me many times how much you dislike visitors while you're here. She said you have so much society in London that you consider Langley your *retreat*. And, if my memory serves, she told me also that your Aunt Eugenia is *not* a relation of whom you're especially fond."

"Perhaps I'm not terribly fond of her. However, Olivia, I *did* send for her. You will oblige me by making her feel at home."

"Make her feel at *home*? When she tells me that we may not have the children down for *tea*? When she expects to be dressing for a country dinner wearing a turban and the family *diamonds*? When she thinks it *improper* to visit the nursery except for an hour before luncheon?"

"Good heavens, has she already suggested all *that*?" Strickland asked, feeling half amused and half chagrined.

"Don't play the innocent with *me*!" Olivia snapped. "You must have known what to expect when you sent for her to take over the running of the house."

"Take over the running of the house? You must be *mad*. I never—"

"She told me that quite distinctly." Olivia drew herself up, took a deep breath, lowered her voice an octave and, in an almost perfect imitation of his aunt's voice, repeated her words to him. "Running a house, my dear, can scarcely be the province of a *child* like yourself. It will be *my* place to take some of the burden from your *little* shoulders."

"Olivia—!" Strickland said, appalled. "I promise you I *never* asked her to—"

"Then why *did* you send for her?"

He felt his neck redden, and he sat down in his chair feeling deucedly awkward. How was he to explain to this little innocent that what he'd done was necessary? "It's rather embarrassing to explain, my dear," he began.

"Is it, indeed?" she asked scornfully. "I don't see why. You've told me often enough that you don't like my so-called meddling. Well, you needn't feel embarrassed, my lord. I do not *need* an explanation. It is all quite *clear*!"

"Cut line, girl," he interrupted disgustedly, "and come down from your high ropes. You don't have the slightest notion why I—"

"Don't I? I am not such a fool as you think me. I can see quite well what you had in mind. You could not, in good conscience, *bar* me from the house, so you took this paltry means as protection against my *interference*. In *this* way, your Aunt Eugenia can control my behavior—isn't *that* your plan, my lord?—while you will not have to bother about me at all."

"Humbug! Don't be such a little ninny. Let me—"

But a knock at the door interrupted them. The butler put his head in to announce that a carriage had just arrived at the door bearing not only the governess, Miss Elspeth and Miss Olivia's brother, Charles Matthews, but another lady. In the greatest surprise, Olivia and Strickland both hurried from the room. The three travelers stood smiling in the hallway. Charles was holding Miss Elspeth's arm in his, but before Olivia could take note of this strange detail, she recognized the third member of the party. "Cousin *Hattie*, of all people—! What on *earth*—?"

Strickland blinked at the elderly little lady who stood leaning on her cane and looking about her with a mouth pursed in disapproval. "Cousin *Hattie*?" he echoed in a choking voice. His eyes met Charles' for a moment as a gleam of understanding exploded upon his consciousness. "Charles! You . . . you *clunch*! You haven't gone and brought us *another* one?" And he threw back his head and burst into a roar of laughter. The entire assemblage—the butler, Olivia, Charles, Miss Elspeth and Cousin Hattie—gaped at him. Not only did the reason for his merriment escape them, but the inappropriateness of such hilarity from a man who still wore a black armband on his coat shocked them to the core. As his eyes moved from one startled face to the next, he found that their expressions only served to double his hilarity. Helplessly, he laughed and laughed, and the watchers could only shake their heads in bewilderment and tell themselves with a sigh that poor Lord Strickland had taken leave of his wits.

chapter fifteen

Later, just before dinner, Charles was introduced to Mrs. Cardew and suddenly understood what it was that had made his brother-in-law laugh so uproariously. He, himself, though not given to such uninhibited mirth, was hard pressed not to guffaw in Mrs. Cardew's face. But it was not until after the lengthy dinner, when the ladies at last left the gentlemen to their port, that Charles was able to discuss the subject with his host. "It was very good of you, Strickland, to concern yourself with Livie's reputation by inviting a female to stay here," he said, broaching the subject at once.

"Not at all, I should have thought of it before. We can't permit Olivia to become the subject of gossip just because she is good enough to wish to look out for my children. I'm completely cognizant of the fact that I stand very greatly in Olivia's debt. Having my dragon of an aunt in residence is a small sacrifice to make in return."

Charles grinned. "Miss Cardew *is* a bit dragonish, isn't she? And now I've added my cousin Hattie to your *ménage*."

Strickland laughed and sipped his wine. "Yes, worse luck! Although I must admit, Charles, that your bringing her here provided me with the first real laugh I've had in months. Whatever made *you* so suddenly think of providing us with a chaperone? You've never worried about such matters before."

Charles' smile faded as he studied the ruby-colored liquid in his wineglass with thoughtful eyes. "No, I never have. Livie's always seemed like a baby to me . . . at least until very recently. It was Jamie, you know, who thought of this chaperone business."

"What? Your hedonistic little brother James?"

"Yes, indeed. He knows more about proper conduct in society than all the rest of the Matthewses put together," Charles admitted.

"Good for him!" Strickland said, toasting him *in absentia* with the raising of his glass. "Perhaps we should ask *him* how to rid ourselves of one of them," he added with a touch of irony. "I have no wish to house *two* chaperones, but I certainly haven't been able to think of a way to send one of them packing. Both ladies seem to take it for granted that they are to remain . . . and I cannot in good conscience suggest that one of them leave."

"No, I don't suppose you can."

Strickland refilled his glass and frowned into it. "One of them shall be nuisance enough, but to have to endure *both* . . ."

"I'm sorry, Strickland. Truly I am," Charles apologized.

"Oh, I don't blame you, Charles. Not at all. It's your sister I blame."

"You mean *Livie*? But you just said how much you're *indebted* to her!"

"I know, I know. But my indebtedness doesn't make her any easier to bear. You have no idea, Charles, how troublesome she can be. She has an uncanny talent for cutting up my peace."

Charles looked across the table at Strickland with interest. "*Has* she?"

"Need you ask? She's lived with *you* for all of her life. Certainly you must know her better than anyone."

"She's never been the *least bit* troublesome at home."

Strickland's expression was anything but believing. "Never been troublesome? *Impossible*! Why, here at Langley she's been turning the household upside down! She's completely upset my routine by coaxing me to go out with the children every afternoon (not but that I don't admit it's done a world of good for my relationship with my son), she challenges every decision I make in regard to their upbringing, and she even has been nagging at me to retain the tutor to whom I've given notice . . . and *this* after she'd made vociferous objection to my hiring him in the first place!"

"That was very presumptuous of her, I must say," Charles murmured, pretending to an engrossing interest in his wineglass but keeping a fascinated eye on his brother-in-law.

"Presumption is a mild word for her. The chit can be a *termagant* when her temper is aroused. You should hear her at the dinner table! I only wish to consume my meal in peaceful contemplation, but every evening she finds something to quarrel over. It can be anything at all—from my opinion of Madame de Stael to the rise in the price of corn. You should have heard her ripping up at me this afternoon for inviting Eugenia here!"

"Well, you see, she doesn't know *why* you've sent for your aunt to stay. Nor does she understand why *I've* brought our cousin Hattie."

"No, she's quite naive in these matters, isn't she? I say, Charles, *you* wouldn't undertake to explain things to her, would you? I'm not very adept, myself, at dealing with such young innocents."

"Yes, of course I will. I should have spoken to her about these things before, but she's so clever about most subjects that it always takes me by surprise to realize she's ignorant in matters like these. But I shall have a talk with her. There are one or two other matters I'd like to discuss with her as well."

Not long after the gentlemen joined the ladies in the drawing room, Cousin Hattie excused herself and hobbled off to bed, the journey from London having quite exhausted her. Strickland, with a meaningful nod to Charles, bore his aunt off to the library for a game of *vingt-et-un*, leaving the brother and sister alone. Olivia didn't give her brother a moment to collect his thoughts. "Whatever *possessed* you, Charles," she demanded, jumping up from the sofa as soon as the door had closed behind Strickland, "to bring Cousin Hattie here for a visit. *Here*, of all places...and when you *knew* I would be too preoccupied with the children to trouble myself over the amusement of guests!"

"I had the same motive for inviting Hattie that prompted Strickland to invite his *aunt*," Charles said calmly, leaning back in a wing chair, taking out his pipe and filling the bowl with tobacco from a pouch he always carried with him.

"What motive?" Olivia asked, startled.

"Your reputation." Charles paused to light his pipe, and then leaned forward to explain to her bluntly that the world frowned upon those living arrangements in which a man and a woman who were not married to each other took residence under one roof.

Olivia stared at him. "What nonsense!" she exclaimed at last, her voice suffused with disdain. "Do you mean that both you *and* Strickland decided, quite separate from each other, that I have need of a *chaperone*? Why, the house is full of chaperones! There's Mrs. Joliffe, the housekeeper, there's Fincher, and dozens of servants, to say nothing of the governess and the children—"

"Servants and children are not considered appropriate chaperones," he informed her. "Not by the ladies and gentlemen of the *ton*, at any rate."

"Good heavens, Charles, this is quite unlike you. *You* know and *I* know that Strickland would never . . . er . . . *misuse* me. Therefore, what does it matter *what* the ladies and gentlemen of the *ton* believe?"

"In the first place, my dear girl, it matters *very much* what the *ton* believes about my sister! Reputation is a priceless jewel to a woman. To *anyone*! Didn't Publius say that *a good reputation is more valuable than riches*?"

"If you are going to spout quotations at me, Charles," she said impatiently, taking an angry turn about the room, "I can think of one or two myself. How about *Reputation is often got without merit and lost without fault*?"

"I don't wish to bandy quotations about, my dear," Charles said imperturbably, leaning back in his chair and puffing away at his pipe. "The fact remains that your good reputation is essential to your future, whether you like it or no. Now, as to the second (and, I admit, more delicate) point—that of Strickland's 'misusing' you—how can you be certain he would not?"

"*Charles*! That's a *dreadful* thing to say! Miles is not the sort of man who . . ." Suddenly, remembering her discovery of Miles' adultery and the details of the embrace that night in the library, she blushed a fiery red.

"Exactly!" Charles said knowingly, reading his sister's face with ease. "You yourself once described him to me as a *libertine*."

"I was mistaken," Olivia declared promptly. "Please don't think of that, *ever again*. Miles would *never* take advantage of my presence in this house, chaperone or no chaperone."

"How can you be so certain of that?" her brother asked, observing her closely.

"I'm just certain, that's all." She dropped her eyes from his face and sat down on the sofa. "Besides, he doesn't even *like* me."

"I would not be so certain of *that*, either, if I were you," Charles said enigmatically.

Her eyes, questioning, flew to his face. "Why do you say that? Did he *say* something to you about me?"

Charles shrugged. "Not exactly. It's just a feeling I have."

She felt a twinge of disappointment. If her brother had an inkling that Strickland felt some affection for her, she would have liked to hear his evidence to support that theory. But no amplification of his comment was forthcoming, so she pushed her disappointment aside and remarked scornfully, "Oh, pooh! You know nothing more about these matters than I do."

Charles responded by giving her an unexpected and very wide grin. "I've learned *something* about these matters since I saw you last," he announced. "I've learned enough to become betrothed!"

She blinked at him. "What? Whatever are you babbling about, Charles?"

"I'm speaking of *love*, my dear. A certain young lady will be announcing, before very long, her betrothal to your brother Charles."

Olivia could scarcely believe her ears. "Betrothed? *You*?"

You needn't sound so amazed, my dear. One would think I am such an 'undesirable' that no lady with the sense to come in from the wind would *have* me."

"Oh, Charles, I didn't mean—!" She jumped up and pulled him from his chair, catching him round the waist in a bear hug. "Are you telling me the *truth*? Are you really to be married? But when did it *happen*? And who *is* she? Do I know her? Is she lovely? Does she truly *deserve* you?"

Charles took her arms from round him and led her to the sofa, smiling broadly as he pulled her down beside him. "Hush, you goose. One thing at a time. Now, let me assure you that

I only hope *I* am deserving of *her*, for she is the sweetest, kindest, most lovable creature I've ever known. And yes, my dear, you know her, for it was through you that I found her."

Olivia wrinkled her forehead in puzzled concentration. "I cannot think whom you might mean. I remember introducing you to my friend, Miss Shallcross, but you took no notice of her at all."

"It's not Miss Shallcross. It's Elspeth."

"Elspeth?" Olivia gasped. "Elspeth *Deering*? Perry and Amy's Elspeth?"

Charles chuckled at her amazement. "*My* Elspeth, now."

Olivia was speechless. How could this have happened? She had left Miss Elspeth in London only a little above a week ago! Could a man like Charles have fallen in love in so short a time? She studied his face intently. There was no question that he looked quite happy. In fact, she didn't remember when she'd seen him look so well. His back seemed to be straighter, and his eyes shone. "Oh, Charles," she breathed when she'd recovered her breath, "I don't know what to *say*! I've always believed that Elspeth is an admirable young woman . . . but I never *dreamed*—"

"That she would be your *sister* one day? No, I don't suppose you *could* have guessed." He grinned at her mischievously. "Although anyone with half an eye could have noticed how smitten I was when she walked into the house that morning to fetch you back to Langley. It was love at first sight, you know."

"Was it really?" Olivia asked curiously. "I didn't notice it at *all*." Here was another example of her amazing ignorance in matters of the heart. She felt a vague frustration. When would she *ever* learn about love?

Charles, complacent and expansive, spent the next half hour telling his wide-eyed sister about his wedding plans. Elspeth had insisted on returning to Langley Park as soon as she was well enough to travel, unwilling to leave the problem of Perry's emotional state on Olivia's shoulders alone. But she'd promised her ardent lover that, as soon as Perry was in a better frame of mind, she would give her notice. Then, when Lord Strickland had found a suitable governess to replace her, she would be free to marry him. Until then, they would keep their betrothal secret. Charles could only hope that the entire process would not be long. "I shan't be able to contain my patience for more than a few weeks," he confided to her sister, "so I hope I can count on your assistance in freeing the girl from her obligations as soon as can be."

Olivia, as she became accustomed to her brother's news, found herself more and more delighted at the prospect of Charles' forthcoming nuptials. She assured him of her support with the utmost sincerity and wished him happy with glowing enthusiasm.

A little later, Lord Strickland put his head in the door to say that his aunt had retired for the night and that he was about to do the same. "Eugenia has asked me to wish you good night. I shall add my civilities to hers and leave you both to your *tête-à-tête*."

"I believe our *tête-à-tête* is quite concluded," Charles said, rising. "Shall we all go upstairs together, Livie, my dear?"

"You go ahead, Charles. If his lordship can spare me a moment, there is something I would like to say to him before I retire."

Strickland came into the room, giving Charles a questioning glance as the two men passed each other. "Is something wrong?" he asked.

"I don't think so," Charles said, giving him a reassuring wink. "Good night to you both."

When the door had closed behind Charles, Strickland frowned down on Olivia quellingly. "I hope you do not intend to renew your attack on me for inviting my aunt to stay with us. I've heard quite enough on that score."

"No, I don't. Quite the opposite, in face. Please sit down, Miles. My brother tells me that I am *beholden* to you for inviting her. I . . . I feel that I must apologize for what I said to you earlier."

"There's not the slightest need for apology, my dear," he said, nevertheless taking the chair opposite hers. "I quite sympathize with your feelings. My aunt is a managing female, to be sure."

"Yes, but you must let me express my regret at my outburst. I was very foolish and . . . naive. Please accept my thanks . . . belated though they are . . . for inviting her. The act shows a thoughtfulness of my position that I didn't . . . er . . ."

"Didn't expect of such a monster as I am?" he finished, a slight suggestion of his ironic smile making an appearance at the corner of his mouth.

She felt herself flush. "I was *not* going to say 'monster.'"

His smile widened. "I shall not dare to ask what you *were* going to say. Let us leave well-enough alone." He got up and helped her to her feet.

"But I do thank you sincerely for what you did," she insisted earnestly as they walked from the drawing room to the stairs.

He raised an eyebrow at her, suspicious of her unwonted humility. "Even if you have *two* 'companions' to contend with—one of whom has already indicated that she will attempt to interfere with your plans and your schedules and so forth?"

Olivia paused at the foot of the stairs and put up her chin. "As to that, my lord—"

"*My lord*, again?" he teased.

She ignored the interruption. "As to that, I hope you will come to my support when your aunt—or my cousin, for that matter—tries to take over the reins."

"No, my dear, I will not. I shall endeavor to avoid all such female altercations, even if it means hiding in the stables. So be warned."

She tossed him a look of scorn. "Coward! I might have known you would choose a craven's role."

"I confess it openly. Call me coward if you wish, but if you believe that using that epithet will drive me to promise you to put myself in the midst of these women's wrangles, you've completely mistaken your man," he declared, his grin wide and his unsympathetic manner apparently unshakable.

She stamped her foot in irritation. "Very well, sir. But I warn you, I shall *not* be overridden by those two . . . harridans. They may be your guests, but I shall not let that fact deter me. I shall *fight* them . . . every step of the way!"

He met her challenging look with one of wry amusement. "I was certain that you *would*, ma'am," he said drily. And, with a friendly nod, he bid her goodnight and went callously up the stairs to bed.

chapter sixteen

But Olivia did not have to quarrel with her two "companions" at all, for the chaperones, having taken an instant dislike to each other, were too busy bickering between themselves to pay much attention to Olivia and her doings. Not an hour would go by when Eugenia would not make some pronouncement which Hattie would negate. "I always take eggs and lightly salted lamb for luncheon," Eugenia would state, intending to order Olivia to so inform the cook.

"One should never eat eggs or meat for luncheon," Hattie would counter, her thin lips pursed in disapproval and her eyes fixed on her omnipresent needlework. "At that time of day, they become putrescent in the stomach and one suffers from alkaline corruption. *I* always eat a great deal of fruit and cheese for the afternoon meal."

Eugenia would redden and her impressive bulk would start slightly to quiver. "Balderdash!" she would exclaim in her masculine voice. "I have been eating eggs and meat for all these years, and my digestion is excellent. One needs eggs and meat for the proper balance between the radical heat and the radical moisture of the body."

"Radical heat? Radical moisture?" Hattie would cackle in disparagement. "There's not a medical man in the whole of Christendom who still believes such antiquated bibble-babble."

"*My* doctor believes in it, and *he* has been an advisor to Princess Caroline herself!" Eugenia would exclaim.

And so the argument would lengthen, involving all the theories they'd ever heard in regard to nutrition and medicine, and including all the royal personages whose names could be dragged in to support their claims. Meanwhile, Olivia would quietly inform the cook to go ahead and prepare the menu that she and the cook had long ago decided upon.

While Aunt Eugenia and Cousin Hattie argued about the meals, Olivia and Strickland took the children on their daily outings. While the chaperones debated about the propriety of including young children at the tea-table, the children were already present, unmindfully drinking their chocolate and eating their jelly sandwiches. While the two elderly ladies bickered about what card games would be most entertaining for the family after dinner, the rest of the members of the household had already dispersed to do what they wanted.

Olivia managed, during the next few days, to retire early. She had a great deal to think about, and the thinking was best done in the privacy of her bedroom. The most immediate problem was the status of the tutor, for his fortnight of grace was rapidly coming to an end. Strickland had listened politely to Olivia's arguments in favor of retaining him on the staff, but his lordship had made no decision on the matter. Beyond her favorable assessment of the tutor's scholarship and her feeling that Perry was attached to him, Olivia could think of no other justifications for keeping him on. She only hoped that Perry's need for a sense of continuance and stability would be sufficient reason for Strickland to countermand his earlier dictum.

She also thought about Perry's progress. The boy had lost the terrified look that she'd seen at the back of his eyes when she'd first arrived, and he seemed to be more comfortable in his father's presence than ever before, but he was still rather silent and withdrawn. Olivia had never heard him stand up to his father. The boy had never—even in the smallest way, like making an objection to wearing his goloshes—rebelled against anything his father said to him. It was Olivia's secret goal to build up the boy's spirit to the point where he would have the courage not only to rebel but to be strong enough to face his father's wrath without backing down.

Another subject that occupied her mind was her brother's betrothal. She remembered with remarkable clarity that Clara had told her, "You're not the sort to be a matchmaker, Livie.

You haven't the knack." Clara had been quite right—she had no talent in matters of the heart. Never in her wildest imaginings would she have believed that her brother would be attracted to Miss Elspeth. Not that there was anything wrong with the match; Elspeth Deering was a gentlewoman with a sweet nature, well-reared and well-educated. She was in no way foolish or vulgar. But she hadn't the sharpness of mind that Charles had. She was always so indecisive, so vague, so vacillating in her thinking that at times one could not even follow what she said. Often her sentences verged on incoherency. How could a man like Charles—a scholar and a writer, a man capable of incisive thought and exact expression—become enamored of a woman with so wispy a mind? She wished Clara were here to explain it to her.

"People don't take to each other in such neat, comfortable patterns," Clara had said. And she'd been right about *that*, too. But then, how *did* people "take to each other"? What made them lean in one direction and not in another? Charles had met dozens of eligible ladies in his adult years. Why, of all of them, did *Elspeth* attract him?

Olivia had gone so far as to *ask* Charles that question. He had been her teacher in so many subjects, perhaps he could teach her something about the subject in which she was most deficient. But he had only shrugged and replied that he didn't know. "All I remember is that her nose was red with cold," he'd said. "It is such a very small nose, and it was so red it looked clownish. There sat this young woman in our hallway, her feet planted together on the floor in perfect decorum, her hands in her lap clutching a single glove, a proper but horridly dowdy hat sitting bravely on her head . . . and that silly red nose making a mockery of all that rigid and respectable propriety. In ordinary circumstances, I suppose I would have laughed and gone about my business. But that morning, the sight of that cold little nose touched me. I had the most overwhelming desire to . . . to *protect* her. To take care of her *always*. Isn't that strange? The feeling has never left me since."

Olivia had been moved by the story, of course, but it had not been particularly instructive. A pathetic little red nose seemed an imprecise explanation for love . . . and a woefully inadequate motive for marriage. Olivia could think of only one other reason for her brother's attraction: Miss Elspeth's beauty. Olivia had noticed from the first that Elspeth had a lovely face. But the beauty was hidden behind the distracted expression, the wispy hair and the helpless, fluttery manner. Charles, sensitive and perceptive, had managed to penetrate through the superficial disguise to the lovely core. The red nose had drawn his attention to the less-obvious attractions behind it.

But was physical beauty the secret of love? Was *that* all one needed in order to feel drawn to another—the attraction of a *face*? It could not be, for she had found Morley Crawford as handsome a fellow as any she'd met, yet she'd never felt the slightest inclination to *love* him. There must be something more to it.

Again she had to put the puzzle aside. The subject was too complex to yield an answer on the basis of vicarious experience. Books didn't help her; her brother's experience didn't help her. She realized that, until she felt the emotion firsthand, she would never truly understand love's secret nature.

Meanwhile, there were things to do and think about which were of much more immediate importance. She had to find a way to save Mr. Clapham from discharge, she had to find a replacement for Elspeth, and she had to find a way to convince Elspeth to come down to dinner with the family. Elspeth had always taken her meals with the children and, wishing to keep her betrothal a secret until the proper time, was reluctant to change her custom. "It will give the secret away entirely," she protested when Olivia had first invited her. "What other reason could you find for making such a . . . you know . . . change in our customary . . . ?"

"But I don't *need* to find a reason," Olivia had insisted. "I've always felt that you should dine with the family. There are many households in which the governesses are treated more like family than like servants."

"Oh, no, Miss Olivia. I don't think you can be right. I've never heard . . ."

"And you must stop calling me *Miss* Olivia, Elspeth. Charles calls me Livie, and so must you."

"Oh, dear, I don't think I can ever become used to . . ."

"Yes, you can," Olivia assured her firmly. "You'll be surprised at how easily you'll become accustomed to it."

But Elspeth was too shy to agree to *any* of Olivia's suggestions. The astounding and enormous change in her life was too recent for her to be able to face all its ramifications with equanimity. She adored her Charles with enraptured awe, and she could scarcely believe that he loved her and wanted to make her his wife. It was enough for her to think of their moments together . . . of their strange meeting . . . of the quick growth of their mutual affection... of his sudden proposal of marriage. She would sit in the schoolroom gazing absently at the opposite wall, a slight smile on her lips and a flush on her cheeks, reliving every moment of that miraculous week in London. (Poor little Amy had to tug on her sleeve to get her attention.) Those memories were enough for now. She couldn't yet cope with more.

But Olivia was determined to make Elspeth take her place in the family, and since Charles was planning to return to London in a day or two, Olivia hoped to prevail upon Elspeth to join the family at dinner before Charles' departure. She didn't think she could succeed unless Mr. Clapham would also be invited to dine, and *that* was the difficult nut to crack. How could she convince Lord Strickland to invite Mr. Clapham to *dine* with them if she couldn't even convince him to *re-hire* him?

But circumstances soon took the matter entirely out of her hands. The fact that Charles and Strickland were getting on famously set off a chain of events that were to have unexpected repercussions in the pattern of life at Langley.

Charles presence was good for Strickland. In the three days of Charles' visit, the two men rode together in the mornings, played chess in the afternoons and had long talks about the happenings in London and abroad in the evenings. It had been a long while since Strickland had paid attention to political events, and it was Charles who rekindled his interest in the outside world. For the first time since his wife's death, Strickland began to think about returning to his political activities. The talks brought the brothers-in-law to a closer affection for each other than either of them had had before. In the warmth of that closeness, Charles revealed to Strickland his anxiety concerning his young sister. "She's almost twenty-one, you know," he said, shaking his head in perplexity. "I know it's hard to realize that she's a full-grown woman already, but there it is."

"Yes, but why does that concern you?" Strickland asked with interest.

"It's her lack of attention to her future that worries me," Charles admitted, puffing away at his pipe. "She has made no serious attachments to any man in all these years, and I'm convinced that the fault lies in the way of life I've permitted her to follow. In London, she does not go about a great deal in society, you know. And now . . ." He hesitated, not certain if he should go on.

"And now she has buried herself here at Langley in order to take care of a pair of children not her own, is that what you were going to say?"

Charles gnawed at his pipe stem unhappily. "Well, yes, I suppose it is. I can't help wondering when she will set about to plan for her *own* future."

As both men lapsed into silence, Charles felt impelled to reveal that he'd taken a giant step to alter *his* future, which was why the subject of Olivia's had begun to trouble him. "I'm about to be married, you see," he admitted.

"Married? Are you indeed?" Strickland responded heartily. "So that explains it."

"Explains it?" Charles echoed.

"The glances I've seen cast between you and Miss Elspeth. It *is* she whom you intend to wed, is it not?"

"Yes, but . . ." Charles let his pipe fall from his mouth in amazement. "How can you possibly have *guessed*?"

"It was not difficult. I've seen you run up to the nursery. And I've noticed you gazing at her when she comes down to tea with the children. And Miss Elspeth herself has never been in better looks. Smelling of April and May, the pair of you. I suspected that something was brewing between you. It took only your statement about marrying to make everything fall into place. But tell me, old fellow, why on earth do you keep your good news *secret*?"

Charles repeated Elspeth's reasons, but Strickland found them silly indeed. The logic of his comments struck Charles as sound, and shortly thereafter he went looking for his be-trothed to urge her to consider making the announcement pub-lic.

Strickland, meanwhile, found himself quite troubled by the conversation. He wondered guiltily how long he could continue to accept Olivia's help with his children. Charles had been quite right to be concerned about her—she was indeed putting aside her own life in her devotion to her sister's children. The girl really ought to be pursuing her own goals—she had a right to children of her own.

But he couldn't encourage her to leave . . . at least, not now. In the first place, the children were still recovering from the loss of their mother. In addition, the tutor was about to go, and Miss Elspeth would soon follow when she married. With all these losses, the children should not be asked to endure the loss of their beloved Aunt Olivia as well.

He sighed in chagrin, wondering why life was becoming so oppressively difficult of late. If he had a more generous nature, he supposed, he would urge Olivia to leave Langley and return to London to pursue her own life. But he could not deal such a cruel blow to his children at this time. Besides, Olivia herself would resist such a suggestion—she was too attached to the little ones to consider leaving them now.

He consoled himself with the thought that Olivia was still very young and unusually innocent for her age. She had many years ahead of her to concentrate on her own life. In the mean-time, she could spare some time for the well-being of his motherless babes. He thrust his feelings of guilt from his con-sciousness and concentrated his thoughts on his more pressing problems. One of them was the situation of the tutor. Olivia had been very persuasive in her reasons for wishing him to reconsider the discharge. Perhaps the girl was right. The tutor's crime had not been so very heinous, after all. He'd encouraged Perry in his tendency to daydreaming and imaginary wander-ings, but the fellow had been satisfactory in other respects. Strickland would go up to the schoolroom at his next oppor-tunity and tell the fellow he'd changed his mind. As much as he disliked dealing with these petty problems of household management, he would take care of it. His children's welfare had become, since his wife's passing, his most pressing responsibility, and he had no intention of shirking it.

The following day was a significant one on the calendar of events at Langley Park. It was Charles' last day before leaving for London and, as far as Mr. Clapham knew, the last day the tutor would spend on the estate. In the minds of both men was a determination to use the last day to accomplish a desired goal; for Charles, it was to convince Elspeth to announce their betrothal to the family before the day ended; for Mr. Clapham, it was to say a farewell to Miss Olivia with such fervor that she would remember him always.

Fortunately for them both, the day was unusually mild for winter, and Lord Strickland sent word up to the third floor that he would ride with both the children that afternoon. This left Miss Elspeth free to spend some time with Charles—to walk arm in arm with him over the snow-edge paths through the winter-faded gardens. Mr. Clapham was also free to act on *his* plans to arrange a last encounter with Miss Olivia, if only he could find a way to lure her to the third floor before Perry returned from his ride.

Before Strickland left for the stables, he met Olivia on the stairs. He told her briefly that he'd decided to keep Mr. Clapham on. Olivia was so delighted with the news that she refrained from giving Strickland her usual warning about Perry's sensitivity to his father's criticism of his riding prowess. (It had been she who'd encouraged Strickland to ride with the boy, convincing him that Perry's lack of skill in horsemanship could be overcome by a bit of parental approval. Each time he took the children out to ride, Olivia found the opportunity to remind him that Amy's talented horsemanship should not be overly praised or used to shame her less-gifted brother.) Strickland, relieved to have been spared the oft-repeated lecture, clattered hurriedly down the stairs, while Olivia turned upward, wishing to be the first to break the news to Mr. Clapham that his position was saved.

She had not gone up more than a flight, however, when she was confronted by a red-faced, infuriated Eugenia. "*There* you are, Olivia," she declared, her bosom quivering with agitation.

"I have been looking for you this past age. Do you know what your demented cousin has told me? She wants my *bedroom*! Did you ever hear of such brazen effrontery? *My* bedroom! She says that hers is too drafty, as are all the others on the north side, and no other room will do for her but *mine*. You must *speak* to her, Olivia, for she has pushed me beyond my patience!"

It took Olivia the better part of an hour to settle the squabble. She showed her pursed-mouthed cousin every available bedroom in the house, but Hattie found fault with each one of them. It was not until Olivia hit on the happy idea of offering her the room Charles was about to vacate that the crisis was averted. "*That* room," Hattie acknowledged in sour satisfaction, "is at least possessed of a sufficiently large fireplace. But you mustn't tell that Cardew woman it is larger than hers, or she'll try to have it from me!"

That matter settled, Olivia made her way to the schoolroom. Mr. Clapham was pacing back and forth in frustration, having already given up all hope of seeing her alone. When he discovered that it was indeed *she* who stood smiling in the doorway, he gave her such a glad greeting that Olivia was startled. "I don't see why you are in such high spirits, Mr. Clapham," she remarked, "for you do not yet know my *news*."

"My spirits have nothing to do with your news, ma'am," he said, a bit breathlessly. "It's *you*, yourself, who's cheered my spirits."

"Oh? Why is that?"

"I have been wishing to see you . . . to say something to you before I . . . that is, on this, my last day."

"But it *isn't*—" she began.

"Please let me say it while I have the courage," he begged in nervous eagerness. He took a step toward her and grasped both her hands.

"Mr. Clapham, what *are* you doing?" She tried to pull her hands free.

"Do you remember that day you fell off your horse?" he asked, looking intently into her eyes.

"I would rather *not* remember," she said with asperity, struggling to free herself. "And I hope, Mr. Clapham, that you don't intend to do anything so foolish as—"

He winced. Her tone was not encouraging, but a kind of hysteria drove him on. "I know it's foolish, but I can't help it. Don't you know . . . haven't you ever realized how much you . . . how often I've dreamed of . . . ?"

"Please, Mr. Clapham, release my hands at once. If you persist in this idiotic behavior, you'll ruin *everything*!"

"Everything I care about is ruined anyway! Nothing, after today, will mean anything to me. It was only the promise of a glimpse of you that gave my days their color. It was only the dreams of you that gave my nights their balm. Oh, Miss Olivia, I . . ." Carried away on the crest of his romantic longings, he swept her into his arms. "Let me have one moment more to remember!" Shaking with excitement, he pulled her against him and kissed her passionately.

She pushed against his chest with the flat of her hands with all her strength, but he was like a man possessed. She was so tightly enveloped that she couldn't move or breathe. She wanted to scream in vexation. She'd tried so hard to keep his post for him, and now he was creating a situation in which it would be impossible to keep him in their employ. Despite her annoyance, however, she was aware of his rapidly beating heart and trembling arms and couldn't help but feel a sense of power to have been able to cause a man so completely to lose control of himself. He must have found her as beautiful as Charles had found Elspeth. For a fleeting moment, the thought pleased her.

But this behavior was really the outside of enough! His grip was becoming quite painful, and if she couldn't take a deep breath very soon, she was very much afraid she would burst. Wasn't there anything she could do to make him break his hold? Her arms were pinned quite helplessly against his chest, but she could move her foot. Perhaps if she kicked him . . .

But before she was able to translate thought to action, he loosed her abruptly. She saw that he was gaping at the doorway, aghast. She turned quickly and found herself staring into Strickland's stunned and darkly furious eyes.

"My l-lord, I . . ." Mr. Clapham stammered.

"I beg your pardon," Strickland said, his voice rasping and

icy. "I had no idea the schoolroom was being used as a meeting place for lovers. If I had, I would have approached with a louder clatter."

"*Miles!*" Olivia exclaimed, outraged.

His eyes, which had been fixed on the tutor's whitened face, traveled slowly to hers. She felt herself flushing hotly under his frozen scrutiny. "So *this* is why you pleaded his cause with such fervor," he said nastily, his hands clenched tightly, as if he were trying to hold himself back from some rash act of violence. "Why didn't you tell me the truth, ma'am? I would have been perfectly willing to advance the cause of true love."

"Oh, Miles, don't be idiotic," Olivia snapped. "Mr. Clapham only—"

"There's no need to explain anything to me, my dear. I am not your guardian."

"You don't understand, my lord," Mr. Clapham said bravely. "What you s-saw . . . was entirely my f-fault. I . . . I completely lost m-my head—"

"Yes," Strickland said in his most sardonic style, "and quite understandable, too. Miss Matthews is the sort of young lady who seems to *encourage* men to do so, isn't that right, ma'am? I seem to remember a time when I *myself* . . . but that is quite beside the point. Am I to wish you well, ma'am? Is a betrothal in the offing?"

"Really, Miles, must you persist in this taunting? Mr. Clapham has *explained* that there is nothing between us," she said angrily.

"Oh, *has* he? That is not what I heard him say. And that is certainly not what I *saw*. If my eyes did not deceive me, I would say that there was a *great deal* between you."

"Your *eyes* may not have deceived you, sir," she said, embarrassed and infuriated, "but your *brain* seems to have done so. This . . . incident . . . has been nothing but a horrible mischance—"

"I don't see why you should say that, ma'am," his lordship said, a sneer disfiguring his face with chilling malevolence. "There is nothing horrible about the 'incident' that I can determine. It's all rather amusing, in fact. First your brother becomes betrothed to my *governess*, and now *you* seem to have an attachment for my *tutor*. Tell me, my dear, would your brother Jamie care to join the group? We have an upstairs maid who might suit him very well."

She stared at him in horror, and then swung her hand furiously to his face, slapping him with vicious rage across the cheek. The sound reverberated from the walls with terrifying loudness. Olivia gasped, her distended eyes taking in the blotchy red patch spreading on his cheek. Appalled at her own behavior and devastated by his, she burst into tears, brushed rudely past him and ran out of the room.

Strickland remained looming in the doorway. His sneer was quite gone, leaving behind only a look of threatening menace. The tutor's eyes dropped to the floor. "You've c-completely misjudged the m-matter, my lord," he said, not able to conceal his inner quailing.

"Take yourself out of my sight!" Strickland growled, not wishing to hear another word.

The tutor drew himself up. He'd made a mull of everything—his relationship with Miss Olivia, his prospects for the future, everything. But he would make his exit from this house with some shred of dignity. "Very well, my lord," he said as steadily as he could. "I shall collect my things and leave the premises at once."

His lordship was staring somewhere in the middle distance, his eyes blank, but at the tutor's words he brought them back into focus. "What's that you said?" he asked abstractedly.

"I said that I shall be off the premises at once," the tutor repeated.

"Who said anything about leaving the premises?" Strickland barked. "You will go nowhere, do you hear me? She wants you to remain, doesn't she? Well, if she wants you here, *here you'll stay!*"

chapter seventeen

It was Charles, with his calm reasonableness, who finally managed to straighten out the tangle. After he'd learned the details from his weeping sister, he sought out Strickland and, by using considerable patience and repeating the facts as logically as possible, eventually convinced his stubborn and angry brother-in-law that Olivia was not in any way attached to the tutor. However, when Olivia learned from Charles that Strickland intended to keep the tutor on, she burst into tears again.

Olivia, using Charles as a go-between (for she could not bear to discuss the matter with Strickland face-to-face), informed his lordship that, under the circumstances, she would find it quite impossible to visit the schoolroom in future if Mr. Clapham remained on the staff. He had *twice* lost his self-control, she informed her brother-in-law, and she would not subject herself to the humiliation of a possible third experience of that kind. Reluctantly, therefore, fully aware that Perry was fond of the tutor, she nevertheless had to recommend that Strickland let him go after all.

It was this message which truly convinced Strickland that the girl was sincerely indifferent to Mr. Clapham, and it was not without a small touch of wicked satisfaction that he informed the tutor that he was to leave the premises after all. He handed Mr. Clapham a letter of recommendation which, in its praise of his scholarship and his affectionate handling of his charges, guaranteed that he would be able to find another post, but his lordship pointed out drily to the tutor before leaving him to his packing that he had better keep his affectionate handling of the *other* members of the households where he would in future be employed more strictly in check.

With that last sardonic admonition ringing in his ears, Mr. Clapham left Langley Park, his emotions a mixture of bitterness and relief. The recommendation insured that he would find a satisfactory post, for which he was profoundly grateful. But as far as *women* were concerned, he swore to himself that never would he permit himself to become emotionally involved with one again. Plato had been quite right about love being a grave mental disease; he would not soon again permit himself to be reinfected.

Dinner that night was a disappointing affair. Although Charles had succeeded in convincing Elspeth to join the family at the table, his announcement of their forthcoming nuptials to Cousin Hattie and Aunt Eugenia did not cause an outpouring of good will. Eugenia, in obvious disapproval of so unconventional a betrothal, remarked that she wished them well, of course, but added that they "should not expect a sanguine acceptance from the *ton*. An unequal match, while sometimes considered acceptable by the less exacting members of *country* society, is much frowned upon in *town*, I'm sorry to say."

Cousin Hattie, pursing her mouth in disagreement, immediately responded. "What utter rubbish! I, for one, am quite delighted, Charles, to see that you have the character to ignore the difference in your stations. If all men looked for *character* in their betrotheds rather than wealth and social position, London society would be all the better for it."

At this point, Olivia leaned toward her cousin Hattie to assure her that Elspeth was every bit as well-born as Charles; while, at the same time, Strickland informed his aunt Eugenia coldly that *any* society, town or country, with an ounce of discernment would welcome into its circle persons of such obvious value as Charles and Elspeth. The betrothed couple looked gratified by this sincere defense, but the spirit of jubilation, which they had every right to expect to flow over the assemblage at such a time, was quite missing. Olivia and Strickland were at pains, all evening, to keep from looking at each other or exchanging words; Hattie and Eugenia were, as usual, quite at odds; and Charles and Elspeth had to be content to gaze across the table at each other and sigh.

Shortly after dinner had ended, Strickland excused himself and retired. Gaskin followed him into the bedroom, but Strickland told him to go to bed. The valet, already disturbed by the lack of occupation, left with ill grace, but Strickland didn't even notice. He threw himself down on his bed without removing anything but his coat in excessive perturbation of the spirit. The scene in the schoolroom had disturbed him more than he'd been able to admit to himself. But now, several hours later, with the matter settled and the tutor dispatched on his way, Strickland still felt shaken. There was little question in his mind about what had upset him. He had found Olivia in a man's arms, and he'd felt *murderous*. He didn't know which one of them he would have liked to murder, but he knew *why* he'd wanted to kill. It had been naked, unrestrained, violent *jealousy*.

For the first time, he had to admit to himself that the girl meant something more to him than he'd supposed. He had habitually thought of her as an irritating nuisance inflicted upon him by marriage. But somehow, at some moment in the past, that feeling had changed. He could not have told when or how, but there was little question *now* that he was strongly attracted. How Clara would laugh if she knew! She'd said many times that he and Olivia had more in common than he realized. Clara had even predicted, that last night, that . . .

But no, it was foolish to dwell on it. Clara had been so ill. In her right mind she would not have been the sort who would have wished to control people's lives from the grave. In any case, this attraction toward Olivia was not to be encouraged. The girl obviously disliked him completely. In every way she indicated her disapproval of his habits, his viewpoints, his politics and his character. She thought of him as a jaded Tory libertine, and he supposed that was just what he was. How could an idealistic, radical little bluestocking have any interest in a man who stood for everything she hated and, even worse, who was too old for her in both age and experience.

Perhaps, if things had been different—if he had just met her and could have consciously attempted to make a favorable impression on her—he could have managed to win her affection. He could have charmed her with his easy manners and assured style...he could have made light of their political differences and disparaged the difference in their ages. It would not have been an impossible task—he'd won admiration from young girls before. But he and Olivia had fallen into the habit of disagreement. There was too much in their pasts which had set them at odds. He could never win her now.

Besides, the girl deserved better. She was young and innocent; she should have a fresh-faced, clean, openhearted young man to love her—one who was not encumbered with memories of past love or jaded by the vestiges of past dalliance. And she should not be permitted to bury herself away from society for too long, or she might be too late to *find* that deserving young man. It was not good for her to remain here at Langley...and it was not good for him either.

But how could he convince her to leave? She felt as strong a responsibility for the children's welfare as he did. Even if he forced a quarrel upon her and drove her away, she would soon feel impelled to return to the children. She would return from time to time in any case. And each time she came, he felt certain that her nearness would create an ache in his insides as strong as the ache he felt at this moment, an ache which would only emphasize the already painful loneliness of his life. What he needed was someone to act as a buffer between himself and his sister-in-law—someone who would love and care for the children too. Obviously, neither Eugenia nor Olivia's cousin Hattie would be satisfactory. It had to be someone more like Clara herself. Good lord! What he needed was...a *wife*!

Of *course*! That was *it*! He had to marry again. A new wife could take over where Clara had left off. It would be the answer to every problem. But the thought was repugnant to him. Could he face a relationship of such intimacy with a woman he didn't love? The answer, he told himself sternly, was *yes*. Even with Clara, the last few years had not been particularly satisfactory, but they had managed. He would manage again.

Finding a wife would be no very difficult matter. There were a number of London ladies who had flirted with him in the past when he'd appeared at social events without Clara on his arm. They had made it clear that they would have welcomed his advances *then*. Now that he was free to remarry, his advances would be all the more welcome. He was too wise in the ways of the world not to realize his value on the Marriage Mart. He had titles, wealth, an acceptable appearance and a certain measure of prestige. Those were just the sort of superficial qualities which most women wanted. He would have no trouble at all.

As he began to think of the various eligible ladies in his circle, he fell asleep. He dreamed that Perry and Amy were leading him up a rugged mountain path, higher and higher until it became dangerously steep. Above him was a ledge which promised a haven of safety. He lifted Amy up to it without much difficulty, but Perry was too heavy. Terrified that he would drop the boy, he shouted for help. Two arms reached out over the edge, lifted Perry from his grasp and disappeared from his view. He reached up and grasped the edge just as the road beneath his feet crumbled away. Hanging by his hands over a deep ravine, he tried desperately to pull himself up but found himself unable to heave his enormous weight. The veiled head of a woman leaned over the ledge and peered at him. "My hand . . . take my *hand*," he begged, reaching out to her. She laughed and grasped it. "Trust me," the woman said in Clara's voice. "Let go and I shall lift you." He did as she bid and found his body floating free and weightless in the air beside the ledge. With his free hand, he reached for her veil and snatched it away, revealing the face of Olivia, her mouth a sneer. She laughed cruelly and let go of his hand. At that moment his body felt heavy as lead, and he began to fall head over heels into the ravine, the sound of her laughter following him down . . .

He awoke with a start. His candle had burned out and the room was in blackness. The constriction of the waistband of his breeches reminded him that he had not yet undressed. Wearily, he pulled himself up and unbuttoned his shirt, aware that a feeling of depression seemed to have settled into his bones. The pain was less sharp than the grief he'd been experiencing during the past months but was somehow more oppressive. The weight on his spirit seemed to exude a threat of permanence—a pervasive heaviness that he knew had settled in to stay, if not forever, then at least for a long, long time.

* * *

Charles left the next morning after whispering a warning to his betrothed that, if she didn't settle her business and return to him before the month was out, he would return and drag her bodily from the premises. He left behind him a household gloomier than it had been when he'd arrived. Eugenia and Hattie were engaged in a bickering war that was carried on throughout the day, and Olivia and Strickland seemed more strained and distant with each other than they'd ever been before. It was only in the presence of the children that they pretended to friendliness.

Olivia did not find this state of affairs at all to her liking. Before the arrival of her brother and the two "chaperones," she had been well on her way to achieving a comfortable kinship with Strickland. They had even laughed together. If only that fool of a tutor had not instigated that dreadful scene. Charles had assured her that Strickland was convinced that she'd spoken the truth when she'd said that there was nothing between herself and the tutor. Then why was Strickland still so distant? Was he still smarting from the slap she'd given him?

Whenever she remembered that slap, the palm of her hand burned. She did not know what had come over her. He had been infuriatingly scornful in his remarks, of course, but the situation he'd come upon was certainly deserving of scorn. Her reaction had been unwontedly violent, and she was at a loss to explain it. Everything about her relationship with Strickland always seemed to be fraught with unexplainable tensions and excitement. Why couldn't they develop a peaceful, friendly *rapproachement*? Why couldn't she see him at the table or pass him on the stairs without this strange acceleration of the pulse and constriction of the chest? Was it guilt for having struck him so angrily on the face? Should she apologize?

For a few days she mulled over the problem, but at last, after another dinner during which the only conversation had been the irritating exchanges between Eugenia and Hattie, she felt she could stand it no longer. She went to the library where Strickland had, every evening, been secluding himself and knocked at the door. Invited to enter, she found him packing a number of ledgers and papers into a carrying case. "What is this?" she asked in surprise. "Are you packing?"

"Yes," he said, not pausing in his work. "I had intended to inform you before you retired for the night. I am leaving for London in the morning."

Olivia felt her heart sink. "But . . . why? Has something happened?"

"No, nothing out of the way. I have some business to take care of that I've been putting off for too long. And I want to find a new tutor for Perry. And there are a few other matters which need attending."

"But what about the children? Won't they be disturbed by your absence?"

"No, I don't think so. I spoke to them about it this afternoon, and they were quite complaisant, especially when I promised to bring back an armload of surprises for them. Amy was quite easily persuaded to part with me as soon as I promised to bring her a strand of red beads."

Olivia had to smile. "She's developed quite a passion for beads of late. She loves to put three or four strands around her neck and admire herself in her glass. Beads will be the very thing for her. But was Perry equally agreeable?"

"Yes, he was. He says he'll surprise *me* when I return by showing me how much his riding has improved in my absence."

"I hope you're not pushing him too hard in his riding, Miles. We don't want him jumping over fences before he's ready," Olivia said, frowning.

"You needn't worry," Strickland answered mildly. "I've warned Higgins to keep a close watch on him when he goes out."

"Well, you seem to have taken care of everything," Olivia muttered in some asperity, "and without consulting *me* at all."

He looked up at her with eyebrows raised. "You sound as if you disapprove, my dear. But I don't understand you. Didn't you yourself, not two weeks ago, suggest that I return to London and use my influence to obtain the release of Leigh Hunt from imprisonment?"

"Yes, but you told me in no uncertain terms that you believed he *deserved* to be imprisoned for insulting the Regent in print."

"I said, ma'am, that the *Regent* believed so. I, myself, believe that Prinny was mistaken to have taken the nonsense so seriously."

"Then you *will* help him?" Olivia asked, gaping at Strickland with pleased surprise.

Strickland gave a quick, snorting laugh. "You flatter me, my dear, if you believe my influence with the Prince is so strong. I *shall*, however, speak to his highness if the opportunity arises. I may even pay a call on Hunt in the gaol. But beyond that, I can promise you nothing."

Olivia felt a surge of pleasure. When she had first discussed the plight of the much-abused Hunt brothers, Strickland had been completely indifferent. "They have abused the freedom of the press" he'd said, "and I have little sympathy for them." Had she managed to convince him to take a more moderate view of the matter? Could she have had an influence on him after all? "You promise a great deal, Miles. I'm very grateful."

Strickland shrugged. "I'm not going to London for the sake of the Hunts, you know. And it is extremely unlikely that I can do *anything* for them. So your gratitude is completely misplaced."

"I quite understand that you're not making such a trip entirely on their behalf, but—"

"I'm not making it *at all* on their behalf."

Olivia met his eye challengingly. "I hope you are not making the trip because of *me*, Miles."

"Now, *why*, my dear, should I do *that*?"

She looked down at the floor. "I remember, when Clara was alive, you always used to take to your heels the moment I arrived."

He glanced at her quizzically and then turned to the table and began to fiddle with his papers. "You exaggerate, Olivia," he said brusquely. "And even if I did so then, you surely cannot believe I would do so *now*. I hope you realize that I'm quite sensible of the fact that you are making a considerable personal sacrifice to stay here with the children, and I shall always be grateful to you for it, even if I seem remiss in expressing that gratitude. And I would not run off and leave you in sole charge of them if it were not necessary."

"I see. Then it is not because of me that you're going?"

"No, of course not. What reason have I given you to suspect such a thing?"

"Well . . . you *are* angry with me, aren't you?"

He looked over his shoulder at her in surprise. "Not at all. Why should I be?"

She flushed. "I . . . I *slapped* you . . ."

He blinked for a moment in bewilderment and then burst out in a laugh. "Yes, you did, didn't you?" He rubbed the cheek in painful recollection. "It was, as my pugilist friend, Jeremy Jackson would say, 'a right smart blow.' And one that I completely deserved."

"No, no! I should never have—"

"You most certainly *should* have, my dear." He came up to her in two long strides and lifted her chin with his hand. "I was unforgiveably rude, and no young woman of spirit could have been expected to ignore it. Don't ever apologize, girl, for the spark of fire you have within you. It sets you quite above the ordinary, you know."

Olivia stared up at him in astonishment. He had never said such a thing to her before. Her heart seemed to swell inside her chest in pleasure. His eyes were fixed on hers with a compelling, if enigmatic gleam, and she wondered with a little thrill of alarm if he intended to kiss her as he'd done once before in this very room. A hot surge of blood rushed up to her face as she realized with shame that there would be nothing she'd like more than having him sweep her into his arms as he'd done before.

But he did no such thing. Instead, he seemed to react to her unmistakable blush with a shudder of self-reproof. He dropped his hand from her cheek and turned away abruptly. "Run along to bed now, my dear," he said in a flat, matter-of-fact tone. "I'll never finish going through these papers if we stand here speaking nonsense."

So the bubble inside her burst, her pulse regulated itself, and the joyful feeling in her chest dissipated like perfume sprayed in the wind. He was going away; that was the only reality that had come from all these words. And the fact of his going was more depressing to her spirit than she'd ever expected. "You *have* spoken a great deal of nonsense, Miles," she said glumly as she went to the door, "but you haven't told me the real reason why you're going away."

"You'll know in due time." He kept his eyes on the papers he was stacking into a neat pile.

She paused in the doorway. "I wouldn't be at all surprised if your reason is to make a cowardly escape from the company of your aunt and my cousin. If that *is* your dastardly plan, my lord—if you are leaving me to cope with Hattie and Eugenia all by myself—I shall concoct a most devastating revenge. I shall find a way to coax them to live with you *forever after*, and then I shall run off and leave them to you!" And with that parting shot, she left him to his packing.

chapter eighteen

Olivia and Perry were perched atop the stone wall which divided the upper South slope from the lower South field, watching Amy trundle a toy wheelbarrow about on the winter-faded grass. The boy and his aunt were having one of their frequent "serious" talks. It was an unusually balmy day for early March, and Olivia had decided to permit the children to spend part of the afternoon in the open air, for they had just endured several weeks of cold and depressing rain. While Amy's goloshoes squelched through the soggy grass behind her little red barrow, Perry and Olivia swung their legs in the air and held their faces up to drink in the sun's faint warmth. "If I were truly Gorgana," Olivia said, "I would devise an enchanted spell which would make every day just like today."

"If *I* were Gorgana," Perry argued, "I would make it *snow* every day. I *love* the snow."

"Really?" Olivia asked, turning to study him. "Why?"

"Because it's such great fun. You can play in it, and make snowballs and build forts—"

"Like the fort you and your father built during the last snowfall?"

"Yes. That was the best snow fort I ever saw, wasn't it, Aunt Livie?"

"The best. Did you like building it?"

"Oh, yes, more than anything!"

"And did you like having your father help you with it?"

"Yes, I truly did." The boy pouted suddenly. "I wish he was at home. When will he be home, Aunt Livie?"

"Soon, I think. And you'll show him how well you are riding, and you'll tell him all you've learned about the Plantagenets, too."

"And even the Tudors," Perry added proudly. "I hope he comes before I forget. Do you know, Aunt Livie, when I was a little boy, I was afraid of Papa?"

"Were you, dearest?"

"Yes. Very. He seemed to be so huge, you know. Like the giant on top of the beanstalk. And he always seemed so very angry, too."

"Did he indeed?"

"I suppose he seemed so because I was smaller then. But it's all right now that I've grown."

"I'm glad. It doesn't do to be afraid of *anyone*, Perry, love. There are no *real* giants, you know. Not on top of beanstalks or anywhere else."

"I know." Perry sighed philosophically. "There are no monsters, either. Or ghosts. Only in people's minds, like Sir Budgidore."

"Do you mean to say that you *understand* that Sir Budgidore was only imaginary?"

"Oh, yes. I *always* understood that. It's just that I could see him, sort of. Almost real, if you know what I mean."

"I do, love. Do you miss him now that he's gone?"

"Not very much. After we had that ceremony for him, I stopped thinking much about him. Do you suppose he's gone to the special place where Mama has gone and that they can *both* watch over us?"

Olivia put an arm around his shoulder and hugged him. "No one knows the answers to such questions, dearest. But it's lovely to think so."

Perry's father had been absent almost six weeks when this conversation took place. It had been a time of considerable change for Perry. Olivia had been quite concerned for the boy. His tutor had gone first, and Olivia had noted that Perry had seemed to be very upset by Mr. Clapham's departure. She readily sympathized with the boy's feelings, but after a bit of thinking she began to understand what had been the real cause of the boy's distress. Perry, shaken by the events of the past year, had developed a tendency to cling to routine. He liked everything to stay the same. He clung to the familiar—to *people* he was accustomed to and to *schedules* he had come to expect. Change was threatening to him. Change meant loss.

Olivia, mulling over the matter, knew that Perry would not be able to live a life without change. No one could. Things and people changed all the time; there was no way to prevent it. Therefore Perry would have to learn to accept it. For that reason, Olivia tried to shake him from routine. Some days she would tutor him in his studies at the scheduled hours, but often she would surprise him by calling off the lessons completely. Sometimes she permitted him to sleep late, and sometimes she woke him early enough to watch the sunrise. Sometimes she and Elspeth and Amy spent the entire day with him, and sometimes she encouraged him to spend almost the entire day on his own, to devise his own ways of passing the time.

It was not until Elspeth left for London, however, that Olivia could determine how well her plan was working. For several weeks, Elspeth had been training the maid, Tilda, to take her place. Tilda was only nineteen, and she had not received the kind of education that Elspeth had, but she was warmhearted, cheerful and had had several years of schooling at a charity school in Leicestershire where she'd been raised. She could read remarkably well, and she wrote in a fine hand. If she could not give Amy lessons in music or drawing, it was not a great problem. Music and drawing masters could be hired later. And when Perry's new tutor would arrive, he could no doubt instruct Amy in those subjects in which Tilda was deficient. The primary trait which Olivia and Elspeth agreed was needed in the governess who would replace Elspeth was loving warmth, and that Tilda possessed in good measure.

Elspeth longed to return to London, but she would gladly have postponed the gratification of her desires indefinitely if the children needed her. Olivia, however, did not think that an indefinite postponement of Elspeth's departure would help the children to learn to face the vicissitudes of life. About two weeks after Strickland's departure (Olivia having noted that both Perry and Amy seemed reasonably content in *his* absence),

Olivia convinced Elspeth that it was time for her to take her leave.

To Olivia's great relief, Perry bid the governess a fond goodbye without the slightest sign of inward distress. The boy had, in fact, taken a strong liking to Tilda because of her carefree manner and easy laughter and was thus able to say goodbye to Elspeth without pain. It was the placid, easy-going *Amy* who surprised Olivia. The child did something she had never done before—she threw herself down on the floor of the nursery and screamed, "I want my Elthpeth! I want my *Elthpeth!*" She kicked her chubby legs up and down and pounded her little fists on the carpet, wailing and weeping furiously.

"But she's only gone to marry Uncle Charles," Perry explained to his hysterical sister calmly. "She'll be back to see us."

But his assurances were of no avail. Olivia took him from the room, and the two of them waited until Amy's tantrum had spent itself. Then they reentered, and Olivia, lifting the still-sobbing child to her lap, carefully explained that Elspeth was soon to be her aunt instead of her governess. "Won't it be lovely to have two aunts instead of only me?"

"W-Wiw she bwing m-me thome beads when she c-cometh back?" Amy asked, wiping away her tears with the back of her hand.

And so the crisis passed, the children accepted the altered circumstances of their lives without any other signs of emotional impairment, and Elspeth went off to London to be married. Olivia was unable, of course, to attend the wedding, but she learned all the details of the affair from the various letters she received from the participants.

Charles sent a letter filled with ecstatic exaggerations of a joyful, flawless, ideal ceremony; no bride had ever been so beautiful and no wedding vows had ever been more meaningful. Elspeth's note was all breathless effusion. Olivia read both letters to her chaperones as they sat at the dinner table. But while Hattie and Eugenia set to bickering over the relative merits of a large wedding over a small one, Olivia pulled from her sleeve a letter from her brother James and silently reread it. Jamie had written her favorite account of the wedding—the *only* account which gave her a clear and truthful picture of the event.

It was just the sort of scrambled affair, Jamie had written, *that only our family can contrive—a kind of frenzied misadventure from the start. Elspeth arrived without warning quite late at night, and Charles, with his newly awakened sense of propriety, would not permit her to spend the night under our roof for fear of "compromising" her. Nothing would do but that I should find a suitable hotel for her. But, of course, he didn't want her to stay at a hotel for one night longer than absolutely necessary, so a special license had to be arranged. One needs the signature of a bishop for a special license, you know, so Charles applied to Father. "Of course I am acquainted with a bishop," Father declared and launched into a long tale about a chap he knew at Eton who'd later distinguished himself in the clergy, etc. etc. But as you might have expected, Father didn't quite remember the bishop's name! It took hours of reminiscences and pulling out of old schoolbooks before the name was positively identified. The next day, Charles went in search of the eminent clergyman only to discover that the fellow had been dead for more than a dozen years!*

It was Lord Strickland who came to the rescue. He and Charles have been thick as thieves of late, you know. He took matters into his own hands and procured a special license within a day. He's completely up to the mark, old Strickland, whatever you may think of his libertine qualities, Livie, for if it weren't for him, the entire wedding business would have been a disaster. The best thing that ever happened to this family was Clara's marriage to him—and you may take my word on that.

In any case, with a special license in hand, we all—Father, Charles, Strickland and I—climbed into Strickland's carriage and drove to the hotel to pick up the bride. We found her waiting eagerly, all dressed in her governess's Sunday best—a gray kerseymere gown and the dowdiest bonnet I've ever laid eyes on. Well, Strickland took one look at her and announced that we must all have tea before we set out for church. Before we knew it, he'd hired the hotel's best private parlour and had ushered us to our places round a well-laden tea-table.

Then, assuring us that he would be back before we'd finished the repast, he took himself off.

Within the hour, he returned, carrying a hat box which he presented to the bride with a charmingly humorous flourish. When Elspeth beheld the flowery confection inside, she promptly indulged in what I later learned was her habitual way of dealing with life—a burst of waterworks. But when she saw herself in the glass in her new bridal bonnet, her eyes truly shone. I must admit, Livie, that it was not until I saw her in that hat—a straw concoction with a deep poke and a row of flowers around the crown—that I realized what a pretty thing she is.

When we arrived at the church, the parson was nowhere in evidence. Strickland, of course, was the one who went to find him. But by the time he returned with the parson in tow, Father had disappeared. He was nowhere to be found. After searching the place for more than half-an-hour, I discovered him in a tiny room—a closet, really, like an ambry—behind the vestry, sitting on an overturned pail and reading avidly a yellowed old manuscript he'd somehow come upon. It was all I could do to pry him away from his discovery—he swore it was fifteenth century and "quite revealing of the changes in Latinate style which had come into being after Thomas á Kempis." He had to be reminded that his eldest son was about to be married and that he himself was expected to give the bride away!

The ceremony itself passed uneventfully, Father leading the bride in with proper, if absent-minded, dignity, and your humble servant standing up for Charles in—if I may be permitted to say so—grand style. But after the ceremony, Father delayed the return to the house (where Cook must have been tearing her hair out over the ruination of the wedding feast she'd been preparing for the past thirty-six hours) in order to explain to the parson that a manuscript of such scholarly value as the one he'd discovered should not be so carelessly stowed in an unused storage space. A lengthy discussion of fifteenth-century clerical Latin ensued until Strickland interfered, distracting Father with a promise to provide funds to restore the manuscript to its original condition. He took Father's arm in his and, while asking his advice about whom to consult about the *restoration, managed to maneuver him out of the building.*

Thus your brother was married, after which ordeal we all returned to the house and merrily consumed that part of the wedding dinner which had not been burned or dried out during the delay.

Looking back on it, I must admit that the day had been enormously entertaining. I only wish that you had been there to share in the festivities.

Olivia slipped the letter back into her sleeve and smiled to herself. Her brother's letter had brought the wedding vividly to life for her. It was quite like her family to make a muddle of the wedding in just that style. Charles had always been a sensible, feet-on-the-ground fellow, but love must have made him into the head-in-the-clouds sort. As for her father, however, he could be counted on to make a goodly number of absent-minded blunders. And Elspeth, with her ready tears, was eccentric enough to fit right in. It was only Strickland whose behavior was unexpected. He had been more thoughtful and kind than she would ever have supposed, even though Jamie had been mistaken in assuming that she still thought badly of him. Strickland could be selfish and stubborn at times, but he could be generous too. It had been many months since she'd thought of him as a monsterish libertine. In truth, this evidence of his kindness to her family during the wedding was only one of a number of signs which showed him to be, as Clara had once told her, a man of character.

The man of character had been gone six weeks when, without a word of warning, his carriage drew up at the door. It was followed by another equipage as grand as Strickland's—a traveling coach with shiny blue panels and brass fittings and bearing a crest upon the door which indicated that it carried behind its curtained windows one or more members of a decidedly noble family. The impressive equipage drew the attention of Aunt Eugenia, who remarked to Hattie that Strickland had returned with a gaggle of guests. "Top-of-the-trees, from the look of them," she announced gleefully, her nose pressed to the window of the upstairs sitting room. "Two gentlemen and two . . . no, *three* ladies . . . and all dressed in the first style of elegance. How delightful. We shall have a bit of excitement at last."

"We shall have noise and confusion, that's what we shall have!" Hattie responded acidly. "Nothing but noise and confusion."

While the guests were climbing from the carriages, Olivia was up in the schoolroom where she, Tilda and the children were engaged in learning the rudiments of watercolor painting. Several hours had been happily spent in dabbing dripping colors upon large white sheets of paper and evaluating the effects. There had been much effort, much failure and much laughter. Amy had dabbed more color on her face, hands and apron than on her painting; and even the others were significantly besmirched. In the midst of this absorbing but begriming activity, word reached Olivia that his lordship had just arrived and was asking for her.

With an eager cry, she jumped up and ran to the stairway, the two overjoyed youngsters at her heels. Warning Tilda to take the children's hands on the stairway, she flew ahead of them down five of the six flights of stairs, her heart hammering in delight. She had not the slightest premonition of the sight that was about to meet her eyes. "Miles, you're *back*!" she clarioned as she rounded the bend of the staircase and came to the top of the last flight. "Why didn't you wr—? Oh! Good *heavens*!"

There below her was what seemed to be a crowd of strangers, all looking up at her quizzically. She had a quick impression of gleaming jewels, waving feathers, luxurious furs. Elegantly gowned ladies were handing their outer garments to Fincher as he moved among them. An impeccably dressed gentleman was handing over his beaver while another was shrugging out of his greatcoat. Strickland, who'd evidently been introducing Aunt Eugenia and Cousin Hattie to his guests, had turned round at the sound of Olivia's voice and was looking up at her. "Ah, *there* you are, Olivia," he said in greeting.

Standing among his fashionable friends, Strickland looked the most elegant of all. Olivia had not before realized quite how handsome he was. He was taller than any of the others, and the impressive width of his shoulders was emphasized by his caped greatcoat of soft brown wool. The greatcoat hung open, casually revealing a modish town coat of dark-brown superfine which Olivia had never before seen him wear. To add to the unfamiliar stylishness of his appearance, she noted that he'd had his hair cut in a new and rather dashing style, although the gray at his temples had become a bit more perceptible. He looked every inch a gentleman of marked distinction.

The impressive stylishness of his appearance suddenly made her conscious of the shabbiness of her own. She remembered with horror that she was wearing an old, faded muslin gown which she'd carelessly stained with watercolors, and her hands flew, almost of their own accord to her hair which she surmised was hideously tousled. But her eyes never left his face. His polite and rather distant smile widened to a grin. "Well, aren't you going to say anything? Have you forgotten how to *speak* in my absence?"

She smiled back at him, feeling unaccountably shy. "I . . . it's very good to have you back," she said awkwardly, wondering desperately whether it was necessary to continue on down the stairs to make her greetings or if it would be very shocking to turn and run upstairs to hide.

Her problem was solved by the appearance of the children. They paused for only a moment at her side, for it took only the first glimpse of their father to send them scurrying on down the stairs. Amy leaped from the fourth step right into her father's arms while Perry rushed on, tumbling against him and hugging him enthusiastically about the waist. If Strickland was annoyed by this unusual laxity of behavior, he made no sign. He buried his face in his daughter's neck while he lifted his son up to his shoulder with his other arm, for a moment surrendering to his joy in the reunion. Olivia felt her throat constrict at the sight of it.

But Eugenia would not let the moment pass without comment. "Have you no *manners*, children?" she chided. "Such untrammeled wildness will not *do*! Miles, dear boy, put them down at once and let them make their bows."

But Strickland, meanwhile, had taken a look at their faces. "Good *Lord*," he exclaimed in amused surprise, "what's that you've smeared on your faces? You look like a couple of red Indians."

The guests had crowded round and were exchanging indulgent smiles. Olivia, shamefacedly remembering the perfect decorum with which the children were made to greet their father when Clara was alive, ran down the steps and took the children from her brother-in-law. "I'm sorry, Miles," she said in a breathless undervoice. Then, looking up embarrassedly at the faces staring into hers, she explained, "We've been working with watercolors, I'm afraid. I shouldn't have permitted them to come down in this besmirched condition. I hope, Miles, that you'll forgive me for causing you embarrassment before your friends."

"You needn't worry, my dear," Strickland said, grinning at her. "I've already told my friends that my sister-in-law is an original."

"No need for embarrassment on *our* account," said a familiar voice, and Olivia looked up to see Arthur Tisswold standing nearby. "They are only children, after all." And he took her stained hand from Perry's clasp and bowed over it.

"You're quite right, Arthur," Strickland said, tousling Perry's hair.

"You're quite *wrong*," Cousin Hattie contradicted in her scornful, cracked voice. "Children should be expected to behave like little adults when they are brought into adult company. Tilda ought to take them upstairs at once."

Tilda, who had been waiting on the stairway, bobbed and started down. But Strickland put up a restraining hand. "No need to stand on points, Cousin Hattie. It's all my fault, you know. I didn't send word of my arrival. Now that the damage is done, we may as well make everyone known to each other."

"If you please, Miles," Olivia suggested quietly, "I think it would be better to wait until later to perform the introductions. The children and I would be more comfortable if we could have some time to change. Let me take them upstairs. I'll bring them down in time for tea—which can't be very far off—and you can make the introductions then."

"Very well, if that is what you wish," he said and turned to a strikingly beautiful young woman standing at his left.

"Shall we go into the drawing room in the meantime? I, for one, would be grateful for a warm fire. Lead the way, if you please, Aunt Eugenia. Come along, Leonora. And let me take your arm too, Lady Gallard. Arthur, old man, will you instruct the footman to serve the port?" Smoothly, with a word for everyone, he guided his guests away from the stairs and toward the drawing room.

Olivia, deeply humiliated by her overenthusiastic behavior on hearing of Strickland's arrival and by having permitted the children to be seen by a houseful of guests in all their dirt, led the children up the stairs. Ignoring their questions about why they couldn't talk to Papa and where he could have hidden their presents, she turned them over to Tilda with strict instructions to dress them in their best and to have them ready by tea-time. Then she ran down the hall to her own room. One look in the mirror confirmed her worst fears—she looked a *sight*! Her hair had fallen over her forehead in shocking disarray, a streak of green paint had spread itself across the bridge of her nose and onto her cheek, and her dress—a shabby old thing to begin with—was speckled with orange and purple spots across the bosom and down the front. Even Tilda in her soiled apron had looked better. What must Strickland's guests have thought of her? What must *he* have thought?

She remembered that he had called her an "original." What had he meant by that? If he intended to imply that she was an *eccentric*, her appearance had certainly supported him.

But she had no time for further reflection. She whipped off her dress, washed her face in the basin and pulled on a presentable gown. She brushed her hair vigorously, attempting to achieve a semblance of neatness, although she knew that strands of curls would spring free of the smoothly brushed waves as soon as she walked away from the mirror. Then she jumped up from her dressing table and went up to inspect the children. *Their* appearance, she knew, was more important than her own. The guests would wish to meet Lord Strickland's children, not his sister-in-law.

In all this time, she'd kept herself from dwelling on the guests. But questions concerning them kept niggling at her mind. Who *were* they? Why on earth had Strickland invited them? Didn't he realize how the need to entertain them would steal time away from that which he would ordinarily allot to the children? There was something strange about this state of affairs, and although she had no idea of the answers to her questions, she had a dismaying feeling that there was something *foreboding* about the presence of the guests. Something was going to happen, and she had a strong premonition that she would not like the happening at all.

chapter nineteen

Olivia thought the children looked perfectly splendid. Tilda had dressed Amy in a white dimity gown belted with a wide blue satin sash and tied in the back with an enormous bow. White pantaloons peeped out below her flounced hem and their ruffled bottoms revealed only the tips of her tiny laced half boots. Perry looked almost manly in his brown coat (very like his father's), velveret waistcoat of antique bronze and pale beige smalls with buckles at the knees. Even his boots were like his father's, the leather gleaming and little tassles swinging from the tops. "You are both *beautiful*!" she crowed, folding them into an embrace. "Why do you look so unhappy?"

"We want to see *Papa* . . . to see what he's brought us from London . . . and to *play* with him," Perry pouted. "We don't *like* to talk to guests."

Amy nodded agreement. "Don't like gueths," she echoed.

"Nonsense!" Olivia said briskly. "They are your father's friends, and if *he* likes them, it is very likely you will too."

"Will *you* like them, Aunt Livie?" Perry asked dubiously.

The question caught her up short, and she realized that she had already, without even having been introduced to them, taken them all in decided *dis*like. "Of *course* I will like them," she said mendaciously, but she couldn't meet his eye.

Instead, she turned quickly to Tilda, complimenting the governess on her achievement in so quickly washing and changing the children and even managing to make *herself* presentable. "You are a *treasure*, Tilda," she said affectionately as

186

she hurried to the door. "Now, wait for five minutes—until his lordship will have had a chance to present me—and then bring the children downstairs."

The guests had moved from the drawing room to the large downstairs sitting room where the tea things had been set out. Cousin Hattie was already seated behind the teapot dispensing the brew with unsmiling efficiency when Olivia entered. Strickland immediately came to his sister-in-law's side and took her to meet his guests. There were not so many of them as Olivia had at first supposed. Besides Sir Arthur, whom she already knew, there were only four: Lord and Lady Gallard, a middle-aged couple whose manners were disconcertingly formal; Miss Leonora Oglesby, Lady Gallard's sister, the breathtaking beauty whom Olivia had noticed before; and Mrs. Oglesby, the mother of Lady Gallard and Miss Oglesby, a dowager of imposing size and equally formidable manner. Of the entire group, only Sir Arthur gave Olivia a smile. The rest offered polite greetings, but their eyes seemed to view her as some sort of strange creature whom they would rather not know.

The children, however, were greeted with many smiles and a number of gushing compliments. "Oooh, the little *darlings*!" squealed Lady Gallard.

"Miles, they are *delicious*," Leonora Oglesby said, her voice melodious with enthusiasm.

"I could eat them *up*!" her mother gurgled, opening her arms to them. "Come to my arms, you precious babies, and let me *squeeze* you!"

This last effusion was, for the uncomfortable children, the last straw. Eyeing Mrs. Oglesby with suspicious fear, they retreated to the safety of Olivia's skirts. Amy hid behind those skirts, peeping out at the assemblage with one frightened eye; Perry merely clutched at them with one hand while standing close beside his aunt, erect and brave so long as he could feel her close by. All the attempts of the guests to coax them away from their protector were unsuccessful. It was only when their father set chairs for them—at a sufficient distance from the strangers to encourage them to let Olivia go—that they finally emerged and accepted their cups of chocolate from their great-aunt Eugenia.

Strickland's face gave no clue to Olivia of any displeasure he may have felt at the shyness of his children, but it seemed to her that there was a feeling of relief all around when they were at last excused and returned to the schoolroom. However, Olivia knew that Strickland could not be pleased at their performance and that, sooner or later, he would take *her* to task for it. She wondered how long it would be before that *contretemps* would come to pass.

That evening she dressed for dinner with a perceptible cheerlessness. None of her dinner gowns seemed to be at all comparable even to the traveling dresses the newly arrived ladies had worn to the tea-table. She pulled out the jonquil-colored silk dress she'd worn to the Crawford's ball but soon decided it was not appropriate for a country dinner. Eventually, she settled without enthusiasm on a dark-blue Norwich crape with a high, round neck trimmed with a small lace ruffle, long sleeves puffed at the top and a pretty row of gold-embroidered *fleurs-de-lis* emphasizing the high waist. Next to the jonquil silk, this was the prettiest dress in her wardrobe, and she hoped (without much confidence) that, when compared to the elegant creations in which the visiting ladies would no doubt be draped, it would not appear to be too dreadfully dowdy.

Dolefully, she examined herself in her mirror. From the top of her short and unruly curls to the soles of her well-worn slippers, she looked the eccentric. Why couldn't she have had smooth blond tresses like the lovely Miss Oglesby, or wear stylish gowns like the mint-green Tiffany silk Lady Gallard had worn? Olivia's dress was too dark to be striking and too plain to be fashionable. She may not look quite a dowd, but she appeared to be just what she was—an eccentric bluestocking. Strickland may have termed her an "original," but she knew what he meant.

She went down to the drawing room a bit early, hoping to find a private moment in which to discuss with Fincher the seating arrangements for the dinner. But, pausing on the threshold of the drawing-room doorway, she saw that Strickland had preceded her. He stood just opposite the door, on the other side of a long sofa, obviously going over with the butler a diagram of the seating arrangements. She was about to cross the room to join them when the sound of voices from the corner of the room at her left stayed her.

"Any fool can guess what he intends," Eugenia was saying in what was meant to be a whisper. "Why else would he have invited her . . . and her family as well?"

"It's you who's the fool," Hattie responded acidly. "There are a dozen reasons other than the one you've suggested which could account for a man's wishing to fill his house with guests."

"Not in this case," Eugenia said with authority. "He's brought not only the girl and her sister, but the *mother* as well. Why would he do that, unless he had serious intentions? It's plain as a pikestaff! Strickland plans to *marry* the Oglesby chit!"

The words struck Olivia with the force of a physical blow. Of *course*! Every question that had been nudging at her mind was suddenly answered. It all *fit*! Everything fell into place. *Strickland was going to marry Leonora Oglesby*. She drew in her breath in an audible gasp, her eyes flying to Strickland's face. He, too, had overheard his aunt's last words, and the sound of the gasp from the doorway drew his eyes at once to hers. For a long moment they stared at each other without moving. Her lips trembled and her knees felt suddenly weak. *Is it true*? her eyes asked, their message unmistakable. He felt the color drain from his cheeks and, painfully, he looked away.

That was all the answer she needed. For a moment, she feared she would drop to the floor in a swoon. She saw him take an involuntary step toward her, as if to try to catch her, but she took hold of herself and turned away. She had never behaved missishly before, and if she had any strength at all, she would not do so now.

Somehow she managed to get through dinner. People addressed remarks to her, and somehow she answered them. During the time at the table she tried to remain unnoticed, so that she could surrender to an enveloping cloud of depression and wallow in her misery, but Strickland seemed intent on bringing her to the attention of the others. He related to the guests that, while in London, he'd gone to visit Leigh Hunt in the Surrey gaol at Olivia's behest. "Don't you want to hear what happened, my dear?" he asked her from across the table.

She mumbled an incoherent response which he took for an assent, and he proceeded to tell the others how she'd imagined poor Mr. Hunt dying of ill health in some pestilential hole, imprisoned and kept from all contact with friends and relations, all for having written some foolish slurs against the person and character of the Prince. "But he is *not* hidden away in some slimy cell, Olivia," he said, smiling at her mockingly. "He has a *room*! Yes, indeed, a quite comfortable room, with rose-covered paper on the wall, blue painting on the ceiling, and all his books around him. And his *piano* has been brought in, too! All true, I swear it. He is permitted to have visitors at any time of the day or night, and he receives a steady parade of them. You will be interested to know, Olivia, that the notorious Lord Byron came to see him just as I was leaving. Hunt is free to do his writing while incarcerated, and, more shocking still, he is permitted to edit the very newspaper in which his diatribe first appeared. Thus does our Prinny punish the man who defamed him. What do you think of *that*, eh, my little libertarian?"

Every eye turned to Olivia, waiting for her response. She tried desperately to snatch her mind back from its miserable wool-gathering to concentrate on the present moment. "I think, my lord," she said with as much spirit as she could muster, "that if the Prince has seen fit to give Mr. Hunt so much of his freedom while *inside* the gaol, he might just as well have gone all the way and let him have it *outside*."

Lord Gallard immediately defended the Prince by claiming that the Regent *had* to make an example of the Hunt brothers, while Arthur Tisswold surprisingly defended *Olivia's* position. A lively discussion ensued, during which neither Strickland nor Olivia took any part. Strickland merely leaned back against his chair and fixed his eyes on her with a small smile of approval lingering at the corners of his mouth. Olivia tried proudly to outstare him, but her eyes soon fluttered to her hands folded in her lap. She spent the rest of the time ignoring him—she kept her eyes lowered and her mouth closed and let her misery swallow her up. In that way, without adding another word to the conversation, she lived through the interminable dinner.

As soon as she could escape, she fled to her room. Her

mind was awhirl with chaotic feelings which she couldn't understand, and she forced herself to sit down and think about what had happened with some degree of calm. It was quite plain that the thought of Strickland's possible remarriage had completely unsettled her. But why? Why should she *care* if Strickland was seeking to marry again?

The first and most obvious answer had to do with the children. A new wife for him meant a new mother for them. Would a woman like Leonora Oglesby be a kind and loving mother? She had no reason to believe otherwise, but she had to admit that she felt a distinct—if unreasoning—dislike for the lady. And if the children had a new mother, what would *Olivia's* position be in regard to them? Would she—*should* she—remain here to protect them?

Her stomach began to churn and her head to ache. She lay down on the bed and threw an arm over her tearful eyes. It would be impossible for her to remain here at Langley after Strickland took a new wife—too awkward, too stultifying, utterly *impossible*. She would be miserable in such circumstances. The pain would be too great to bear...

...But *what* pain? *Why*? Why would the addition of another woman to the household cause her *pain*? She had accepted the presence of Eugenia and Hattie easily enough. Why not Leonora Oglesby? Or any other woman Strickland might choose?

She winced as an image of Strickland in the company of a new wife burst upon her inner eye. She could see him quite clearly, walking down the stairs on a sunny spring morning with his willowy, blond wife, his arm about her waist and her gaze fixed on his face in dewy-eyed adoration. She could see him at the breakfast table, his new young wife standing behind his chair, handing him a plate of coddled eggs and York ham and then planting a kiss on his brow as she leaned over to serve him (just as she'd once seen Clara do in the dim past). She could see him with his Leonora, romping with the children through the snow-covered South field, Strickland pelting his new wife with snowballs until she fell, laughing, into a drift and pulled him tumbling down on top of her. These visions made Olivia feel decidedly ill.

She sat up with a cry. All at once the reason for her disturbed emotions burst with crystal clarity on her mind. She wanted all these experiences for *herself*! She wanted the troublesome, irritating libertine, Miles Strickland, to marry *her*!

She ran a trembling hand through her tangled curls. How had this happened? When had her antagonistic feelings toward Strickland taken this unexpected turn? She remembered the kiss in the library that had so disturbed her . . . the discovery of Clara's view of his character . . . the day she had coaxed him out to play in the snow . . . the evening, not so long ago, when he'd told her that her spirit set her "quite above the ordinary." All these were memories which had suddenly become as precious as jewels. And they seemed to represent road-markers on a course which led to . . . Good Lord! . . . was it *love*?

She got up and began to pace about the bedroom in long, nervous strides. *Could* she have fallen in love with him? It hardly seemed possible. He was scarcely the sort of man who she'd imagined would some day win her affections. He was stubborn, opinionated and quarrelsome. He was fifteen years older than she. He was the notorious Tory Hawk whose politics she'd always detested. And worse than all the rest, he had been her sister's husband . . . and an adulterer. Was it possible that love could have leapt over all those deterents and managed to lodge inside her?

No, it couldn't be, for the feeling she had was too painful, too unpleasant and too completely humiliating. If love could make one feel so miserable, who would seek it out? Why would poets sing of it or young girls pray for it? This feeling couldn't be love—it was only a sort of emotional disease.

And yet she'd read of many whom love had made miserable: Virgil's Dido . . . and Catullus . . . Ophelia, Launcelot, Griselda . . . Dante . . . and Isolde . . . and a host of others, real and fictional, who offered testimony to love's pain. So could this disease of her spirit be love after all?

Well, whatever the name and whatever the diagnosis, she was certain of the path to the cure—escape. She had to leave Langley Park. She understood enough about her condition to know that she couldn't endure seeing Strickland wed—to Miss Oglesby or to anyone else. As quickly as she could, she must prepare the children for her departure and for their new life.

As her resolve grew, during the next few days, the children

became more difficult. Each time they were brought into the company of the houseguests, they retreated behind Olivia's skirts. No amount of coaxing, no honeyed words, no promises of mouthfuls of sugary sweetmeats succeeded in tempting the children to approach the visitors. It was as if they suspected, by some childish instinct, that Miss Oglesby and her family had an ulterior motive for wishing to embrace them, and they hung back.

After three days of frustration, Strickland invited Miss Oglesby and her mother to join him in a visit to the schoolroom, hoping that there, in their own special surroundings, the children might feel freer and more relaxed. The visit proved to be as unsuccessful as all the other encounters. Amy backed away from all contact with the visiting ladies and clung to Olivia as if her life depended on the attachment. And Perry, after making a polite bow, resumed his seat and kept his eyes glued to the storybook he was reading. Even Olivia's urgings to Amy to "sit down with Miss Oglesby and show her how you write your name on the slate," or her suggestion to Perry to "read to Miss Oglesby about how Dick Wittington came to London" fell on deaf ears. Strickland, his mouth stiff with suppressed annoyance, took the ladies downstairs. Shortly afterwards, Olivia received word that his lordship wanted to speak to her at her earliest convenience.

She found him staring out of the library window at the slowly greening fields which stretched out below him in smoothly undulating swells to the edge of the home woods. The trees, still bare, were casting long afternoon shadows on the lawn as the still-wintry sun moved toward the west. The light in the room was dim and the atmosphere redolent of tension and gloom. "You sent for me, my lord?" she asked, trying to make her tone brisk and cheerful.

He turned from the window and regarded her with a quizzically raised eyebrow. "Have we returned to *my lord* again? That is a sign that I've incurred your displeasure. What is it I've done, ma'am?"

"Nothing at all. My use of formal address is not a sign of *my* displeasure—only that I've put up my defenses to guard against *yours*," she said with a hesitant smile.

"What makes you think I'm displeased with you?"

"I have a distinct feeling you are about to deliver one of your famous scolds," she replied with alacrity.

"What rubbish! Why should I scold you? You're not some errant schoolgirl, and I am not your father."

She looked at him suspiciously. "Are you trying to tell me that your message saying that you wished to speak to me 'at my earliest convenience' doesn't signify a warning to me to put up my guard?"

"Did the message sound as peremptory as that? I did not mean it so." He came across the room to her, his lips curling in a reluctant smile. "What a disconcerting wench you are, my dear. You always succeed in making me feel like a heartless brute." He paused for a moment and regarded her with some misgiving. "Perhaps you *should* put up your guard, for I *do* have something of a rather unpleasant nature to say to you."

"Oh, dear," she murmured fearfully. "Then perhaps I'd better sit down." She perched uneasily on the edge of the nearest chair. "Very well, you may proceed, my lord. I am . . . quite ready."

He began to pace about the room. Then, pausing, he opened his mouth to speak, hesitated, and clamped it shut again. Resuming his pacing, he muttered a hoarse, "Damnation!" under his breath.

Olivia, although decidedly apprehensive about the substance of this interview, was nevertheless a bit amused by his obvious reluctance to proceed. "If you do not come to the point, and *soon*, Miles, I shall positively faint away," she said, teasing. "Your hesitations and mutterings are frightening me to death."

He gave an appreciative little snort of laughter. "Yes, you're right. I shall plunge in without roundaboutation. But I must say first that you don't deserve . . . that I don't wish you to think . . . oh, *damnation!*"

"Goodness! Now you truly *are* frightening me. This is something *more* than a desire to scold me about the children's shyness, isn't it? What *is* it?" She looked up at him, her brow wrinkled in alarm. "Please, Miles, *tell* me!"

"Very well, then, here's the substance in a nutshell." He dropped into the chair facing hers. "I must ask you, Olivia, to leave Langley at once."

Olivia's breath caught in her chest. "*Leave?* Why? Has

something happened at home? *Father*—?"

"No, no. It's not anything in London. The problem is right here." Seeing the lack of comprehension in her eyes, he got to his feet again and began once more to pace about. "How can I explain this without seeming to be completely lacking in gratitude for all you've done for us? To have to repay your generosity . . . your sacrifice . . . with *this*—!" He paused before the fireplace and stared down into the flames. "Don't you see?" he said more quietly. "The children are too attached to you. How can any other woman hope to win their regard while you—?"

"Oh! I *see*! You are speaking of Miss Oglesby." Olivia's voice was suddenly cold. "Has she asked you to send me away?"

"No, of course not. By what right would she—?"

"She is to be your *wife*, is she not?"

He shook his head. "It is not a settled thing. I have not yet made an offer."

"But you intend to do so?"

There was a moment of silence, during which Strickland continued to stare at the fire. "I . . . don't know. Not if the children resist her as they have been doing."

"And you think it *my* fault that they resist her?" she asked, unable to keep a tremor from her voice.

He wheeled about, strode across the room and pulled his chair close to hers. Without taking his eyes from her face, he grasped her hands in both of his. "There is no question of fault, Olivia," he said, his voice choked. "Don't you understand? The children love you! How can they *help* it? How could *anyone*—?" Abruptly, his gaze on her face wavered, and he lowered his eyes to his boots. "How can they possibly learn to accept someone else when you are near them?" He paused, his grasp on her hands tightening as his discomfort intensified. "I . . . we . . . the children can't expect you to stay here indefinitely, you know. So they must be forced to learn to live without you. Don't you see?"

Forgetting that she had determined, herself, to take leave of the children at the earliest opportunity, she leaned toward him and said softly, "I am willing to stay as long as they need me, Miles."

He cast a quick glance at her face, his expression, for a

fleeting moment, almost hungry with hope. But before she could be certain she'd read it correctly, he looked down again. "Don't be a fool, girl. They will need mothering for *years*. You're a budding young woman. You have your *own* life to live. You have a right to children of your own!"

Olivia's pulse began to race. What was Strickland trying to tell her? Had he brought Miss Oglesby back with him for *her* sake? To set her free from the burden of his children? Could he be as generous as *that*? "I've never planned to have children of my own, Miles," she said gently. "I have no interest in looking for a husband, if that's what you mean by pursuing my own life. I had always intended to devote my life to scholarship, to helping Father and Charles. But while Amy and Perry need caring for, it seemed more important to me to—"

He jumped to his feet and glared at her in disgust. "Don't spout those bluestocking platitudes at me, Olivia. They are the mouthings of a silly child, not of an intelligent woman."

That sort of remark had always been the response of Toryish men who believed that women were incapable of intellectual pursuits. She rose and faced him with sudden hostility. "Don't spout *your* Tory platitudes at *me*, my lord. They are the mouthings of a narrow-minded coxcomb, not of a sensible gentleman."

"Confound it, Olivia," he said through clenched teeth, grasping her by the shoulders in irritation, "you always manage to set up my bristles! Can you seriously pretend that a lovely, vibrant, desirable creature like you can escape matrimony? And do you think I could, in conscience, permit you to remain here in Langley, taking care of someone else's children like a blasted, pathetic *governess*? Forget your foolish, bluestocking pretensions. Forget your self-imposed obligations to children not your own. Go out in the world and find your *true* destiny!"

Breathlessly, she stared at him while a whirl of contradictory feelings stirred inside her. If he truly believed that she was the lovely, vibrant, desirable creature he'd described, why didn't *he* offer to be her destiny? Was he offering her Spanish coin, to make her believe that he'd brought his Miss Oglesby here for *her* sake rather than for his? Angrily, she shook herself loose from his grasp. "Liar!" she accused, her voice trembling with suppressed tears. "Stop pretending that it is *my* destiny which concerns you! It's your *own* destiny that is your concern . . . your destiny and Miss Oglesby's! Isn't *that* it?"

He kept his eyes on her face for a moment longer and then turned away. "What difference does it make?" he asked, his passionate anger spent.

"Very little, I suppose," she said, trying to speak more calmly. "I shall leave in any case. I just want the truth from you."

"The truth, my dear," he said with a sigh, "is that we cannot go on in this present arrangement. It's unhealthy for all of us."

Although she herself had come to the very same conclusion just a couple of days before, she could not now admit the truth of it. Her emotions seemed to have taken control of her tongue. "You mean we cannot go on in this present arrangement because you wish to wed Miss Oglesby. I quite understand, my lord. You have as much right to pursue *your* life as I have to pursue mine."

He threw her a quick glance over his shoulder and then walked to the window. "We *all* have to pursue life . . . even if we'd sometimes prefer to hide away in corners and let it pass us by."

She stared at his back silhouetted in the window by the light of the setting sun. Was he speaking of her . . . or of himself? But there seemed to be little point in continuing to quarrel. "I . . . I suppose I may stay until tomorrow afternoon, so that I can say a . . . a p-proper goodbye to the children . . . ?" She pressed her lips tightly together to keep them from trembling.

"Don't ask foolish questions. You may make whatever arrangements you wish." The words were curt, but the voice was hoarse.

"Very well, then. I shall go and start my packing at once." She went quickly to the door. "I hope you will believe, Miles, that I . . . I . . . wish you h-happy," she said softly.

He nodded his head. She stood motionless, hoping he would turn and face her once more—that by some miracle of the fates he would say something . . . *anything* . . . that would change or alleviate the aching emptiness inside her. But he neither moved nor spoke, and she quietly left the room, perceiving for the first time, and with terrifying dismay, that in spite of what he'd said, she was leaving her life *behind* her.

chapter twenty

Olivia's return to the house in Brook Street was a cause for sincere rejoicing for everyone in the family, but it was not long before she recognized that, although she was held in great affection by each one, none of them had any real need of her. Many of the activities that had been her responsibility—like deciding on the week's menus, copying manuscript pages for Charles or making certain that her father took time from his books to eat his luncheon—had been taken over by Elspeth. And the household had fallen into so comfortable a routine in the months of her absence that she almost felt like an intruder.

This state of affairs was far from comforting. Already crushed by the pains of unrequited love and her very real concern over the happiness of her beloved niece and nephew, she could barely keep up a semblance of equanimity before the family. Before long, she became aware that Jamie was watching her with wrinkled brow and that Charles and Elspeth were whispering about her worriedly.

There was only one thing for her to do. She had to take herself in hand and begin to, as Strickland put it, pursue her destiny. She had to force herself to get out in the world. For that, of course, she needed to seek the advice of her brother Jamie. With some eagerness, he informed her that Morley Crawford had been inquiring after her with persistent interest. With her permission, Jamie advised his friend that he was free to pay a call on her, and within a week Crawford became a frequent visitor to the house on Brook Street.

Olivia tried sincerely to find enjoyment in his company. But she succeeded only at those times when he escorted her to the theater or the opera. There, for a few hours, she was able to forget herself . . . to lose herself in the artificial world of make-believe. And she also found it a relief to be occupied, even if the occupation was as mundane as freshening her wardrobe or planning superficial amusements. But Morley Crawford had neither matured nor changed in the months since she'd last seen him, and it was difficult to maintain a sincere interest in his rather commonplace, boyish conversation.

Morley, however, had found Olivia *greatly* changed—and all for the better. She seemed to have become even prettier than before—slimmer and more mysterious. Better still, she no longer disconcerted him by saying outlandish things and making unconventional suggestions. She was quieter, more restrained and more willing to let him take the lead. Once more he fell head over heels in love. And this time he was determined to court her until she'd agreed to become his wife.

It soon became plain to Olivia that Morley had serious intentions, and, on reflection, she admitted that there was a distinct possibility that she might one day accept him. There was very little else she could do. Strickland evidently had been quite right—her "bluestocking pretensions" had been foolish. A lady of intellectual pretensions was looked on by all the world as queerly eccentric. Even so formidable a bluestocking as Madame de Stael, who was a Baroness wealthy enough to set herself up in grand style, hold *salons* and entertain all the famous writers and thinkers of the time, was laughed at behind her back. If a woman didn't wish to grow into a dried-up old maid, hiding away in the parental household and growing more and more pitiful with time, there was nothing for her but marriage. And if a girl didn't *love* any of her suitors, what matter? Olivia wondered how many of the young ladies of society had married without love, merely for the reason that there was nothing else for them to *do* with their lives. As for herself, if she *had* to marry, she supposed The Honorable Mr. Crawford would make as conformable a husband as any other. He was easy-going and likeable, his character was open and honest, and he had five thousand a year. Many girls would call him a "catch." If Morley Crawford was her destiny, so be it.

• • •

At Langley Park, Strickland was finding *his* pursuit of his destiny more difficult. Sending Olivia away had done little to bring about a closer relationship between his children and the woman he was considering as his next wife. Their encounters were as stiff as ever. He'd tried bringing Perry and Amy, singly or together, to her when she was alone, and he tried it when she was in company with others. He'd tried taking them all riding together. He'd tried showing Leonora up to their bedrooms to tuck them up at night. None of his efforts had resulted in any perceptible growth of warmth. He had one remaining hope: Amy's forthcoming fifth birthday.

He arranged with Tilda and the cook to hold a birthday luncheon. It would be held in the large downstairs sitting room, where everything would be carefully arranged to delight and entertain the children. On the appointed day, Strickland sent Lord Gallard and Arthur out to ride, relieving them of the sort of afternoon they would find unbearably dull—and at the same time relieving the children of having to endure their stilted presences. He checked the room carefully before inviting the participants to make their appearance. As he'd ordered, one side of the room was cleared of furniture so that they could play at ringtoss and spillikins. On the other side of the room, a table had been set up for the luncheon. It was cheerfully decorated with gayly colored confetti scattered all over it (an idea of Tilda's) and had as its centerpiece a huge dish piled high with *bonbons*. The entire room had been decorated with banners and streamers, and every surface held dishes of sweet-meats and cakes. Strickland was quite satisfied that the at-mosphere of the room was as festive as possible. He could only hope that it would remain so after the party had begun.

Leonora, at first, tried her best, and so did her mother and sister. They played at spillikins with enthusiasm and made much pleasantly silly chatter over luncheon. Strickland, sitting next to Perry at the festive table, making tantalizing jokes about the presents that were to be brought out for the two of them, was not discouraged by the results of his efforts. Amy was looking quite cheerful, and Perry had even exchanged some words with Leonora's mother. But after Amy had unwrapped her new doll (which didn't interest her at all) and Perry had glowed with joy at receiving a real pocketknife quite suitable for carving wood, a climactic incident occurred to spoil everything.

Leonora, determined to succeed in attracting the birthday girl to her lap, held out a brightly painted top. "Here's something *else* for you, Amy, my little love," she said, her melodious voice sugary with temptation. "Come here to me, and you shall have it . . . all for your very own."

But Amy had spied on the wrist of that outstretched hand a bracelet of garnet stones. *"Beadth!"* she breathed, her eyes eager. "What pwetty beadth!" She slid off her chair and ran toward Leonora with arms outstretched.

Leonora could not let the opportunity go by. She scooped the child in her arms, lifted her to her lap and again offered the top.

"No, thank you," Amy said politely, "I wike the beadth."

Leonora didn't quite understand. "Are you saying *beads*? What beads?"

"Thethe," Amy said, reaching out for the bracelet. Her hand flew out to grasp the glittering stones, making contact with them just at the moment when Leonora realized her intention. With a hasty, instinctive jerk, Leonora pulled her hand away, causing the delicate catch of the bracelet to break and the trinket to fall from her wrist to the floor. At the same time, she dropped the top, which rolled across the table to Perry's place. "Oh!" she cried, disconcerted. "My *bracelet!*"

"Shame on you, child!" Aunt Eugenia scolded.

"I *want* it!" Amy said, sliding off Leonora's lap and scrambling on the floor for it.

"Then may *I* have the top?" Perry asked politely. But no one was paying any attention to him.

"Amy, get up from the floor and return Miss Oglesby's bracelet!" Strickland ordered firmly.

Amy was sitting on the floor holding the gold-set stones and looking at them admiringly. *"No!"* she said with a pout. "It'th *my* birfday, and I *want* them!"

"Spoilt little imp!" Cousin Hattie muttered, not looking up from her needlework.

Perry, having heard no refusal of *his* request, picked up the top and carefully wound the string around it. Meanwhile, Leonora's mother had risen from her seat and come round the table to stand behind her daughter's chair. "Oh, my lord," she said eagerly, giving her daughter a meaningful poke in the back, "let the child *have* it. They are only garnets, after all."

Leonora nodded in agreement. "Yes, Miles, please. It *is* her birthday."

"On *no* account may she have it! We must not encourage such rudeness."

"Quite right, Miles," Eugenia agreed, and for once no rejoinder came from Hattie.

Strickland strode over to his daughter, leaned down and forcibly took the trinket from her grasp. Amy glared at him, astounded and outraged. "But I *want* it!" she wailed.

"One does not get everything one wants, my girl," he told her, handing the bracelet to its owner, "even on one's *birthday*."

Amy was not accustomed to denial. She burst into frustrated tears and threw herself face down on the floor. "I don't *care*! I want the pwetty beadth! I *want* them!" And she began to scream and kick her heels, her fists pounding furiously on the floor. Strickland stared down at her dumfounded, never before having witnessed one of her tantrums. Leonora, horrified, bit her lips and mutely held out the bracelet for Strickland to reconsider, while the others watched the scene aghast.

Perry, in the meantime, was paying not a whit of attention to the scene being enacted on the other side of the table. Amy's tantrums were not new to *him*. Completely absorbed in his top, he spun it out on the table and watched with delight as it careened along the edges of the plates in its path across the table.

"*Please* take—" Leonora was saying as the top spun off the table's edge right into her lap, giving her a shocking start as well as a rather painful prick on her upper leg. She jumped up with a cry, glanced at the place from which the missile had come and saw Perry, his arm stretched across in his effort to stop it, in a position that suggested he'd *thrown* it at her. This, in addition to the shrieking of the little girl at her feet, completely undid her already frayed nerves. "You horrid, *dreadful* boy!" she cried angrily. "You did that on *purpose!*"

"Perry!" Strickland barked, appalled.

"But I *didn't!*" Perry exclaimed, retreating to his chair. "I was only—"

To Strickland's horrified eyes, it seemed as if the room was in complete chaos. Amy was screaming. Mrs. Oglesby was leaning over her and begging her uselessly to stop crying. Eugenia was urging him in her booming voice to give the tot a good spanking, while Hattie was muttering that whippings never did anyone a bit of good. Lady Gallard was berating Perry for making mischief while his sister was so upset. Poor Leonora looked as if she would break into tears at any moment. And Perry's face was set in stiff, angry lines, as if an explosion was about to break from that direction as well. "I have had *enough* of this!" Strickland shouted in disgust. "Amy, stop that caterwauling and get up from the floor *at once!*"

Amy just kept on screaming. Strickland was completely at a loss. What was he to *do* with this hysterical child?

Tilda, who had kept in the background during the entire scene, stepped forward and came to his side. "Miss Olivia says that children won't stop their tantrums when people fuss over 'em. It's best, she says, to leave 'em alone in their rooms 'til they cry it out," she told him quietly.

He looked at her appreciatively. "Very well then, Tilda. Take her out of here at once. I'll be up later to deal with her."

Tilda knelt down, scooped the child up under one strong arm and carried her, yowling and kicking, from the room.

The silence that followed their exit was thick with tension. "Perry," Strickland said, turning to the second culprit in rigidly suppressed anger, "you will come over here and *apologize* to Miss Oglesby!"

Perry's chin set firmly, and his hands clenched into two tight fists. "I . . . I'm sorry, sir, but I *won't!* I'm not a dreadful boy! I didn't throw anything . . . and I w-won't apologize. It's *she* who's dreadful!"

Lady Gallard gasped, Leonora dropped down in her chair in despair and Strickland flushed red in chagrin. "Young man, your conduct is *inexcusable!* But I will give you one last chance. Will you do as I *say*, or shall I be forced to . . . take measures?"

Perry met his father's eye bravely, although his lips quivered slightly and his knees began to tremble. "No, sir, I *won't*," he said, his back stiffly erect.

"Very *well*! You may go to your room and wait there until I come to you."

Strickland watched as the boy marched firmly from the room, his shoulders back and his head proudly high. All at once, his anger seemed to melt away. The boy had always seemed to him too shy and spineless; this was the *first time* Perry had ever stood up to his father! Perhaps the boy had more pluck and character than he'd supposed. There was no question in Strickland's mind that the child had behaved abominably, but he couldn't prevent a bit of fatherly pride in the child from creeping into his chest.

After the boy's departure, Lady Gallard rose from her chair. "I . . . I think I'd like to take a bit of air while the sun is still warm," she said tactfully. "Would you care to stroll in the gardens with me, Mama?"

Mrs. Oglesby, after a fearful glance in Strickland's direction, nodded and followed her elder daughter from the room. Eugenia, about to give voice to her reactions to the scene just played, felt a restraining hand on her arm. "We should take a bit of air, too, Eugenia," Hattie said meaningfully, getting stiffly to her feet. Eugenia, after a glance at Leonora, blinked, nodded, and followed Hattie out of the room.

Leonora, who had been sitting with her eyes downcast and her hands clutched nervously in her lap, looked up at Strickland penitently. "I . . . I'm so ashamed. I am not adept with children. I never know how to speak to them, or—"

"It was not your fault. I should never have subjected you to—" he began.

"*Please*, don't . . . ! It was as much *my* suggestion as yours to come here." She lowered her eyes, and the tears slid down her cheeks. "It won't work, will it, Miles?"

He was silent for a long moment. "No, Leonora. I'm very sorry . . ." But in truth he felt relieved.

When at last he climbed up to the third floor, about an hour later, he found that all was silence. He knocked first at Perry's door, but no answer came. He opened it and found it empty. Angrily, he shouted for Tilda, but the governess was as surprised as he that Perry was not in his room. They both turned immediately to Amy's room. The birthday girl was discovered to be standing on a chair before her dressing-table mirror, preening before it in admiration of the several strings of colored beads which she'd hung about her neck. There was no sign, other than a dirt-streaked face, that she'd shed a tear. Her eyes were clear and content and her manner calm.

But Strickland was too preoccupied to puzzle over the child's abrupt change of mood. "Where's your brother?" he asked brusquely.

"He'th gone to Wondon," Amy said, gazing raptly at her reflection.

"*London*? What are you *talking* about?"

"He thaid he hath to find Aunt Wivie and bwing her back."

Strickland and Tilda exchanged alarmed glances. "And did he say how he intended to *get* there?" Strickland asked.

"He'th going to *walk* until he cometh upon a hay-wagon— wike Dick Wittington."

"Oh, good God! Tilda, run down and tell Higgins to saddle Pegasus! Tell him I'll be down in five minutes. And as for you, Amy, my girl, get down from that chair before you break your neck. You are not to leave this room, is that clear?"

"Yeth, Papa," she said, climbing down with placid obedience.

"Just remain right here until my return. I shall have a few words to say to *you* later."

There was no sign of Perry along the driveway. Even when Strickland had galloped out through the main gate and had peered down the road toward Devizes, all the way to the horizon, he didn't see a sign of him. It was not until he'd ridden over the hill that he discerned a small figure trudging gamely eastward, and he was able to breathe a sigh of relief. When he'd almost come up to him, he brought the horse to a stop, slipped down and, leading the horse by the reins, walked quickly along the road until he'd caught up with him. Perry looked up, saw his father, put his chin up and, wordlessly, kept on walking.

"I hear you're planning to go to London," Strickland re-marked, falling into step beside his son.

"Yes, I am."

"It's a longish way off, you know."

"I know."

"It will soon be dark, too."

Perry cast his father a mulish glance. "I don't *care*. I'm not going home! You'll only make me 'pologize to that...that lady you brought home. And I won't! Not *ever*!"

"But suppose no wagon goes by. Dick Wittington had a bit of luck on that score, you know."

"Then I'll *walk*!"

"But you'll have to sleep under hedges—"

"I don't care."

"And eat nothing but berries—"

"I *like* berries."

"And it might take you weeks and *weeks*."

Perry's step faltered. "W-would it?"

"I'm afraid so. However, if you agree to come home with me, I would be willing to ride to London in my carriage and fetch Aunt Livie *for* you. With four horses, I could be there in less than a day."

"Would you do that?" the boy asked in surprise.

"Yes, I would."

Perry stopped and considered. "Would you give your word to go *tomorrow*?"

"Yes, if you wish me to do so."

"All right then. I'll come home with you. But only if you don't make me 'pologize."

Strickland rubbed his chin. "As to that, Perry, I think you should reconsider."

"No, I won't reconsider!" the boy said stubbornly, resuming his walk eastward. "I didn't do anything but spin the top. It slid off the table by *accident*. And she called me 'dreadful' for it."

"I don't think she meant to say that, you know. And a true gentleman is never rude to a lady, even if she says things that are quite provoking."

Perry paused again and looked up at his father suspiciously.

"But *you've* been rude to ladies. I've heard you shout at Aunt Livie—"

"Have you? Well, I was very wrong to do so . . . and I'm certain that I must have apologized later."

"Oh." He bit his lip in thought. "Very well. I'll 'pologize."

"Good boy! Shall we ride back, or would you rather walk?"

"Let's ride, please. I didn't want to say so, but my feet feel as if they've done enough walking for today."

Suppressing a smile, Strickland tossed the boy into the saddle and climbed up on the horse behind him. Turning the animal around, they began a slow amble along the road toward home. "Will you *really* go to fetch Aunt Livie tomorrow?" the boy asked uncertainly.

"I've given my word. But I can't promise that she'll agree to come back with me, you know. She may not wish to come."

Perry turned his head around to scrutinize his father's face. "Why not? Doesn't she love us any more?"

"She loves *you*, Perry, very much. And Amy, too. I think, however, that she doesn't much care for *me*."

"Oh, I don't think you can be right about *that*, Papa," Perry said reassuringly. "It was *she*, you know, who told me you are not a monster."

"*Did* she, indeed?" his father said drily. "That was very kind of her. Did you believe that I *was*?"

Perry leaned forward to pat the horse's mane. "Once I did. When I was smaller. You seemed so huge, you see . . . almost like the giant on top of the beanstalk. And you were angry all the time . . ."

"I see. Then I'm very glad your Aunt Olivia told you I am not a monster."

"So am I. I would have been afraid to really talk to you if she hadn't."

Strickland tightened his hold on the boy, feeling an amazing surge of fatherly affection. "What do you mean, *really* talk?" he asked curiously.

"I mean what Aunt Livie calls 'serious talk.' About thoughts and feelings and things of that sort."

"Are we having a serious talk now?"

"Oh, yes. Do you like it?"

Strickland felt a constriction in his throat. "Yes," he said huskily. "I like it more than anything."

Perry nodded. "So do I." Contentedly, he leaned back and snuggled into the curve of his father's arm as, slowly and peacefully, the horse plodded homeward.

chapter twenty-one

It was after dark when the carriage drew up at the house in Brook Street, and Strickland alighted feeling as nervous and suspenseful as a schoolboy. But he didn't ask to see Olivia. He asked for Charles.

He was shown into his brother-in-law's untidy study, and Charles, in delight at seeing him, jumped up from his desk and, stumbling over a pile of books, rushed over to seize his hand. "What brings you back to London, Miles?" he asked, slapping Strickland heartily on the back. "Though whatever it is, I'm glad it's brought you here."

"You may not be so glad when I tell you why I've come," Strickland warned.

"Oh?" Charles studied him curiously. "Well, sit down, old fellow, and tell me what it is."

Strickland removed the books and debris from the room's easy chair, while Charles leaned against his desk and pulled out his pipe. "Do you remember the day when you told me your concerns about Olivia's future?" Strickland asked.

"Yes, I do. It was the day I confided to you my intention to marry Elspeth.. Why do you ask?"

"You see, Charles, I have been thinking about Olivia's future myself."

Charles' eyebrows rose, but he lowered his eyes and pretended to be absorbed in filling the bowl of his pipe. "Have you?" he asked mildly.

"Yes. And I've been wondering...what you would say about *me* as a...a suitor for her."

Charles flicked him a quick look. "I would say, of course, that it was entirely up to Olivia. She's a girl of very independent mind, as you no doubt are aware."

"Of course I realize the final decision must be hers. But do you think I should ask her in the first place? Don't you think I'm too old for her? Too dissipated . . . too cynical . . . too deucedly *unworthy*?"

Charles grinned. "Such unwonted *humility*, Miles! I hadn't thought you capable of it. Can you have fallen so deeply in love as all *that*?"

"Completely over my head, if you want the truth. I'm almost out of my mind over it." He looked up at his brother-in-law with a sheepish smile. "Well...what do you think?"

Charles tossed his pipe on the desk and got to his feet. "I think, old man, that you should ask her at *once*! I've been *expecting*...but never mind that. Come along, and I'll take you to her." Throwing an affectionate arm about Strickland's shoulder, he propelled him eagerly out of the room and down the hall.

Olivia was sitting in the library with Morley Crawford, who had come unexpectedly that evening to pay a call. Dissatisfied with the progress of his courtship, he'd hoped to come to a better understanding with the girl he intended to marry. They had chatted in a desultory manner for some time, but at last Morley had boldly taken a seat beside her on the sofa. Moving as close to her as possible, he'd reached for her hand. "What lovely hands you have," he'd murmured softly.

Olivia had almost laughed aloud. She had a quick recollection of the evening, many months ago, when she'd heard him say those very words. It had been a ruse...the first step toward an embrace. She also remembered how her outspokenness and teasing had embarrassed him the last time, so she kindly stifled her tendency to giggle. "Thank you, sir," she said and, recalling his instructions of that long-ago night, fluttered her lashes at him.

He found the gesture irresistible. "Oh, Olivia," he breathed and gathered her into a passionate embrace.

Olivia did not resist. She had not let him kiss her properly the last time. Perhaps this time he would be more successful. If she were really going to agree to wed him, she supposed she ought to learn to enjoy his embraces. She relaxed against him and closed her eyes, trying to surrender herself to the "mood" he'd once told her was so important. But her feelings remained unstirred, and after a while she decided that this would not do. She could *not* marry him. Perhaps, if Strickland had never kissed her—if she had not experienced the exhilaration that could occur when one's emotions were involved in the kissing—she could have convinced herself that *this* embrace was quite satisfactory. But under the circumstances, she couldn't fool herself.

She pushed at his chest, and he lifted his head. His eyes were misty with passion, and his breath came in quick gasps. "Olivia, my own *dearest*—"

"Please, Morley," she said, covering his mouth with her fingers. "I must talk to you. You must not go on with this—"

He kissed her fingers tenderly and withdrew her hand. "Don't talk yet, my love. Only let me..." With eager enthusiasm, he pulled her close and kissed her again.

It was at that moment that Charles burst in with Strickland in tow. "Livie, my dear," he chortled, "look at who has—good *God*!"

Morley, red as a beet, leaped to his feet.

"*Miles*!" Olivia cried, aghast.

Strickland winced. "Not *again*!" he muttered.

"I...I'm terribly sorry," the humiliated Crawford stammered. "I don't know wh-what...I'm afraid I quite l-lost my head."

"It's a symptom that seems to afflict many young men who find themselves in proximity to Miss Matthews," Strickland remarked drily.

"Please don't be nonsensical," Olivia pleaded, rising. "What are you *doing* here, my lord? Has anything happened to the children?"

"No, my dear. There's nothing I've come to tell you that is important enough to have interrupted your . . . er . . ."

"I beg to differ, Miles," Charles cut in firmly. "It seems to me your . . . er . . . mission is *very* important. I'm certain that Mr. Crawford will not object to leaving you to your discussion, will you, Crawford? Come along, old man, and let me offer you a drink of brandy in the drawing room. You look as if you could use it." With an iron grip on Morley's arm, Charles led the unhappy fellow inexorably toward the door.

Morley threw a helpless look over his shoulder at his beloved, but she was not even looking at him. Muttering a sheepish goodnight, he permitted himself to be led from the room.

When the door had closed behind them, Strickland turned to Olivia with an expression of wry amusement. "Am I to wish you happy *this* time, my dear, or was this *also* an instance of an unfortunate mischance?"

"Don't be infuriating, Miles. Morley is just a . . . friend."

"Is *that* what he is? In that case, girl, it seems to me that somebody should instruct you in the proper manner of entertaining friends. There is a limit, you know, to the amount of . . . er . . . *friendship* a well-bred young lady should permit."

"Are you quite finished with your jibes, my lord? Or must I endure this sort of treatment for the rest of the evening?"

He held up his hands in surrender. "My apologies, ma'am. Perry warned me about my tendency to be rude to ladies. I forgot myself."

"*Perry* warned you?" she asked, puzzled.

"Yes, my dear. It is on his behalf that I've come. He wants you back at Langley, you see. In fact, we *all* want you back."

Olivia felt her stomach knot. She sank down on the sofa in considerable perturbation. "*Do* you?"

"Yes, we do. However, there is a problem to overcome first."

"You mean Miss Oglesby, I suppose. I don't think—"

"I do *not* mean Miss Oglesby. She and I have agreed that we should not suit. She has returned to her home with her family. No, my dear, the problem is that my aunt Eugenia and your cousin Hattie are leaving us, and—"

"*Leaving* you? Are they *really*?"

"Yes, indeed. You will never credit it, but they've decided to take up residence *together*. Hattie intends to dispose of her London rooms and move in with Eugenia as soon as arrangements can be made."

"Miles, you're *joking*! They fight with each other *constantly*!"

"Yes, isn't it amazing? Apparently, there's nothing either one of them enjoys so much as a good quarrel."

Olivia broke into a peal of laughter. "What a fortuitous circumstance for *you*, my lord," she said when she'd recovered her breath, "to have rid yourself of both of them at once."

"Yes, but therein lies the problem. If there are no chaperones in residence at Langley Park, it will not be at all proper for you to come home—"

"*Home*?" she echoed, a bit breathlessly.

"Not at all proper," he repeated, "*unless* . . ."

"Unless?"

"Unless you married me, of course. It would be a brilliant solution to all our problems. And would make everyone ecstatically happy besides."

She gazed up at him, almost too shaken to speak. "W-Would it make *you* happy, Miles?"

"More than anything," he said softly, taking a seat beside her. "Of course I realize that I'm quite old . . ."

She clasped her hands tightly in her lap to keep them from trembling. "Yes, I know," she murmured, her eyes demurely lowered.

"And an incorrigible Tory . . ."

"Yes, you are."

He leaned a little closer. "And a disreputable libertine . . ."

"Quite so."

His face was disconcertingly close to hers. "You know, Olivia," he murmured, "there *is* something dangerous in a man's finding himself in proximity to you. *I* am beginning to lose my head *myself*!"

She was aware of only the slightest movement on his part before she found herself locked in his arms, his lips on hers. Her head seemed suddenly to be swimming in dizzying joy, while delicious little bubbles of excitement started a dance in her blood. There was certainly *something* this man knew about the nature of kissing that the other men who'd embraced her did not. *Perhaps he ought to give instruction*, she thought fleetingly, but immediately afterward, all thought deserted her, and she surrendered her entire being to the heady delight of the embrace.

The sound of a rattling doorknob drove them apart. With a whispered "Damnation!" he leaped to his feet in time to see Jamie coming in the door. "I say, Livie," Jamie was saying, "what have you done to Morley—? Oh, Strickland! *You* here?"

"Obviously," he responded tersely.

Jamie stuck out a welcoming hand. "Good to see you! What brings you to town? Has Liverpool got himself into a fix?"

"I've come, you jackanapes, to make an offer to your sister. And I would be eternally grateful if you would take yourself off and let me get on with the business."

Jamie's mouth opened in gaping surprise as he looked from one to the other. "Oh?" he inquired, not quite sure what to make of the situation. Then, with a shrug, he turned back to the door. "Very well, I'll go. But I wouldn't waste my time over it, Miles, if I were you. She don't like you above half."

When the door had closed behind him, Strickland resumed his seat and grinned at her. "*Don't* you like me, my love?"

"Not very much," she murmured, playing with a button on his coat, "although I must admit that your kisses are quite extraordinary." Then, her smile fading, she held him off with one trembling hand. "Do you *truly* love me, Miles?" she asked, her eyes searching his face. "It scarcely seems possible. You've always said you *dislike* bluestockings."

"I do. All but one." And he kissed her again to prove the point.

"But, Miles," she persisted when she could speak again, "what brought you to me *now*? Why didn't you speak of your feelings at *Langley* instead of sending me away?"

"Because, my dear girl, I was convinced that you thought me a *monster*. You've called me that a number of times, you know. It was not until Perry revealed to me that you'd said I was *not* a monster that I had the courage to declare myself." He smiled down at her with a sudden touch of hesitancy in his glance. "You haven't answered me, ma'am. *Will* you come home with me?"

"Oh, my dear, you've thrown me into the greatest turmoil!" she responded, moving away from him in an effort to think. "I don't know *what* to do." She could see a glimmer of fearful pain jump into his eyes, and, tenderly, she lifted her hand to his face. "I *do* love you, you know. Quite desperately. But... we are so different, you and I. We shall be so much at odds..."

That she loved him was all he needed to hear. Nothing else had any importance. "Not so very much," he assured her, rubbing his cheek against her hand. "Only about politics. I've quite put my libertinish activities behind me. And as for the political differences, I think we shall quite enjoy debating parliamentary actions."

But not all *her* doubts were resolved. "Then there's... my *guilt*, you know."

"Guilt?"

"You *were* my brother-in-law, after all. Doesn't this make you feel . . . somehow . . . traitorous?"

"To Clara, you mean? She will be rejoicing, I think." He took her gently into his arms again. "She predicted this would happen, you know."

Olivia gazed at him wide-eyed. "*Did* she, Miles?"

He smiled down at her. "I thought, when she said it, that the illness had affected her *mind*. But she was quite lucid about everything else, so I must conclude that she was expressing her true feelings."

"Oh, *Miles*!" She threw her arms about his neck in a completely uninhibited rush of happiness. "Then I have nothing else to say but *yes*!"

She lifted her face to be kissed again, but again the opening of the door interrupted them. Strickland again got to his feet, his face a study of amused irritation. Sir Octavius padded in, his spectacles low on his nose, a sheaf of papers in his hand and a puzzled expression on his face. "Livie, have you seen my *Euthyphro*? There's a quotation concerning the definition of holiness which I must—Ah, *Strickland*! Paying us a visit, are you?"

"No sir, not exactly. I've come for a very special purpose. I want to ask your permission for your daughter's hand."

"What? Her hand?" Octavius asked absently as he wandered about the room picking up books and putting them down.

"In marriage, sir. I wish to marry your Olivia."

"Oh? Well, old fellow, you'd better ask *her*. I don't know

anything about those matters. Can't fix my mind on fripperies, you know. Ah! *Here* it is! Could have *sworn* I put it on my desk." He began to look through the pages for the desired quotation.

"Then may I assume, sir," Strickland persisted, "that, if she agrees, I have your consent?"

Sir Octavius looked up from the page. "To marry my daughter? Yes, yes, I suppose so." Suddenly his brow wrinkled and, peering out blankly from above his spectacles with puzzled eyes, he muttered, "That's strange! I had the most peculiar feeling for a moment that you'd asked me that very same question some time ago. Do you think, Olivia, my love, that I might be becoming absent-minded?"

MS READ-a-thon— a simple way to start youngsters reading

Boys and girls between 6 and 14 can join the MS READ-a-thon and help find a cure for Multiple Sclerosis by reading books. And they get two rewards — the enjoyment of reading, and the great feeling that comes from helping others.

Parents and educators: For complete information call your local MS chapter. Or mail the coupon below.

Kids can help, too!